To Connie,
Hope you enjoy this one as much as the others. Thanks,
Carl

ALSO BY DARRYL BOLLINGER

A Case of Revenge

The Medicine Game

THE PILL GAME

A Novel

DARRYL BOLLINGER

JNB
PRESS

This book is a work of fiction. Names, characters, places, and incidents are the product of the author's imagination or are used fictitiously. Any resemblance to actual events, locales, or persons, living or dead, is coincidental.

Copyright © 2014 by Darryl Bollinger

All rights reserved

JNB Press
Tallahassee, FL

www.jnbpress.com

Printed in the United States of America

First Trade Edition: January 2014

ISBN 978-0-9848432-4-4

In memory of my seventh grade teacher, Mrs. Neal, who taught me to think.

Chapter 1

The skinny blonde girl peeked around the side of the weathered marina building, watching the middle-aged man get out of his gleaming white Lexus SUV. He wore khaki shorts, a blue and white striped shirt, and deck shoes. She absent-mindedly twirled a lock of her shoulder-length hair as she watched him reach into the vehicle, pull out a duffel bag, and sling it over his shoulder. His hair was almost the same color as hers, though his tan was a bit darker. He locked the vehicle and started toward the docks.

She scratched the inside of her arm, and regarded the simple tattoo underneath her fingers. It was a heart, with the name *Peabo* inside. She shook her head. She regretted the tattoo, but the cost to remove it was more than she could afford.

She stooped to pick up two green Publix grocery bags stuffed with paper but containing mostly nothing. She glanced at her reflection in the window before she stepped out onto the boardwalk running along the seawall. When she turned sideways, she could see the outline of a cell phone in the back pocket of her short jean cutoffs. She tugged the bottom of her halter top down and brushed her hair out of her face.

She fell in step following the man with the duffel bag and walked down the main dock as if she belonged, stopping just behind him at the locked gate. She watched as he punched in his security code and opened the gate. When he noticed her carrying two grocery bags, he paused and held the gate open as she passed through.

"Thank you," she said, flashing him a smile.

He returned the smile. "Looks like you've got your hands full. Need any help?" His eyes took a quick trip down the length of her body and back.

"No, thanks. I appreciate it, though."

She brushed by him, then stopped and set one of the bags down on the dock. With her free hand, she grabbed the cell phone out of her back pocket and put it next to her ear.

"Hi. What's up?" she said into the phone. She smiled at the man as he closed the gate, and gave him a little wave.

He stood there, waiting for her to get off the phone. She kept up the imaginary conversation, hoping he would leave, but he didn't budge. She heard the gate open and turned around to see another man coming out toward them. He wore a cap that bore the same Clearwater Beach Marina logo as his shirt. As he approached, she could see *Manager* underneath the emblem on his chest.

Shit, she thought, *not good.* She struggled to keep the conversation on the phone going while her mind raced to come up with another plan.

The manager, an older man, spoke to her new friend while watching her with a wary eye. "Afternoon, Mr.

Padgett. Going out for the weekend?" he said, looking down at the younger man's bag.

The man nodded. "Hi, Don. You doing okay?"

Don continued to scrutinize her. "Doing well, thanks."

"I'll be with you in just a minute," she said to the man she now knew as Padgett, flashing him another big smile. She also pulled her shoulder up slightly, which exposed more of her bare stomach beneath her cropped top. She watched Padgett's eyes, and he didn't miss the gesture.

"I was just helping her with her bags," Padgett said to the manager.

Don shifted his glance from her to Padgett and back. He gave Padgett a slight nod of understanding and said, "Let me know if you need anything. Have a good weekend." He turned and walked back toward the gate.

As soon as Don was out of earshot, she told her imaginary caller goodbye and said she'd see him in a few minutes.

She turned her full attention toward Padgett, cranking up the voltage on her smile a notch higher.

"I'm so sorry," she said. "That was my boyfriend. His last patient took longer than expected, so he's running behind."

"Patient? So he's a doctor, I take it?" Padgett said, already putting some distance between the two of them.

She nodded, almost as if embarrassed by the disclosure. She picked up the other bag. "Thanks again for helping, but I can manage just fine."

"No problem. Nice talking to you." He turned and walked away, disappearing down one of the finger docks on her left, behind the boats lining each side.

She headed to the opposite side of the marina, out of his view. Her eyes darted back and forth, checking out the boats as she walked. She observed the area, looking for anyone out on their boat or people coming and going on the dock. The marina manager had spooked her.

She took a deep breath, smelling the salt air, and looked up. The sky and clouds seemed more vivid here, and she felt more in tune with her surroundings. She didn't know why she was so drawn to the ocean, since she had lived her entire life in Harlan, Kentucky and that was a long way from salt water.

Boats were much easier to break into than houses and took less time to search, she thought, regaining her focus. They rarely had alarms and if a dog was onboard, it was obvious.

She favored sailboats. She didn't know how to sail; it wasn't something anyone did in a small town in southeastern Kentucky. Her family didn't have the money to afford a decent car, let alone a boat. Sailboats looked sleek and fascinating with all of the ropes and gadgets.

The powerboats were usually backed in to their slips, but sailboats were parked nose first. She was always amused by the boat names, and wondered where people came up with some of them. It was like they tried to emulate a picture of something you would see on a magazine or television show. She read the names of the sailboats on the opposite dock mixed in with the names of the powerboats on her dock. *Wind Chaser. Fishin Fool. Follow That Breeze. The Office. Cloud Dancer.* Lame, she thought, shaking her head as she continued walking.

She slowed a bit as she saw an attractive sailboat ahead at the dock on her right. It was cream colored, with a dark green top over the back and matching covers around what she guessed were sails. The boat was clean and polished, and looked like it was well taken care of. People who didn't take care of their boats usually didn't have anything worth stealing.

She stiffened when she heard a dog barking, then realized it was over on the main boardwalk. That was another problem on the water; sound carried. She hated stealing. If she got caught, she knew she'd go to jail. But, she had few choices. She convinced herself that if she was smart, the risk was small. It beat the hell out of dancing. She scrunched up her shoulders and tried to relax. A few more minutes of scouting and she'd leave.

As she got closer, she saw a shiny grill hanging off the back rail and the boat looked lived on. She glanced around as she passed, cataloging the other boats nearby. The setup looked good. There were a couple of fishing boats opposite, and several smaller boats on the other side of the sailboat.

When she got to the end of the dock she turned around to see what it looked like from that angle, checking out the name. *Left Behind*. That was different. She wondered about the story behind the name. It was unique, and not dumb like the others.

There was a large boat between the end of the dock and *Left Behind*. That was good, since it blocked the view from the end. She turned to the left, and there was a stone jetty on that side. Again, perfect, no access to that, so no way for anyone to observe the boat from that direction.

She had to find a mark soon. What little money she had was almost gone. She'd had a job dancing before, but didn't want to do that again. After only a week, she'd quit, although the money was good. It wasn't so much taking her clothes off—that didn't really bother her—she got tired of the drunken men pawing and touching her all over like they owned her. It was disgusting to think about doing it again, but she was getting desperate.

That damn moron Peabo had ditched her, and she'd been wandering around looking for a way to score some quick cash. She'd started dating him when she was thirteen, and he was the only boyfriend she'd ever had. He was in business, as he would tell people, and would travel from Kentucky to Tampa to pick up a load of pills to take back home to sell.

They had been in Clearwater Beach all week, and late Friday afternoon were threading their way back through Clearwater to get on I-275 and go back to Kentucky. Shorty, Peabo's friend, was driving, and had asked for another beer. She made the mistake of saying he didn't need another one while he was driving.

The next thing she knew, Peabo told Shorty to pull over. When the SUV stopped, Peabo jumped out, opened the back door and yanked her out, throwing her bag out next to her. Then they drove off and left her on the sidewalk in downtown Clearwater.

Since she was more familiar with the beach, she picked up her bag and walked across the causeway to more well-known territory. She only had forty-three dollars in her pocket and that wouldn't last long.

That was three days ago, and she hadn't heard from Peabo since. He'd done that kind of crap before, but usually came back or called within a couple of hours. This was the first time he'd gone this long without contacting her.

Damn, it was hot, she thought, as she got back to the park next to the marina. Back home was hot, but not like this. It was June, and she wondered what it would be like in another couple of months.

She sat on the picnic table and lit her last cigarette that she'd bummed off a guy earlier. She leaned back and took a drag, waiting and watching.

Chapter 2

Jack Davis sat in the cabin of his sailboat, *Left Behind,* tapping his fingers on the table. His wife, Molly, was changing clothes and getting ready for the evening. It was their first social event involving his new job, and he wanted to make a good impression. His boss, Dr. Devo Drager, had invited them to a party at his house on Bayshore Boulevard, *the* address in Tampa if you were somebody. He'd never been there, but knew it was a pretty exclusive area and he felt uncomfortable. Just not his thing, even though he knew he had to do it.

Dr. Drager had started ten years ago as a solo practitioner in a small office in Clearwater. The practice had done well, and he now oversaw twelve clinics with seventeen doctors and 150 employees throughout the Tampa Bay area. His income and reputation had grown commensurate with the growth of Drager Clinic to the point that he was now an A-list personality in the area.

Jack had left Fort Myers after exposing the chief executive officer of HealthAmerica, a large for-profit hospital company, for fraud involving a counterfeit, hi-tech biopharmaceutical drug. Though the CEO had avoided jail time, his career with HealthAmerica was over.

Jack's best friend, Richard, had been murdered during the process and Jack's future with the hospital chain was finished as well.

He decided he needed a change from the hospital business and corporate America. Although he owned a boat slip in Fort Myers, he wanted a complete change of scenery, and sought a job elsewhere in Florida. A friend had referred him to Dr. Devo Drager, and Drager had hired him as chief financial officer with Drager Clinic, a multi-specialty clinic concentrating in pain management.

Molly walked out of the forward berth. She looked stunning, in a simple, black sundress that contrasted against her long red hair.

"Wow," he said, surveying her from head to toe.

She held out her arms and spun around. "You like?"

He grabbed her and pulled her close, kissing her.

She pushed him away, smiling. "Later, Tiger."

"You look scrumptious," he said. "Why don't we skip Drager's party and just get naked?"

She grinned and her green eyes sparkled, flattered by his attention, but holding him at bay. "You're going to have to wait. You said this party was important, so we need to get moving."

He moved closer and ran his fingertips down her back, starting at her neck and stopping on her waist. "We could be fashionably late, you know?"

Molly laughed. "Stop it, before I have to douse you with some cold water. We've got to go." She turned and started toward the steps, pulling him along.

The girl sat on the picnic table at the park, pretending to be looking at something else. A man and woman walked down the dock, holding hands. They had stepped off the sailboat she was looking at earlier.

The woman wore a black sundress, nothing fancy, but nice looking in an elegant way. She was slim, a tad shorter than the man, and her red hair stopped just above her shoulders. Her boyfriend or whoever wasn't bad-looking either. He had casual light brown hair and was laughing as he held her hand. The khaki slacks and blue blazer looked good on him, and the two made a handsome couple.

She watched them get in their car and drive away.

"So, who all's coming to this party?" Molly asked, as Jack drove across Gulf to Bay Boulevard toward Tampa, coming up on the Courtney Campbell Causeway. Traffic was heavy, but worse on the westbound side. He could see the orange ball of sun in his rearview mirror, low in the sky.

"Not exactly sure. Drager said it was just a small gathering, but knowing him, I wouldn't count on it."

They were almost to the bay, when Jack slammed his hand on the steering wheel, startling Molly. "Shit," he said, shaking his head.

"What?" Molly said, turning toward him. "What's the matter?"

"I forgot the directions," he muttered.

Molly looked at the clock on the dash. "We're halfway there— we can't turn around now, we'll be late. I thought you said he lived on Bayshore. Don't you think we can find it?"

Jack shook his head. "I have no clue where his house is or what it looks like. I don't even have the address—it was on the directions."

"Can't you just call him or something? It'll take us forever to go back with this traffic."

Jack reached for his phone and pressed the button to select Drager's number. The call went straight to voice mail. He shook his head and put the phone back in the console.

"Voice mail," he said. "We've got to turn around."

It was almost dark when the girl walked up to the gate, this time carrying only one shopping bag. Not seeing anyone, she punched in the code she saw the guy enter earlier. The gate opened, and she went in.

She knew the security guard didn't come on duty till around nine, so she had at least an hour to go through the boat. She strolled out to the dock where *Left Behind* was tied up. When she got to the intersection of docks, she heard music and stopped.

People were laughing, and it came from the same general direction as the music. *Where were they?* She scanned the area and realized the sounds were coming from her left. A small group of people were out on the back of a large boat docked at the marina. She turned her head back to the right, toward *Left Behind,* trying to imagine the sight line. *Would the people on the boat be able to see her?*

This was unexpected. If someone saw her and called security, she was trapped. She glanced back at the gate. No one was there, but that could change any minute. She couldn't just stand there and act like she was lost. She looked toward the sailboat, turned right and walked that direction.

When she got to the boat, she risked looking back toward the party boat. The sight line wasn't perfect, but adequate if someone onboard happened to look toward where she stood. She heard the gate slam, and saw a couple with drinks in hand walking down the main dock. They were talking and laughing and did not appear to see her. Yet.

Warning bells went off in her head and the smart side of her screamed "Get out!" She remembered how little money she had left, held her breath, and stepped onto the boat. It rocked slightly, and she hunched down in front of the cabin door, making her profile as low as possible.

There was a brass padlock on the door. She reached in her back pocket and pulled out the thin case containing a lock kit. Her boyfriend had taught her how to pick locks, and she was good at it. He had learned in prison—one of the more useful skills he'd picked up there. She selected the proper tools and glanced around once more to make sure no one was watching before turning her attention back to the lock.

It was a popular, simple model. Most burglars these days took a brute force approach; it was easier and faster than picking a lock, even if it was noisier. As a result, most of the locks at the big box stores were designed to thwart bolt cutters or crowbars, not picks. For someone like her, who knew what to do, it was a simple task to pick a lock. In less than ten seconds, she had it open.

She chanced another quick glance back toward the party boat. The couple must have gone there, since they were no longer in sight. No one else was out. She took a deep breath and entered the sailboat.

The cabin was clean and the owners had been considerate enough to leave a small light on in the galley. That, coupled with the small LED flashlight she had, provided more than enough light to navigate.

She quickly passed through the main cabin, stopping only to put a few items in the shopping bag she carried. There was a safe in the main cabin, but it was bolted to the boat and had a combination lock, so she moved on, looking for small, valuable things she could easily turn into money.

When she got to the forward cabin, she was pleased to find a jewelry box setting on top of a chest. She opened it, finding an assortment of earrings, rings, necklaces, and two watches. She raked the jewelry into the shopping bag and moved on. In the top drawer of the chest, she rummaged through male underwear and found three hundred-dollar bills. She dumped the money into the bag and looked around to see what was next. There was a small closet on the side of the boat, and she decided to give it a quick once-over before moving back to the main cabin.

As she went through the closet, she heard voices outside and froze. The voices were getting louder. She turned her flashlight off and risked a peek out the tiny window. The redhead and her boyfriend were walking down the dock, toward the boat. *Shit, now what?* Frantic, she looked around the boat. She was trapped. Nowhere to run, nowhere to hide. She felt the boat sway slightly as someone stepped aboard.

***

"Stop," Jack said to Molly, as she stood on the dock next to the boat. He'd already stepped into the cockpit, but held his hand up blocking Molly.

"What?" she said.

He lowered his voice and pointed toward the companionway. "It's open." The unlocked padlock was hanging on the hasp.

"Call the police," he said, keeping his voice down.

Molly pulled the cell phone out of her purse, and dialed 911. She grabbed his arm and whispered, "What if they're still inside? We should go to the office."

He thought about it. She was right. If the intruder had a weapon, it could get ugly in a hurry.

As he turned to look at the cabin, a skinny girl with blonde hair came crashing out of the companionway, knocking him to the side. On his back, crunched up against the seat, he watched as the girl jumped up on the dock and tried to sidestep Molly. She stepped aside as the girl ran past. At the last minute, Molly stuck out her leg and tripped the girl, who went flying down to the dock on her stomach.

In a flash, Molly grabbed the girl's arm and twisted it behind her back, hard enough that the girl screamed. She was still flaying about as Molly kneeled on the girl's back, knee between her shoulder blades, holding on to the girl's arm.

The sight of Molly, in her black sundress, on top of the skinny blonde in shorts, was a picture he wouldn't soon forget. The girl struggled, but just when it seemed she might dislodge Molly, Molly twisted her arm a little harder and that was it.

Still groggy from hitting his head on the cockpit bench, Jack made his way up on the dock.

"You think you could give me a hand here?" Molly said, not taking her eyes off the girl.

Jack couldn't help but laugh. "Looks like you're doing pretty good to me—better than I managed." He pulled out his phone and called 911. He explained the situation to the operator, and hung up.

He went back to the cockpit and got a line from the locker. It was probably unnecessary, but he wasn't sure about what to do with the girl and he didn't want her to get away before the police arrived.

With Molly still sitting on the girl's back, he proceeded to tie the stranger's ankles together, then took her free hand and tied it to the one Molly had twisted behind her back. He was careful not to tie it too tight. He didn't want to hurt her, only prevent her from running away.

They turned the girl over on her back. She looked to be in her teens, with long, stringy blonde hair. Her blue eyes darted about like a caged animal, looking for a way out. He didn't recognize her and wondered if she was local. She wore a halter top, shorts, and sandals, one of which was lying on the dock below her foot.

"What's your name?" Jack asked.

The girl stared at him, ignoring his question.

"Guess she doesn't want to talk," Molly said.

"I don't care whether she does or not. The police will be here soon, they can deal with her," Jack said.

"Wren," the girl said, in a small voice.

Jack looked at her for a moment before speaking. "Well, Wren. What were you doing on our boat—besides breaking in and trying to steal things?"

The blue eyes darted to Molly, over to Jack, and then back to Molly. "I'm hungry. I was trying to get something to eat."

She was far from being overweight, he thought. A couple of pounds less, and she could pass for anorexic.

Molly picked up the Publix bag which had fallen on the dock in front of the girl, and opened it. As she pulled out some of the items in it, she said, "Yeah, I can see. Lots of food in here."

She held up a necklace that had come from her jewelry box. Molly's eyes narrowed as she looked back at Wren. "I don't see any food in here. What were you doing, looking for stuff you can turn into cash so you could buy drugs?"

For the first time, Wren looked remorseful and almost defiant. "I don't do drugs. I told you, I was hungry. Yes, I was looking for stuff I could turn into money, but to get food, not drugs."

Jack shook his head, not buying her story. "You can ask for food, you don't have to steal."

The girl shot Jack a glance. "What would you know? You've got a place to live, a nice boat. You've got money. You don't know what it's like to live on the street."

"You live on the street?" Molly asked, her tone shifting.

Wren nodded. "Didn't have a choice. My boyfriend kicked me out."

"Kicked you out? Where were you living?" Molly asked.

Wren hesitated, then said, "We drove down from Kentucky. He was going to get a job, then we had a fight and he kicked me out of the car. I been staying in the park over there." She nodded toward the park on shore.

"You've been living in the park here at the marina?" Jack asked.

He looked that direction, not believing someone would be sleeping there. Two uniforms from the Clearwater Police Department were walking out on the dock, hands resting on their weapons, scanning the area as they approached.

"What seems to be the problem here?" asked the taller officer, a man wearing a nametag that read Owens. He looked down at the girl tied up on the dock and kept his hand resting on top of his pistol.

Jack spoke. "I'm Jack Davis, who called." He pointed to Wren, lying motionless between them. "We left to go out to dinner, forgot something and had to come back. When we got here, we saw the boat was open. While we were discussing what to do, she ran out of the boat with this bag of our things she'd stolen." Molly handed the Publix bag to him.

"How'd she get tied up?" the female officer, Frost, asked.

"I tripped her when she tried to run away, and we tied her up," Molly said.

Officer Owens looked in the bag and handed it to his partner. "Do either of you know her?"

Jack and Molly both shook their heads. "Never seen her before," Jack said.

"This your boat?" Owens asked, still looking at Jack and Molly.

Jack nodded.

Officer Frost asked Wren, "Is this what happened?"

Wren shrugged and answered, "I guess."

"We're going to need some ID from everyone and take statements," Owens said.

He looked down at Wren, then at his partner and nodded. Frost explained to Wren that she was going to pat her down and cuff her while they got things sorted out. While she helped Wren to her feet, Officer Owens took Jack and Molly's IDs and copied the information down.

Officer Frost looked at Wren. "Got any ID?"

"My back pocket," Wren answered.

She reached into Wren's pocket and removed her phone and driver's license, then reached into the other pocket and removed the case containing the pick set. She opened it, shook her head, then turned her attention to the driver's license, reading the information.

"Wren Lawson?"

Wren nodded.

"You still live in Kentucky?"

Another nod.

"What're you doing in Clearwater?"

"I rode down here with my boyfriend. He was looking for work. We had a fight, and he kicked me out."

"What's his name?"

"Peabo."

"Peabo have a last name?"

"Watson."

"Where is he?"

"Don't know."

She quizzed Wren about Peabo, but Wren wasn't giving up a lot of information about him. Frost held up the pick set and asked, "So, you want to explain this?"

Wren shrugged, not saying anything.

"It'll be easier on you if you tell me what happened."

The girl hesitated as if she wasn't going to cooperate, then seemed to decide it wasn't worth it and told Frost what happened.

The two officers finished taking statements and verified that Jack was indeed the owner of *Left Behind*. They dusted the boat for fingerprints, and when they were finished, huddled, and then read Wren her rights.

As they walked Wren down the dock, she turned to Molly and said, "Please. Keep my stuff for me. It's in the park under the picnic table."

Molly nodded. They stood on the dock and watched the officers leave with Wren. Once they were out of sight, they stepped back on the boat to change clothes.

"Shit," he said, stopping in front of the companionway. "I forgot to call Dr. Drager." He pulled his phone out and dialed the doctor's number. Still no answer. He left him a message, explaining what had happened.

They went below and changed, then walked up to the park by the marina to look for Wren's things. Not exactly sure what they were looking for, they walked around each of the picnic tables, looking underneath. When they got to the third one, under a tree, Molly found a rolled-up sleeping bag hidden under the table.

"This has to be it," she said.

Jack picked it up and put it on the table. He reached for the cord that secured it and started to untie it.

"Stop," Molly said.

Jack froze and looked up at Molly. "What?"

"Don't open it."

"Why not?"

"It's her personal stuff. We have no right to go through it."

Jack shook his head. "You've got to be kidding! We caught this girl stealing from our boat, and now you're saying we have no right to go through *her* things?"

Molly set her jaw. "Just because she was stealing doesn't mean we should violate her privacy. She asked me to keep it for her, and that's what we're going to do."

Jack exhaled, still shaking his head. "Whatever," he said, as he picked up the bundle and they walked back to the boat. "She was lying to us, you know?"

"About the boyfriend?"

"Yeah, there's more to that story than she was letting on. Sounded fishy to me."

"He sounds like a prince."

When they got on the boat, Jack went below to put the bundle in the aft cabin, and he stepped back up to the cockpit. Molly was sitting silently, staring out across the bay.

"You're quiet. What's the matter?" he asked, sitting next to her.

Molly looked at him. "Just thinking about that poor girl. How old do you think she is? Seventeen? Eighteen?"

"Poor girl? She was stealing from us! Sorry, but I don't have a lot of sympathy right now."

She reached over and took Jack's hand. "I'm not condoning what she did. But I keep thinking about how alone I was when I left Boston. I was fortunate, I had an education and a little money saved up. This poor girl has nothing. I just feel sorry for her, is all. Maybe we shouldn't have called the cops."

Molly's words touched Jack's heart, as he remembered her story about leaving her first husband, Ambrose Clark. He'd been abusive, even threatening to kill her, and she'd told him how difficult it was to leave.

"I feel sorry for her, too, but I'm not sure what we can do," he said. His temper had subsided, and as Molly pointed out, they didn't lose anything.

"Maybe we can find a social service agency that could help her when she gets out. I'll check at the hospital," Molly said.

He nodded. Molly had slipped into the role of advocate. He'd seen it before. While that was good for Wren, it was trouble for him.

Chapter 3

Jack stretched his arms up over his head, then strapped the iPod to his upper arm. He picked up his socks and running shoes and climbed out into the cockpit.

Though warm, it wasn't hot this morning. A slight breeze was stirring and the humidity was down—just right for running. A brown pelican sat silently on the piling to his left, seeming to pay no attention to him. Seagulls, birds he dubbed *flying rats*, squawked overhead.

The water was calm, and the sun was just starting to peek over the buildings across the bay in downtown Clearwater. A few puffy white clouds were scattered overhead against a cobalt sky. Not a lot of traffic was moving on the causeway yet, with most beachgoers sleeping in.

He liked to start his day off with a run. It was cooler then, less traffic and distractions, and got him going for the day. It was his way of waking up and engaging the brain, transferring the night's workload from the subconscious to the forefront.

Molly had already left for work an hour ago, so he had the boat to himself. He put the earbuds in and switched on the iPod. The tiny device contained an assortment of everything from blues to classic rock, his favorite genre. The haunting, opening riff of Driving Towards the Daylight by Joe Bonamassa flooded his ears and Jack grinned. Bonamassa was one of his favorites, and this was a great song to start the day.

He put his socks and shoes on, singing along, stood, yawned, and extended his arms out to his side. He stepped off the boat and walked down the docks for a few minutes letting his muscles warm up.

When he got to the main dock, he stopped to stretch, then set his watch and started running. He had a five mile loop that he ran most mornings, across the causeway, through a section of downtown Clearwater, then back across the causeway to the Clearwater Beach Marina. The bridge just before Clearwater not only provided a beautiful view of the area, but presented a slight hill to break up the otherwise monotonous, flat terrain of the Florida coast.

As he chugged toward Clearwater, he thought about the clinic. Drager had hired him because he wanted to make his expanding organization more efficient. But it was a challenge without decent information. Since there wasn't much reporting in place, Jack had decided to start there.

Before he realized it, he was across the bridge in town. He turned left on Fort Harrison Street and ran down by the sprawling Church of Scientology complex. As usual, there was a cadre of people in dark slacks and white shirts going from one building to the other.

He didn't know much about the Scientologists, only that it had been started by L. Ron Hubbard, and Clearwater was their spiritual headquarters. They called it

Flag Land Base, and it included the renovated Fort Harrison Hotel.

They tended to keep to themselves, and from what he gathered, didn't interact much with the rest of the community. He did know that they had quite a physical presence in Clearwater, owning fifty buildings in the downtown area.

At Pierce Street, Jack turned left, running along the back side of the Harrison Hotel. A block later, he turned left again on Osceola Avenue, approaching Court Street in front of the Pinellas County Courthouse.

He saw a homeless man standing on the corner, panhandling, and thought about Richard. A professional killer, disguised as a street person, had murdered him late one night on the streets of downtown Fort Myers. Richard was involved in the discovery that an expensive, new cardiac drug was losing its effectiveness—a discovery that Jack had brought to Richard's attention.

He turned right at Court Street and headed back out toward the beach, picking up his pace. Soon, he was on the bridge, headed toward the Gulf. The view from the crest was magnificent, one he never tired of seeing. He could see the turquoise waters, the ribbon of white sand, and the large pink building to his left that was the Hyatt.

Back at the marina, he walked around for a few minutes letting his body cool down. At the dock, he stopped and stretched, the breeze off the water feeling good. He walked out to the boat, grabbed his things, and went to the marina building to shower.

Jack had a meeting scheduled this morning with Dr. Winston Andrews, the physician in charge of Bayview Clinic, the largest clinic in Drager's empire. It had taken him weeks to get an appointment with Andrews, with the doctor coming up with one excuse after another. He knew that Dr. Andrews was the first doctor Drager had brought onboard years ago, and it was critical that Jack get Andrews's support.

As he drove east down Gulf to Bay Boulevard, he slowed and looked carefully as he got close to the street for the clinic. Bayview was near the intersection of McMullen Booth Road and Gulf to Bay. He had not been there before, but knew it was on the right, close to the water.

He saw the sign up ahead, signaled, and turned into the parking lot. Like the other clinics he'd visited, it had an attractive, well-maintained façade. The parking lot was almost full, but Jack found a spot two rows from the building and parked.

He clipped his Drager Clinic badge to his shirt and walked into the entrance. The large waiting room was packed, with only a couple of empty seats. It looked like a typical medical office, with rows of sturdy chairs against the walls and a couple of islands interspersed throughout, containing more seats and a few small tables scattered about with reading material. The clientele ranged from young kids to gray-hairs and everything in between. If this was the norm, he thought, no wonder this clinic had the highest revenue.

He went over to the glass window separating the receptionist from the waiting area and tapped on the glass to get her attention. The heavy-set black woman looked up at him and smiled as she pulled the glass back. Her badge read *Tabitha*.

"May I help you?" she asked. Her voice was pleasant, and she seemed eager to help.

Jack pointed to his badge and said, "Hi, Tabitha, I'm Jack Davis with Drager Clinic and I have an appointment with Dr. Andrews."

She squinted as she looked closer at his identification. Apparently satisfied that he was who he said, she nodded and told him to come through the door on his left.

He turned and before he could get there, she appeared, opening the door for him.

"You must be new," she said as the door shut behind him. "Come on back to Dr. Andrews's office and I'll try to find him. How long have you been with Drager Clinic?" she asked as she led him down several hallways, deep into the office maze.

"About three months. Have you been here long?"

"Ten years. I came with Dr. Andrews when he joined up." She ushered him into a small, but well-furnished office.

A sleek modernistic desk was in the middle of the room, with only a thin, flat panel computer display on one side. A tall, mesh-back executive chair sat behind the desk, with two, shorter versions parked in front. The requisite medical texts and journals lined the bookcase on the side wall, and Jack could see a park out the window at the rear of the office.

"Have a seat and I'll tell him you're here," she said as she turned and walked out.

Various certificates lined the wall, including a diploma from Emory University School of Medicine and Board Certification. A picture of a tall man with bushy eyebrows and thinning red hair shaking hands with Devo Drager sat on a shelf. Next to it was a picture of the same man with a tall woman and a little girl who looked to be about seven or eight years old.

Jack heard a voice behind him and turned to see an older version of the man in the picture walking through the door. He stood to greet the doctor.

"Mr. Davis," he said, as he extended his hand. "I'm Dr. Andrews." They shook hands and Andrews motioned to the chair Jack had been sitting in. "Please, have a seat."

They chatted for a few minutes, then Andrews folded his hands together on his desk and leaned forward. "So, what can I do for you?"

Jack pulled a copy of a spreadsheet out of his folder and pushed it across the desk to the doctor. Andrews slid the page toward him, but kept his eyes on Jack, waiting for a response.

"I've been trying to set up a little better management reporting system for Dr. Drager. As you know, there wasn't a lot in place—"

"I was under the impression that you were hired to extend our efficiencies to the other offices."

Jack felt his face flush at the rebuke. "That's true, but we need good information in order to determine what measures are effective."

"We have the highest revenue per patient of any of the clinics, and I'd say we've done extraordinarily well with what reporting we have."

Jack cleared his throat, surprised at Andrews's adversarial tone. "You have, and I'm not suggesting otherwise. I'm just trying—"

Andrews leaned forward in his chair. "What are you trying to do, then, Mr. Davis? Please. Enlighten me."

Silently, Jack counted to five before responding.

"Look, Dr. Andrews. I am trying to determine how we can make the entire organization more efficient. You're right—that's what Dr. Drager hired me to do. I'm sure there are things that you do better here than the other clinics, and we'd like to replicate those."

He paused as he chose his words. "This clinic has the highest revenue numbers and volumes. I'm just trying to understand what's behind the numbers and why."

Andrews pursed his lips and nodded. He leaned back in his chair before speaking.

"You don't have a clinical background, do you?" Andrews asked.

Jack shook his head.

Andrews nodded with a condescending smile. "I didn't think so. Given that, I'm not surprised at your question. Pain management, while based on hard science, still contains a fair amount of, shall we say, art. We know a lot more about it now than we did even a few years ago, but in the end, it's still a very subjective process."

Jack cocked his head, and Andrews continued. "Take orthopedics, for example. If you've fallen and come in with a pain in your arm, it is a relatively straightforward process to take an x-ray and determine whether or not there's a break in a bone somewhere. And the treatment is again, pretty standardized for the diagnosis." Andrews chuckled. "Of course, my orthopedic friends would probably disagree with my over-simplification, but I think you can follow what I'm saying."

This time Jack nodded, as Andrews kept going. "Now, when a patient comes in and complains of a pain in their arm, but there's no obvious reason for it like a break, then the diagnosis becomes significantly more problematic. Is it muscular? Neurological? Psychological? Maybe it's a combination, and many times it is. Even someone like yourself, with no clinical training, can see that the possibilities are numerous and exceedingly complicated."

Andrews leaned forward, putting his elbows on his desk. "So, I think you can understand that the volume of visits could fluctuate wildly, depending on the severity and type of pain, as well as the type of patient. Statistical correlations on what I call cut-and-dried diagnoses are much more meaningful than with pain management, which is more esoteric.

"You're not the first to point this out, I might add. I fight this battle with insurance companies constantly." He sat up a little straighter and puffed his chest out. "I've spoken at many conferences and have written numerous articles on this subject. Of course, most of them have been in clinical journals."

Andrews rose, indicating he was done. "I wish I could help you, but you'll find that what we do just doesn't lend itself to ordinary financial modeling of the type you're accustomed to doing. Someone who doesn't have a clinical background typically has a hard time understanding this."

Jack stared at him for a minute, but realized there was nothing else to say. He nodded, and picked up his file. "I'd appreciate it if you'd look over that report when you get time," he said, pointing to the still unread piece of paper in front of Andrews. "Maybe you will notice something that may strike a chord."

He stood. "Thanks for your time, Dr. Andrews. I look forward to working with you."

Andrews smiled, not offering his hand, and said, "Have a nice day, Mr. Davis."

That went really well, Jack thought as he walked out of the office. Andrews had kicked his ass, and he was furious.

"I got my ass kicked today," Jack said to Molly. He was still seething about his meeting with Andrews. Molly had just joined him out on the deck of *Left Behind* after work.

"What happened?" she asked, as she took a sip of wine.

"I met with Dr. Winston Andrews this morning. He's the head of the Bayview Clinic—our largest—and apparently goes back to the beginning with Dr. Drager. According to Dr. Drager, his clinic is the best in the entire organization, so I need to win him over. Oh, and did I mention that Andrews is one pompous and arrogant prick?"

Molly laughed. "Not like he's the first you've had to deal with."

He shook his head. "I know—that's what pisses me off. I walked into the meeting naively thinking we were on the same side. Didn't take long for him to carve me up into little pieces and hand them back to me on a platter."

"What now?"

"Regroup. Lick my wounds and figure out where to go from here."

"Why don't you take it to Dr. Drager?"

Jack shook his head. "Not yet. I need to make another run at it. I don't want to play that card until I have to, otherwise, word will get out that every time I don't get my way, I go running to the boss. Plus, it'll undermine my credibility with Dr. Drager."

He was mad at himself for not doing his homework. He knew better, having worked for large corporations before. Now that he worked for a smaller, privately-owned company, he'd let his guard down. That wouldn't happen again. The next clinic on the list was Palm Harbor, and he'd have his act together before walking in there.

Chapter 4

Jack walked out of the forward berth into the main cabin. He felt silly in slacks and a blazer. This was way overdressed for restaurants in this area of Florida, where you could go out to eat anywhere in the Bay area without a jacket. But, it was his birthday, and Molly had insisted on getting dressed up, since she was taking him out to dinner.

She had retreated to the aft cabin to get ready, so he sat and fidgeted, waiting for her. In a few minutes, he heard the door open, and she walked out. She wore a stunning green dress, cut low in the front and back, with an enticing split that seemed to go all the way up to her waist. He stood and walked over to her, admiring what he saw.

"Worth the wait," he said.

She grinned and twirled in front of him. "So, you like?"

"Oh yes," he said. He reached out to pull her close and give her a kiss.

"Easy, birthday boy," she said as she pushed him away, still smiling. "Later. We have dinner reservations, so we need to leave."

They walked up to the parking lot and Molly stopped, holding out her hand. "Keys?"

He fished in his pocket, retrieving the keys to his Mini, and handed them to her. "Why not your car?" he asked.

She walked toward the red Mini, clicked the button on the key fob and opened the passenger door for him. "Because, I never get to drive yours, and since I planned this evening, I get to decide."

He shrugged and got in. He couldn't help but watch as she entered the car, the slit in her dress revealing a nice section of her thigh. Seeing him look, she smiled and shook her head. "Don't worry, I'll tend to you later."

She drove through Clearwater and east toward Tampa on the Courtney Campbell Causeway, maneuvering the little car through the traffic.

"I don't suppose you'll tell me where we're going?" he asked, knowing the answer before he even opened his mouth.

She gave him an exaggerated grin and shook her head. Once in Tampa, she made her way downtown, turning right on Armenia and making her way over to South Howard Avenue, where she turned right again. That wasn't much help, as there were quite a few good restaurants in the trendy area known as SoHo.

Molly passed several of their favorites without slowing down. At the lower end of South Howard, just below the Crosstown Expressway in an area that once was a bit on the sketchy side, she slowed and switched on her turn signal.

The non-descript building on their left had a simple white sign with black letters indicating Bern's Steakhouse, an institution in Tampa. Now he knew why Molly insisted on dressing up for the occasion. While not required, Bern's clientele seemed to be a little dressier than in most places.

She turned in and pulled up under the portico. Jack felt pretentious for valet parking a bright red Mini amongst all the luxury sedans, but the former parking lot across the street was now occupied by a three-story building, so parking would have been problematic.

The waiting area was crowded when Jack opened the door to the restaurant. There was a steady buzz as people milled about waiting to be seated. Servers dressed in dark suits and white shirts shuffled to and fro, while patrons stood around, waiting for the hostess to call their names.

It was a fascinating place for people watching. Women were dressed in everything from thigh-high dresses with six-inch stilettos to prom dresses, while men sported tuxes to blazers to golf shirts. He noticed one man wearing a traditional blue blazer and tie, white slacks, and flip-flops for shoes. The clientele seemed to be preoccupied with trying to outdo one another with the hippest trends, as if they were there for a fashion magazine photo shoot instead of dinner.

Molly stopped at the hostess stand to tell them she had reservations for Davis, party of two. The hostess nodded, held up one finger, and told them it would be just a minute.

He always marveled at the décor, jokingly referring to it as early bordello. With dark, deep red patterned wallpaper, ornate picture frames housing various paintings of a bygone era, and a two-story mirror opposite the entry, that had been Jack's initial impression long ago when he'd first dined there. Neither the décor nor his impression had changed over the years. Fortunately, the legendary food and service had also remained the same.

Molly leaned over to whisper in Jack's ear.

"I forgot something," she said.

He gave her a puzzled, sideways glance and saw that she wore a mischievous grin.

"What?" he asked, trying to think of what they had left behind.

She smiled and whispered, "My underwear."

Jack's eyes widened, and he looked Molly up and down, as if he could see through the dress. He was still staring when the hostess motioned to them and escorted them back to be seated.

"You're bad," he whispered as they passed through the crowded restaurant. "Now that's all I can think about."

As they passed a dining room, Jack thought he heard someone call his name. He stopped, backed up, and looked inside a small room with only six tables. In the far corner, Dr. Devo Drager waved and called his name again. Jack grabbed Molly's hand and tugged her with him over to Drager's table.

"Jack, what a nice surprise," Dr. Drager said. His wife, Ivana, was seated with him at the table for two.

Devo rose, and greeted Molly with a kiss on each cheek. Ivana followed suit with Jack, then kissed Molly as Devo and Jack shook hands.

Jack noticed that Devo wore khakis and a blue blazer, matching his outfit. He was relieved that Molly had prevailed on his choice of attire. In the dim light, Jack could see the tight lines on Drager's face, remnants of the many plastic surgeries he had undergone.

Jack thought back to his interview with the doctor. He was intrigued by the tight skin on his face and the traces of scars just visible. He wanted to ask him about it, but was too polite to say anything.

As if reading his mind, Drager had told him the story about being involved in a horrible car accident as a teen, suffering third-degree burns over much of his body. He asked Jack if he had ever been burned. When Jack replied that he'd experienced only minor burns, Drager proceeded to tell him how painful third-degree burns were. Unimaginable was the word he used. When he recovered, he decided to become a doctor and do what he could to try to minimize the suffering that others endured.

He had lost count of the plastic surgeries, he told Jack. Then he rolled up his left sleeve and Jack saw a hideous, disfigured arm that didn't look human. Jack gave Drager a puzzled look, and the doctor told Jack he insisted that the surgeons leave the arm alone. He wanted it as a reminder, so he would never forget. And if he ever got too smug, all he had to do was look down at the arm and the memories would flood back.

Back in the present, Jack looked at Ivana Drager. She was a tall, striking blonde, and wore an iridescent blue dress, cut very low in front to showcase her ample chest. She, too, exhibited the traces of surgery, though in her case, it was for vanity's sake and extended below her face.

Drager spoke to the young girl that had been leading Jack and Molly to their table. "Can we add a couple of seats to our table?"

The hostess started to protest, but a tall, well-dressed gentleman appeared and stepped in between her and Drager. "Dr. Drager. Mrs. Drager." He gave each of them a slight nod. "So good to see you this evening. Is there anything I can help you with?"

Drager, reaching out to shake his hand, said, "Hello, Henry. Yes, thank you." He nodded toward Jack and Molly. "We just saw our associates here, and would like for them to join us at our table. Would that be possible?"

Henry gave a slight nod. "Absolutely, Dr. Drager. No problem at all." He turned to the hostess, and told her to bring two additional chairs and two more place settings. The tone of his voice indicated it was not up for discussion, and he dismissed her with a stern look.

Turning his attention back to the doctor, he smiled and asked, "May I bring you and your party a complimentary glass of champagne to enjoy while we make the changes?"

"Thank you, that would be nice," Drager answered.

Henry left, passing the young girl bringing the chairs over, who trailed another server with additional place settings. By the time Jack and Molly were seated and comfortable, Henry reappeared with four glasses of champagne.

Jack looked at Molly and gave a slight shrug, helpless. He realized Molly was blushing, and frowned. His frown soon turned into an impish grin when he realized the source of her discomfort, remembering what she'd told him in the lobby. *Nothing that could be done*, he said with his eyes, and knew she agreed.

Devo raised his champagne glass in a toast.

"Naroc," he said.

"Naroc," everyone repeated, raising their glasses. Jack had learned during his interview with Drager that the term was Romanian for "cheers" or "good luck."

The tuxedoed sommelier appeared and engaged in a brief conversation with the doctor about the merits of the two wines Devo was considering. At last, he settled on the 1961 Chateau Figeac, a Bordeaux that Jack recognized in name only.

The sommelier disappeared and Devo turned his attention to his guests. "I'm so glad you could join us for dinner," he said. "It's been too long. And we missed you at our house the other evening."

"Thank you for inviting us to share your table," Molly said.

"I'm sorry we missed coming over to your place," Jack added.

"Well, I understand. It was good you were able to apprehend the thief. A girl, was it? Is she still in custody, I hope?" Drager asked.

Molly looked at Jack and then back to Drager. "It's a sad case, actually. Her boyfriend from out of state dumped her here with no money or job."

Ivana looked confused. "But she stole from you, yes?"

Jack tried not to roll his eyes, but he was curious as to how Molly was going to handle this.

"Yes, but we recovered everything," Molly said.

Before Drager could pursue it further, the sommelier returned with the wine, smiling and presenting the dusty bottle to Devo for his approval. The subject of Wren was forgotten as the doctor turned his full attention to the wine. Drager inspected the label and nodded his approval. Everyone watched as the sommelier removed the cork and decanted the wine. He poured a taste for Drager, who gave it the proper consideration and pronounced it good. The sommelier set the decanter on the table and left.

They enjoyed an assortment of appetizers with the champagne, and when the main course appeared, the sommelier returned to pour the Bordeaux. The wine was exceptional, Jack had to admit, and he wondered how much it cost. He was glad he wasn't picking up the tab.

Devo asked Molly where she was from, and she told him Boston. One of his favorite cities, he told her, and they proceeded to compare notes on the place.

"Winston is from Boston, too, isn't he, darling," Ivana said.

Jack tensed at the mention of Dr. Andrews.

Drager nodded. "Yes, he moved from there to Chicago, where we met. He told me you came by to see him," he said, looking at Jack. Drager brought the glass of wine to his face, breathing in the bouquet before drinking.

Jack studied his face, trying to determine what he was thinking. *So Andrews had already ratted*, he thought.

"Yes, I did." He decided not to elaborate, and see where Drager was going. Drager dropped it and changed directions. "You are from Florida, yes? Jacksonville?"

"Yes, I grew up in Jacksonville. Hard to leave Florida," he said with a nervous laugh. "I like the weather and don't think I would ever want to live anywhere else."

"Do you have brothers and sisters?" Ivana asked.

He stiffened, and felt Molly's hand on his under the table. "No," he said. He thought about his brother, Ray. Ray had been addicted to prescription painkillers. Twelve years ago, he overdosed and died, but the memory haunted Jack.

He heard Ivana's voice say that she had never been to Jacksonville. Relieved to be able to shift the conversation away from painful thoughts, he proceeded to tell them a little about the city.

After dinner, they went upstairs to the dessert room. Bern's had a separate area for desserts and after-dinner drinks. Over dessert and coffee, Drager regaled them with stories of coming to America and struggling to get through medical school. The only son of poor immigrants, he had to work while putting himself through school.

At the end of the evening, they stood out front of the main entrance, waiting for their cars. Jack wondered why Drager bothered with driving, since their house was only a few blocks away.

The Drager's green Bentley was first to arrive, so the doctor and Ivana bid their goodbyes and left. The red Mini was next up, and looked like a toy compared to the Bentley. Jack herded Molly to the passenger door.

"Hey," she said. "I'm chauffeuring you tonight."

He bolted to the driver's door. "I'll drive. You made the arrangements and all, so I'll drive home."

"Well, that was a bust for the nice, romantic dinner for two I had planned for your birthday," she said, as the valet closed Jack's door. "And, I was just a little uncomfortable in there. I didn't expect to be having dinner with your boss with me half-dressed."

Jack laughed. "Hey, I want a rain check on dinner. And a bottle of Bordeaux, too," he said. Drager had of course insisted on picking up the tab.

Now Molly laughed. "Believe it or not, I was prepared to splurge for a nice Bordeaux. I'd asked for the sommelier to come over when I made the reservation. Of course, I doubt I could've afforded the one that Dr. Drager picked out."

He reached over and put his hand through the slit in Molly's dress. "I need to verify what you told me before dinner. Are you trying to drive me crazy?" he asked, as he turned north on South Howard, heading home.

She grinned and tilted her head back against the headrest as he touched her with his fingers.

"You complaining?" she asked, closing her eyes as he stroked her.

"Not at all."

Good thing the Mini had an automatic transmission, he thought, his right hand still busy. He glanced over at Molly, who was enjoying his fingers. Several times on the way home, he stopped and started, teasing her. By the time they reached downtown Clearwater, she was pleading with him to quit torturing her. He relented, and just before they got to the Clearwater Beach Causeway, he finished what he'd started. Based on the expressions of the couple in the car next to them at the traffic light, he was sure they'd heard her and knew what was happening.

She had barely caught her breath by the time they pulled into the marina parking lot.

"I love your fingers," she said. "They're magic."

Jack smiled. He loved pleasing Molly, and found her incredibly sexy.

As soon as they got on the boat, Molly took his hand and led him below to their forward berth, illuminated only by the ambient light through the hatch and several small portholes. Once inside, she unbuttoned his shirt, taking it off and throwing it on the floor. Then, she unbuckled his pants, slid them off, and pushed him back on the bed.

"My turn," she said, as she unzipped her dress and let it fall to the floor. True to her word, she had on absolutely nothing underneath. Jack licked his lips and watched as she crawled up on the bed, straddling him. He could feel her body just touching his as she kissed his neck, then his chest. Now it was Jack closing his eyes as Molly continued to work her way down his body, determined to even the score from the ride home.

Chapter 5

Peabo Watson was behind the wheel of a black Cadillac Escalade, driving south on I-75 just north of the junction of I-275 and I-75 near Tampa. A cigarette dangled from his mouth, and he was tapping the steering wheel in time to the country and western music blaring from the radio. His real name was Buster, but for the last ten years he had been called Peabo, after Peabo McAllister, the World Wrestling Federation champion. Someone had told him he resembled the burly, scar-faced wrestler and the name had stuck. He never liked Buster—he thought it sounded like a little kid—so he was happy for the new name.

He was on his way to Tampa to score another load of painkillers to take back to Kentucky. Running pills was a lucrative business and relatively low risk. He could buy 30 milligram OxyContin for five bucks apiece and sell them back home for a hundred or more each, not a bad markup. His mentor in the business had turned him on to 30 milligram OxyContin and told him to stay away from the larger doses, since they attracted more attention. With 30s, it was easier to stay under the radar.

It was also a simple business. He recruited people off the street to get prescriptions for the medicine, then get them filled. Having a physician that didn't look too close and was willing to not be too critical about prescribing the powerful painkiller also helped. The other key was having a pharmacy that was equally lax. Once that structure was in place, the only thing left to do was find people to get prescriptions, not too difficult in a beach town in Florida.

That's why he wanted to get Wren back. She could be a royal pain in the ass, but she was good at scoring prescriptions and getting them filled. She was attractive enough to get the male doctors and pharmacists to pay more attention to her looks than her medical history.

She was also good in the sack. He was her first, so he'd taught her to do whatever he wanted, and she was a quick study. Peabo had a wide range of tastes, and so far, she hadn't disappointed him.

He knew the girl was in love with him, but it was one-sided. To him, it was business and sex, nothing else. Last trip, he got tired of her yapping and threw her out of the car. Now, he was back for more pills. He needed her, and she was the best operator he had.

He looked over at Shorty, who was born Robbie, passed out in the passenger seat. Robbie had grown up with Peabo and Wren in eastern Kentucky. As kids, Robbie was always the littlest one, earning him the nickname. As a kid, Peabo was bigger and meaner. On more than one occasion, he had protected Shorty from bullies.

In their teens, however, Shorty hit a growth spurt and quickly surpassed the rest of the group. He didn't stop growing until he hit six-four and two hundred seventy-five pounds, but the nickname stuck.

Unfortunately, Shorty's brain didn't keep pace with the rest of his body, but he was loyal and unquestioning. Since Peabo had taken over the business, Shorty had settled into the role of sidekick and enforcer.

Peabo had thought about not bringing Shorty to Tampa this trip. Shorty was using too much of the product, which was trouble, but with Wren out of the picture, he needed him. As a rule, Peabo didn't use the drugs he sold, again, something that was drilled into him by Billy, his mentor. It was hard enough to run the business without getting messed up on the product. He'd seen too many people in his position lose everything that way or end up in jail, and he was determined not to make that mistake.

Shorty was a smooth talker, though, and good at recruiting people to get scripts. Peabo knew he was going to have to cut him loose before long, but figured he'd be good for another trip or two.

His plan was to get back with Wren, then leave Shorty in Kentucky. She was smart, and didn't use the pills that much, preferring booze instead. The only problem with Wren was her mouth. She tended to get a little sassy, but he figured her skills in the sack more than offset the inconvenience. Besides, her mouth was good for other things, he thought, as he remembered the last time they were together.

It was almost dark when they got to the split, where I-75 and I-275 parted ways on the north side of Tampa. Peabo stayed right on 275 and headed south toward Highway 60, which led across the bay to Clearwater.

South of Tampa International Airport, he exited the interstate and took Highway 60 west. Just before continuing towards Clearwater on the Courtney Campbell Causeway, he decided to continue north on Veterans Expressway for a few miles. When he came to the Gunn Highway exit, he slowed to leave the toll road. Shorty stirred and opened his eyes just in time to see them breeze through the SunPass lane at the toll booth.

"You didn't pay the toll," he pointed out to Peabo, as the camera lights flashed in the side rearview mirror.

SunPass was Florida's version of prepaid tolls, and required an electronic device in the vehicle so the system could deduct the proper amount from the owner's account. Without the transponder, cameras took pictures of the license plate, and a citation eventually found its way to the owner.

Peabo shrugged. "Too many cars in line. Besides, what they gonna do? I got Kentucky plates, and I don't think they'll send out the cops to look for us since we didn't pay a fifty-cent toll." He laughed. "I got one of them tinted license plate covers, so their camera can't get a picture of it anyway."

He turned into a combination gas station and convenience store and McDonald's restaurant, pulling up to the gas pumps. "I'll get us something to eat while you fill it up," Peabo said, as he got out of the car and headed toward the building.

In a few minutes, Peabo emerged with a six-pack of beer and a McDonald's sack. Shorty had finished refueling the Escalade and was leaning against the car with arms crossed, a cigarette in his mouth. Peabo started to say something about the wisdom of smoking next to the gas pumps, but shook his head and got into the driver's seat.

They pulled to the back of the parking lot, where Peabo stopped and shut off the car. They sat in the Escalade with the windows down, eating their dinner. It was dark in the corner, at the edge of the light bathing the parking area. Peabo liked to eat in the car here, because he could drink a beer with his dinner, which he couldn't do inside the fast food restaurant.

"Pretty cool, huh? A Micky Ds with beer," Peabo said, taking a swallow from the can. "And open twenty-four hours."

Shorty nodded. "Yeah, but it's a long way to come for a hamburger. Why'd we come over here, there're plenty of Micky Ds in Clearwater? And plenty of places to buy beer." He had obviously figured out they were nowhere near Clearwater.

Peabo was finishing a bite out of his sandwich and about to answer his buddy when they heard a sound coming from behind the eatery, somewhere through the trees. It sounded like a roar.

"What the fuck?" Shorty said, dropping a French fry in his lap. He turned to look out the window toward the trees at the edge of the asphalt.

Peabo laughed, grabbed a couple of French fries and shoved them into his mouth. Still chewing, he told Shorty, "It's probably a lion."

Shorty looked at him like he was from outer space. "Yeah, right. Seriously, what the hell was that?"

"Telling, you, dude, a lion. No shit."

"A lion? Behind a Micky Ds in Tampa? You're full of it!"

Peabo laughed. "I'm serious, man. There's a place back there, like a dog pound kinda place, for all these big ass cats these people have rescued. Lions and tigers and shit."

Shorty studied him, trying to decide if Peabo was pulling his leg. After a few seconds, he realized Peabo was serious.

"How the hell you know about that?" Shorty asked.

"Billy took me there a few times. He loved that place, every time we'd come to Tampa, he'd wannna go there. We'd come to this McDonald's, eat a hamburger, and drink a few brews. He had a thing about lions. Damndest place you ever saw. We should go there sometime."

Shorty shook his head. He had worked for Billy too, but didn't know about his ex-boss's thing for lions.

"Hell, whadda I want to see lions for?" said Shorty, stuffing the remainder of a hamburger in his mouth.

"They're pretty cool. You ever seen one up close?" Peabo asked.

"Where the hell would I see a lion in Harlan, Kentucky?"

Peabo disregarded his question and said, "Maybe we'll come back and go over there one afternoon before we go home."

Shorty shook his head again. "Man, this is one weird town. Lions and stuff in one neighborhood, and in another, one night, you're lying in your bed and a damn sinkhole opens up and swallows your ass." He was referring to the news on the radio as they neared Tampa. Sinkholes were a common hazard in the area. "Then you got hurricanes, plus all these people—I'm ready to go back home."

"We won't be long, soon as we get what we came for, we'll be headed back."

They finished their dinner, and drove over to Clearwater Beach. When they got across the causeway, they pulled into the Clearwater Beach Marina parking lot, across from the beach at Pier 60.

"Time to go fishing," he told Shorty, which meant finding people to make office visits for them tomorrow. He liked working the beach. Although the clinic was in Clearwater, there were more transients in Clearwater Beach, and Billy had taught him the importance of spending as little time as possible near the clinic and pharmacy. Those were danger zones, Billy said, and you had to be careful.

As they walked toward the strip of restaurants, shops and bars, Peabo pulled out his phone and called Wren. No answer.

They always walked past Hulk Hogan's beach shop on Mandalay to pay their respects. The well-known wrestler, a legend in Kentucky, lived in Clearwater Beach, and had a store right on the strip, where various memorabilia from his career was displayed. They stopped and took turns taking pictures of each other next to the statue of Hogan out front. The two grown men looked like a couple of kids, clowning around, draping their arms around the figure and displaying what they perceived as gang signs for the phone camera.

Much later that evening, which turned into early the next morning, they staggered back over to the parking lot at the marina. They had closed down the beach bars and recruited ten people to go to the clinic tomorrow and get scripts, not a bad start. Three or four of them wouldn't show up in the morning at the assigned meeting place, so they'd be lucky to end up with six people.

Peabo would pick them up at the Waffle House and drive them to the clinic, off of Gulf to Bay on the other side of downtown Clearwater. There, Shorty would give them a CD containing an MRI and the money for the office visit. They'd watch them go in to the clinic, not letting them out of their sight. They had been burned before, and handing a street person over a hundred dollars in cash was a shaky proposition. As soon as the person walked out with the script, they would immediately take them to the pharmacy in the next block to get the script filled.

When they handed over the pills, Shorty would check and count them, then give them a hundred bucks and they'd be done. Peabo had learned the hard way to check everything and not trust anyone.

"Where we going?" Shorty asked, as Peabo reclined back in the driver's seat and made no effort to start the car. "I thought we were going to get a room back at that motel where we stayed last time?" referring to the Two Palms Motel a couple of blocks off the main drag.

"It's late, no sense getting a room tonight. We'll get a room tomorrow night. Just me and you, I figured we could sleep here. It seems pretty quiet and it'll do for a few hours."

Shorty grunted, and reclined his seat.

Peabo closed his eyes. What he didn't tell Shorty is that he wanted a room tomorrow night for Wren. Shorty could stay out partying while he and Wren had a little private time to catch up on things.

Chapter 6

Jack drove over to Palm Harbor, just north of Clearwater, to see Dr. Marshall. Tina Marshall, M.D., was in charge of the Palm Harbor Clinic, located on US 19. She had been with Drager Clinic for only two years, coming from Philadelphia, where she did her fellowship at Thomas Jefferson University Hospital.

When he got to the clinic, Jack told the receptionist who he was and that he was there for a meeting. She asked him to have a seat in the waiting room, and she'd let Dr. Marshall know he was there.

He found an empty seat near the outside window, facing the reception area and the door he assumed that led to the exam rooms. The room was smaller than Bayview's, and not as crowded. It had a quieter feel to it, with more subdued furnishings and an older group of patients, at least those here today.

As he sat there, he recalled Dr. Marshall's picture on the Drager Clinic website. It showed short brown hair, a round, almost baby face, and penetrating brown eyes. She was not glamorous, but pleasing to the eye, the kind of person you wanted to get to know better. He wondered what her connection was to Drager.

Connie, Drager's administrative assistant, told him that Drager had met Marshall at a pain management clinical meeting in New York. When asked if there was anything else he should know about Dr. Marshall, all Connie would say was that she was a "go-getter."

In a few minutes, the door next to reception opened and the small, gray-haired lady that greeted him at the desk stood there and called out, "Mr. Davis?" He followed her through the labyrinth of exam rooms to the back part of the building and into a small, sparsely furnished office. "Dr. Marshall will be with you in a minute," she said as she turned to walk out.

He had just started to look around, yet to sit, when he heard someone behind him and turned to see Dr. Marshall coming through the door. She looked harried, and wasn't carrying as much weight as she appeared to be in the website photo. Her hair was a bit longer and her face thinner. She was taller than he realized, and he decided her picture didn't do her justice.

The brown eyes were familiar, well represented by the photograph. They twinkled and bore into him as she extended her hand. "Mr. Davis," she said, "Tina Marshall."

"I'm not old enough to be mister—just Jack. Nice to meet you, Dr. Marshall," he said, taking her hand. It was smooth, and surprisingly warm to the touch.

"Please, call me Tina. Have a seat." She walked behind the desk and sat. "What brings you here today?"

Sitting in his chair, Jack placed the file on the desk, and folded his hands in his lap. He'd crafted a new approach after the Bayview fiasco.

"Just trying to understand the business, I guess you could say. My background is finance and hospitals, so I've been visiting the clinics to get a handle on exactly how this business works. My self-orientation, I guess you could call it," he said, laughing.

She laughed with him, and nodded. "Good to see the orientation package hasn't changed since I started. I had to look up the address for my clinic. When I got here, they had to call Devo to verify I was the new doctor."

Her smile was infectious, and Jack grinned. "Glad to know it's not just me. How did you end up in Tampa?"

"I met Devo at a conference in New York. I was finishing my fellowship at Jefferson Hospital in Philadelphia, wanted to move south, and he offered me a job. You?"

"Long story, but I'll spare you and give you the abridged version. I spent most of my career in the hospital industry, wanted a change, so here I am."

"That's really an abbreviated version. Sometime I'd like to hear the unabridged version." Her brown eyes were so intense it almost made him uncomfortable.

He shifted in his seat. "I've been working on some new management reporting for Dr. Drager and the clinic directors—routine stuff, like volumes, revenue, etc. I'm struggling trying to correlate volumes with revenue."

She grimaced. "*New* management reporting? How about *any* management reporting?" she said, leaning back in her chair. "I'm not surprised about your struggle to correlate volumes with revenues—I used to have these discussions with the CFO at Jefferson. There's a loose relationship, but not as tight as most accounting types would prefer."

Jack smiled and nodded, "I'm finding that out. What I'm trying to do is see if there are any issues at the clinics that might help us develop an early warning system. Make sure we're not missing any revenue or losing any charges, productivity, that sort of thing." He watched her closely for any reaction. "I also want to see if there are any best practices that we could implement at all of the clinics."

Pulling the same one page report out of his portfolio that he gave to Dr. Andrews yesterday, he turned it around and handed it to her.

She took it and studied it for a minute, then looked back up at him.

He leaned forward and pointed to the line representing Dr. Andrews's clinic. "For example, as you can see, the revenue numbers for Bayview Clinic seem to be extraordinarily high given the volumes and number of physicians. Is it because of the type of patients they have? Are they that much more efficient? I don't know."

She looked across the page and raised her eyebrows as she digested the numbers. Jack knew her numbers were four lines down the page and not as high as Andrews's clinic.

She wrinkled her forehead and tilted her head slightly. "Have you talked to Dr. Andrews?"

He hesitated, prepared for the question. "Briefly." He threw his hands aside in a casual gesture. "To be honest, he was—shall we say—less than forthcoming once he found out I had no clinical background." He noticed a thin smile crease Dr. Marshall's lips. "Anyway, I was just using his clinic as an example. Obviously I'm not here to talk about his practice."

"I'm not surprised at his actions," she said. "Winston's very competent, but he can be an insufferable snob sometimes. He thinks that anyone without MD after their name is mentally inferior." She relaxed and looked back at the report, her eyes moving down the page. She looked up at him and asked, "What do my numbers suggest?"

He knew she was testing him, and again, he was expecting her question. He shrugged his shoulders. "At first glance, the revenue numbers appear a little high, based on the volumes. You see fewer patients per physician, but, that's why I'm here, to understand."

She nodded and leaned forward, pointing to the report. "I'd agree. But I think you need to drill down a level or two, and look at what type of procedures and patients are represented here. Maybe it's an efficiency issue, maybe not."

She was sharp, he thought. Not defensive but naturally curious, she was someone he could work with. "That's my next step. You seem to have a good grasp of the financial side of things." He'd been thinking about talking to Drager about getting one of the physicians to work with him, and decided the one sitting across from him would be excellent.

"Maybe you'd be willing to work with me? I need a physician—someone with a clinical background—to work with me," he said. A frown crossed her face, so he held up his hand before she could answer. He continued, "I know you're extremely busy, but this is important, and I promise I won't take much of your time, maybe an hour or so a week."

She put her hand on her chin and looked down at the numbers while she considered his request. She was taking a long time, too long.

He pushed for the close. "This is one of Dr. Drager's top priorities, and I really could use your help on it."

She considered it for a few more seconds, then said, "Let me think about it. I have to admit, though, I'm curious."

He smiled and stood with his hand extended. "Thanks, I'll take that as a positive sign."

She reached up to shake his hand, reflecting his smile.

Jack gathered his things. "I know you've got a busy clinic today, so I'll get out of your hair." He pointed to the report in her hand. "That's yours to keep. Thanks again, Dr. Marsh—Tina. I'll be in touch."

He headed back to the office, disappointed that he didn't get Dr. Marshall's agreement to work with him.

Chapter 7

By the end of the week, Jack had visited six of the clinics on his list. Dr. Andrews was the most defensive and uncooperative, and Dr. Marshall the most accommodating. The other four fell somewhere in between.

True to his word, he did some additional analysis on the top-level numbers for Dr. Marshall. She'd called and agreed to work with him on the management reports.

He'd also done some research on Dr. Winston Andrews, trying to figure out a way to win his support. While he found it hard to believe that Andrews was simply that much more efficient than the other clinics, he needed Andrews on his side.

There was plenty of information available on the good doctor, who traveled in the same orbit as Dr. Drager. They had both come from Rush Hospital in Chicago, which is apparently where they met. Drager was the first to move to the Tampa area, and less than a year later, Andrews joined him. They belonged to many of the same social organizations and made frequent appearances in the local society pages. Andrews lived in an opulent mansion on Davis Islands, a popular in-town neighborhood not far from Bayshore Boulevard, where Drager lived.

Both were the toast of the town, and involved in many charitable causes along with their wives. Jack was starting to appreciate the kind of income the doctors were generating, based on their lifestyles. He'd seen that kind of affluence in the corporate ranks, but didn't realize it was also possible in the realm of the individual physician, too.

He finished getting ready for his monthly meeting with Dr. Drager, put his reports in a manila folder, and walked down the hall to Drager's office. He stopped to chat with Connie, and as soon as Drager's telephone line was clear, she motioned him in.

Drager Clinic's administrative offices were located on the third floor of an office building in the tony, Rocky Point area of Tampa. A clinic operated on the ground floor, where Dr. Drager still carried a full patient load, but he preferred to take his meetings upstairs in the corporate office where there were less distractions. When he was seeing patients, he wanted to give them his undivided attention.

Drager managed his empire from a large corner office with a magnificent view of Tampa Bay. The furniture was minimalist and uber modern, reminding Jack of Winston Andrews's office. The chrome and glass desk, supported by thin, arching columns of stainless steel, stretched out in the middle of the office. To the right was a matching conference table, with mesh back chairs floating over single black posts.

The doctor was at his desk, making a few notes on a single notepad on the desktop. He had thick, wavy, almost black hair, neatly combed to one side. Although he was not very tall, his shoulders were broad and gave him the appearance of someone larger. As always, he was impeccably dressed. Jack had never seen him in anything other than a crisp, white shirt, expensive tie, and cufflinks. His harsh features seemed almost discordant with the tailored clothes. Devo Drager could be called many things, but handsome would not be one of them.

He rose and stepped from behind his desk to greet Jack. "Come in, come in," he said, motioning Jack to sit at the conference table. He asked Jack if he wanted something to drink as he poured himself a glass of water from a pitcher on the middle of the table.

Jack shook his head, and opened the folder, handing Drager a copy of the report he'd prepared for him.

Drager ignored the report for the moment, looked at Jack and said, "We enjoyed dinner the other evening at Bern's. Your wife is a delightful person, and it was nice getting to know her."

Jack shifted in his chair when he thought back to Molly's "forgetting" her underwear. "Yes, it was very nice. Thank you for asking us to join you. We enjoyed getting to know Ivana as well."

"I'm still sorry you and Molly weren't able to make it over to the house. We'll have to reschedule. It must have been quite a shock to find someone in your boat. Thank goodness no one was hurt."

"Yes, we were very fortunate."

Drager nodded. "At least she's in jail, yes?"

"Oh yes, where she belongs," Jack said.

Drager nodded again, an approving smile on his face. "Good. So, how is progress?" he asked, looking at the report.

"Good," Jack answered. "I've met with the directors at the six biggest clinics and prepared drafts of management reports that I think you'll find interesting."

Drager turned his palms up with a quizzical look on his face.

Jack pushed another report across the table. "First, I wanted to discuss this. I'll get right to the point. I think we've got a problem at the Temple Terrace clinic."

Drager looked right at Jack. "What kind of a problem?"

"Dr. Hayek appears to be billing Medicare for procedures not done."

Drager cocked his head. "Appears?"

Jack regretted his choice of words. Devo Drager liked his news straight and without sugar-coating, something Jack was still getting comfortable with after years of working in a political, corporate environment. "Let me rephrase. The report in front of you details over one-hundred-fifty thousand dollars worth of procedures that were billed to Medicare the first four months of this year. The bills were authorized by Dr. Hayek, yet there is nothing in the medical records that substantiates the charges. A few charges with no support could be an oversight. That many constitute fraud."

Drager picked up the report and took a minute to read it. When he finished, he put it down and stared at Jack. "You're sure of these numbers?"

Jack nodded. "Absolutely. I've gone back through them several times, and had an independent review of the medical records."

Dr. Drager reached for his phone and told Connie to have Dr. Hayek come to his office. "I realize he's in

Temple Terrace, but I want him here as soon as he finishes with his last patient this afternoon—no excuses," he said.

He hung up the desk phone and turned back to Jack. "We'll meet with Dr. Hayek later. Now, on to the management reports."

Jack exhaled, wondering about the coming confrontation. He was confident in his report, but was surprised at Drager's summons issued to Dr. Hayek. He continued, "I'm still trying to understand the relationship between volumes and revenue in this business. It seems that they are not as necessarily closely related as I thought they would be."

"How so?"

Drager had a naturally inquisitive mind, and that was one of his favorite retorts. He had a genuine desire to understand things, and was able to get to the core of things quickly, even in areas that he didn't fully understand.

Jack led him through a quick primer of the hospital business, where there was a fairly tight linear correlation between volumes and revenue. He concluded with a comment that Bayview Clinic seemed to be generating much higher revenues than the numbers supported.

Drager nodded and sat back in his chair. "Winston is my most senior partner. He's been here the longest, has cultivated a great relationship with the medical community, and my guess would be that he gets the most difficult and complex cases. I'd wager that his revenue per patient is probably the highest in the entire organization."

Jack nodded in agreement, impressed that Drager had grasped the issue.

"Those patients require more testing and more ... maintenance than most. I would only say this to you, but he is the best. I wish he had been practicing when I needed someone with his skills."

This was quite a compliment, coming from Drager. It further reinforced Jack's understanding that Andrews was the golden boy, and if there was going to be a problem, then Jack better bring his best game.

"That's what puzzles me. As you've pointed out, his revenue per patient is the highest. But, the number of patients per physician is also the highest," Jack said.

A slight frown creased Drager's face. "Interesting," he said. "But the priority is how we can transfer the efficiencies at Bayview Clinic to the other clinics. Imagine the impact on our bottom line if we could accomplish that?"

Jack shifted in his chair, wondering if Drager was trying to tell him something. "I understand, but first, I have to have good information."

Drager waved his hand. "Lynn does a good job with the accounting. I didn't hire you to do accounting. Just make the other clinics work as effectively as Winston's."

Lynn was the corporate controller, who had been with Drager from the beginning. Jack started to disagree with Drager's assessment about her, but decided that wouldn't be wise.

"I'm still trying to get a handle on things, so it's a little early to draw any concrete conclusions. I've asked Dr. Marshall to work with me on refining these reports. Palm Harbor exhibits some of the same characteristics, but since it's significantly smaller, I thought she might be in a better position to have time to work with me."

Drager nodded. "Tina's very capable. She agreed?"

Jack laughed. "Well, she was a little reluctant at first, but she called later and said she'd work with me."

"Good, good. What else?"

"What I consider typical things—centralized purchasing, computerizing inventory. I should have some numbers for you by the end of next month."

"I'm pleased so far, Jack. I hope you are. Just don't lose sight of the primary goal—making the organization more efficient. That's your first priority."

Jack nodded. "I understand."

"Let me know if you need anything. There are probably some on the team that aren't crazy about more scrutiny, so don't hesitate to pull me in if you need." Drager moved the reports to the corner of the table, signifying the meeting was over. "I'll have Connie call you as soon as Dr. Hayek arrives."

Jack went back down to his office, and continued to work on the management reporting system. He lost track of time, and was surprised when his phone rang. It was Connie, and Dr. Hayek was upstairs.

Jack went back to Drager's office, where he saw Dr. Hayek sitting next to Connie's desk, a serious look on his face. Dr. Samir Hayek, the partner in charge of the Temple Terrace clinic, was a small man, with delicate features, olive skin, and jet black hair. He looked down at the floor, his hands together at his waist. When Jack spoke, he lifted his head and shook Jack's hand with a weak grip before rising. Connie ushered them both into Drager's office, closing the door behind her when she walked out.

Drager sat behind his desk, not rising or moving to the conference table. Jack had never known him to take a meeting this way. He motioned to the two chairs sitting in front of his desk. He handed a copy of a document to both Dr. Hayek and to Jack. When Jack looked at it, he recognized it as a copy of the report he'd given Drager earlier on the Temple Terrace billing discrepancy.

Jack watched Dr. Hayek's face flush as he finished reading the report. "I can explain," Hayek said, but Drager's hand went up to stop him.

"Samir, I have only one question," Drager said. "Is it true?"

"There may be possibly billing—"

Drager slammed his hand on the desk. "Stop! I do not wish to hear any lies! It is a simple question, Samir, and requires a simple answer—yes or no."

"I did not think—"

Drager's hand slammed on the desk again, causing Hayek and Jack to jump. He leaned across the desk and his eyes glared at the Lebanese doctor in front of him, reducing him to nothing. "You disgrace me and my organization with your actions. Your services are no longer needed. Someone will escort you back to the clinic to pick up your personal things." With a wave of his hand, Drager dismissed him.

Dr. Hayek stood and said, his voice quivering, "Devo, I—"

Drager shook his head, waved his hand once again, and turned to Jack, ignoring the doctor. Hayek dropped his head, turned, and walked out of Drager's office, humiliated.

Jack was speechless. He'd assumed Drager had summoned Hayek to his office to discuss the allegations, maybe discipline him, slap his hand, but this? In all of his days working for big corporations he'd never seen such a brute display of force. A vein in Drager's temple pulsed with anger, and his face was flushed.

Almost a full minute of silence passed before Drager spoke. When he did, his demeanor was a forced calm and measured. "That was difficult, and I'm sorry you had to witness my lack of control." He paused and took a breath. "I hired Samir five years ago. He was like a son to me."

Drager paused, looked out the window, then returned his gaze to Jack. "That was hard, but I have no tolerance for cheating. It threatens our entire organization, and it must be dealt with swiftly and with strength. There is no other way. I hope you understand."

Jack was still in shock when he got home that evening. When Molly asked how his day went, he described in detail the meetings with Drager and the dismissal of Hayek.

"I had no idea he was going to fire him on the spot," Jack said.

Molly frowned. "Well, your report was true, right? I mean, he did commit fraud."

Jack nodded. "I guess I didn't see Drager taking such quick and drastic action. I figured there'd be the usual round-and-round, eventually resulting in a hand-slap. Drager reduced the poor man to tears, in front of me."

"You said when you came to work with him, you thought he was a man of principle, right? Sounds like he walks the walk."

"I'm not complaining, okay? Hayek screwed up. What he did was wrong, and it could have cost us big time. I just didn't think he'd get the ax. Drager wouldn't even give him a chance to explain."

"Maybe Drager wanted you to see how serious he is about people not following the rules?"

He thought about it. *Or maybe Drager wanted him to witness how he handled people that crossed him.* Either way, it was disturbing, and a side of Devo Drager that Jack hadn't seen before. And one that he didn't want to see again.

Chapter 8

Bird's stomach rumbled as he sat in the back of the Escalade. He was squeezed in between a smelly, fatass named Wes and an older woman named Megan. He'd hoped that the driver, known as Boss, would buy them something to eat before they left the Waffle House, but that hadn't happened.

They were on their way to the clinic for their exam and prescriptions, which they'd take to the pharmacy down the street to fill. Bird, whose real name was Keith, had worked with Boss for several months doing this, so the routine was familiar by now. Bird's friend, a small black guy named Ronnie, had gotten him the gig.

Shorty, Boss's right-hand man, was sitting up front and turned around explaining things to Wes and Meg, who were newbies. The other three, seated in the rearmost seat, were people that Bird recognized from the street and previous trips, so they knew the drill.

Shorty had handed each of them a CD in a plastic case with a label marked Bayview Clinic Diagnostic Center, telling them that their MRI was on the CD should anyone ask and they were to give it only to the doctor when they saw him, no one else. They were also cautioned not to open the case.

Bird knew that underneath the CD was a hundred-dollar bill, which he figured was for the doctor's pocket. Last month, he had stopped in the restroom in the clinic and opened the CD case, curious as to why they had been told not to open it. He wondered what would happen if he took the money, and mentioned it later to Ronnie. Ronnie, who'd worked for Boss more than a year, told Bird that he took the money a couple of times, and nobody said anything. Today, Bird was going to try it. He figured he needed the money more than the doctor.

Shorty gave them the code word, which was Atlanta. There was a different code word each trip. He'd wondered about that, and figured the code word was to keep them from going back to the doctor on their own and getting a prescription.

Bird lived on the street in Clearwater. He was smart and had even gone to college in Tampa for a few years until the voices in his head got too loud and interfered with classes. He quit his job and dropped out of school, moving across the bay to Clearwater and living on the street.

In Clearwater, he'd met a couple of Scientologists and realized they were aliens from another planet trying to take over Earth. The voices told him it was his mission to spy on them and figure out their plan, so he stayed in Clearwater, close to their mother ship downtown. Sometimes, though, he got a little confused, and couldn't remember who he was supposed to tell.

They pulled into the clinic parking lot and parked in a far corner. So as not to draw too much attention to them,

Shorty staggered their leaving a few minutes apart. Wes went first, so Bird was next to go.

When it was his turn, he walked into the clinic, clutching the CD, signed in at the desk and sat down. He picked up the six-month old Sports Illustrated magazine and thumbed through the well-worn pages without interest, but it gave him something to do. The waiting room was full, and names were called on a frequent basis, the person disappearing through the door leading to the exam rooms.

After a few minutes, he heard his name called and he walked over to the desk, where the heavy-set black lady behind the glass had slid it to the side to talk to him.

"Mr. Walker?" she asked, verifying the name on the list in front of her.

"Yes ma'am."

"You're back for your monthly checkup, I see," she said, looking down at the paperwork in front of her. "Has anything changed since last month?"

He knew she was not referring to his condition, but to his payment ability. "No, ma'am."

She lowered her voice a tad. "It says here that you are still on Medicaid."

He nodded. Boss had talked some of the regulars into applying for Medicaid, and they got paid extra, since Doc could collect from the state and from Boss.

"We need to go ahead and get your co-payment of twenty dollars. How will you be paying today?" she said.

He started to answer *my Gold American Express card,* but just handed her the twenty dollar bill that Shorty had given him in the car. She took the money, entered the information in the computer, and printed out a receipt, which she handed to him. "Just have a seat, we'll call you in a few minutes," she said, closing the glass door.

Bird walked back to the same seat and picked up the magazine, still open to the page he left.

In a few minutes, he heard his name called again. He looked up to see a young, Asian woman in a flowery print top, standing at the open door to the back of the office. He put the magazine down and walked over to her.

"Good morning, Mr. Walker," she said with a slight accent.

"Morning," he said.

She led him down the hall, stopping at the scales to get his weight, and then into an exam room, where she indicated for him to sit on the table. She took his blood pressure and temperature, entered it on her clipboard and asked him how he'd been doing.

"Okay, still having back pain." He held up the CD. "I got an MRI like doc asked, and brought it with me."

She reached for it, but he pulled it back out of her grasp. "They told me to give it to the doctor."

She opened her mouth to protest, then simply nodded and said, "He'll be with you in a minute." She turned and walked out, closing the door behind her.

Bird studied the charts on the wall, outlining the heart, the human body, and one listing the signs of a heart attack. He heard footsteps outside the door, the shuffling of the paper chart, and then the sound of the door opening.

The doctor, a tall, gray-haired man in a white lab coat, walked in with a folder in his hands, the same nurse trailing behind him. "Mr. Walker. How are you, today?"

"About the same," Bird replied, handing him the CD.

"Your MRI?"

Bird nodded.

The doctor looked over the notes and scribbled a few comments. "Pull your shirt out, please, I need to check your lower back."

Bird complied, and the doctor moved around behind him, poking and prodding. Bird stiffened, not because it hurt, but because he was playing the game.

"Still some pain, I see?" the doctor asked, now back in front, writing again.

Bird nodded.

"Have you been anywhere since the last exam?"

This was the phrase that Bird was expected to answer with the code of the month. "Atlanta," he said.

The doctor nodded, tore off a page on the prescription pad he produced out of his pocket, scribbled something and signed it, handing it to Bird. "I'm refilling your prescription for OxyContin for another month. Let's see how it does, and I'll see you in thirty days. No strenuous activity or heavy lifting." He turned and was gone. The entire exam took less than two minutes.

Bird walked back to the car with his prescription in hand and piled into the back seat, where Wes was already sitting. A few minutes later, Megan came out and as soon as the others returned, Boss started the car, and drove down the street to the pharmacy, a small, but well-kept building a block away from the clinic. This time, he parked near the front door so he had a clear view of the entrance.

They repeated the same routine as at the clinic. One person left the car at a time, followed five or ten minutes later by the next. This time, Shorty handed them each a hundred-dollar bill and a twenty, but only as they were ready to leave the car. Bird knew this was to pay for the prescription, which was always cash.

Walking back to the car, he saw Wes walking the other direction, his work for the day over. When Bird got back to the car, he handed the pill bottle over to Shorty, who opened it and verified the contents. Once Shorty was satisfied everything was accounted for, he turned and gave him five twenties. Taking the money, he got out and walked away, noticing Megan coming out the front door of the pharmacy.

Business concluded for the day, Peabo turned to Shorty. "I'm ready for a beer." The sun was getting low as they passed through downtown Clearwater, headed to the beach. "Good day, today."

Shorty nodded. "I'm hungry."

Shorty was always hungry. Damn guy could put away some food, Peabo thought. His phone rang. He was hoping it was Wren, but scowled when he looked at the caller-ID. "Yeah," he answered. He listened for a few minutes, then asked, "Which one was it?

"Walker," he repeated. "I'll take care of it."

He pressed End and turned to Shorty. "Walker—that's Bird, right?"

Shorty nodded. "Yeah, why?"

"Scrawny bastard stole doc's Franklin," he answered. He turned the SUV around and headed back toward the pharmacy.

Bird walked down the busy street, only a few blocks from the pharmacy. He'd forgotten about the hundred-dollar bill he'd stuffed into his pocket at the clinic. He sipped on a Red Bull and took a bite of a Slim Jim he'd just bought at the convenience store.

It was getting dark. Traffic was heavy, but it didn't slow him down. He was shuffling along, minding his own business, when someone grabbed his arm. Startled, he looked up into the piercing eyes of an angry Shorty.

"Hey, Bird," Shorty said.

The scrawny man tried to shake his arm loose, but Shorty was too strong. Bird looked over the big man's shoulder and saw Boss a few steps behind. As scary as Shorty was physically, Boss was more frightening. There was something about his eyes. Even in the light of day, they were as dark as a moonless night, with no trace of warmth or emotion. If the eyes were truly the windows to the soul, then Boss was missing that human element.

Shorty guided Bird toward the corner. "C'mon, we'll give you a ride."

"No, that's okay. I can walk," Bird said in a weak voice. The big man holding his arm didn't turn loose.

"You're riding," Shorty said.

They turned the corner, and he saw the black Escalade parked up ahead on the deserted side street. This was not good. The last thing he wanted to do was go for a ride with Boss and Shorty.

When they got to the vehicle, Shorty opened the rear door and pushed Bird into the back seat. The big guy got in, sat next to him, and closed the door. He tried to scoot over, but Shorty grabbed his arm, keeping him close.

"I think you must have lost something in the clinic," Boss said from the front seat, as he started the SUV and pulled away from the curb.

"Empty your pockets," Shorty said.

Bird hesitated, trying to figure out how to get out of his predicament. His drug-addled brain still wasn't sure what they wanted. He reached into his right pocket and pulled out what remained of the five twenties he'd earned from the morning's work and handed it to Shorty. Bird looked up at him, hoping that was it, and for a second, thought everything was fine. Then, before he knew it, the big man had punched him in the stomach with a strong, meaty fist.

He doubled over in pain and gasped for breath.

"I ain't asking again," Shorty said.

It was a few minutes before he could respond. He straightened up the best he could, his gut still hurting, and stuck his hand in the left pocket of his tattered shorts. He felt something, and pulled out the forgotten hundred-dollar bill, more surprised than his hosts.

Shorty snatched it out of his hand. "Well, looky here," he said, holding up the crinkled bill.

Bird could see Boss's eyes in the rearview mirror, and he knew he was in trouble. "I didn't—I forgot—"

"Shut up. You fucked up, Bird," Shorty said, tucking the bill into his pocket. "You can steal from anybody but the boss. You *never* steal from the boss."

The car stopped, and Bird noticed they'd pulled into the marina parking lot at the beach. It was dark now, and there were no other cars nearby. He saw a light pole next to them, but the streetlight was dark over their heads.

"We're going for a little walk. Don't even think about trying to run. It'll just make it worse," Shorty told him.

Bird was scared now. He knew he'd screwed up, and wondered what they were going to do. Whatever it was, it wasn't going to be good. "Look," he pleaded. "I know I messed up. It won't happen again, okay. I promise."

"You got that right—it won't happen again," Boss said as they got out of the Cadillac.

They walked down the sidewalk toward the bay, Boss on one side and Shorty close on the other. Bird continued to babble, but the other two didn't say a word. He realized they were walking down to the place where the sidewalk went under the causeway.

He knew the spot well—it was a good place to panhandle. It was a little spooky, which caused the tourists to be more generous so as to insure safe passage. Now it was late, and no one else was anywhere near. When they got underneath the bridge, they stopped next to the railing by the water. He could hear the bridge rumbling as vehicles passed overhead.

He started to say something, but before he could speak, Shorty had grabbed his ankles and was holding him upside down. Next thing he knew, the big, powerful man had swung him over the rail and his head was inches from the salty smell of the bay. He could feel the warm water lap up against his head, and he could see Boss standing upside down.

"You don't ever steal from me, you hear?" Boss said. "Anybody else stealing from me?"

Bird grunted, but it was hard to speak hanging upside down. Suddenly, he was being lowered into the water, so he gulped as much air as he could. He struggled, trying to pull his face out of the water, but the arms that gripped him lowered him even further. Just as he was about to empty his lungs, he was snatched out of the water.

Choking, and gasping for breath, he realized he'd pissed himself and was shaking uncontrollably.

Boss asked again, "Anyone else stealing?"

"Ronnie," he sputtered, still coughing. "That's the only one I know."

"Make sure he understands," Boss said, as Shorty dropped him once more into the water. This time he didn't have a chance to get a full breath, and the little air he had in his lungs quickly gave out. He inhaled a mouthful of briny water and thought he was going to drown.

Shorty pulled him out again. Bird was sputtering and gagging. Shorty dropped him on the sidewalk, where he was coughing up water. He curled up in a fetal position, trying to catch his breath.

Boss walked over and kicked him in the gut. "Next time, you stay in the water. Don't forget it." The two men turned and walked away, leaving him lying there alone and shaking, whimpering like a baby.

Chapter 9

Thursday afternoon, Molly was sitting out in the cockpit of *Left Behind*, reading. Jack was working late and she was off today. She glanced up from her book and saw Wren, the girl that broke into their boat, walking down the dock toward her.

She stopped when she got there, as if unsure of herself.

Molly marked her book and put it down beside her. She'd expected Wren to come back for her things. Molly had talked to Kim, the head of social services at the hospital, before she called the district attorney's office.

"How did you get through the gate?" Molly asked.

Wren shrugged. "I remembered the code from before."

"I guess you're here for your things?"

"You kept them?"

"How are you doing?"

The girl shrugged again. "Better, now. I got out of jail today. They told me you dropped the charges. Why?"

"How was it?" Molly asked, ignoring the question.

"Okay. At least I had meals and a place to sleep. Noisy, though."

Molly nodded. "Take off your shoes and come aboard. I'll go below and get your stuff. Would you like something to drink?"

Wren slipped her sandals off and stepped onto the boat. "I guess."

"Lemonade okay?"

Wren nodded and sat, taking in the view from the cockpit of the thirty-eight foot sailboat.

Molly went below, grabbed the sleeping bag from the aft cabin, and got two bottles of lemonade from the small refrigerator. When she came out topside, she handed the bundle and one bottle to Wren, then sat opposite her.

Wren studied the cord tying the sleeping bag, then looked up at Molly. "You didn't open it."

Molly shook her head. "No, it was your personal stuff. You asked me to keep it for you, and that's what I did."

The girl looked down at her feet. "Thanks for getting me out." She looked up at Molly. "You still haven't told me why you did it?"

Molly took a sip of her lemonade and looked at Wren. Pitiful was the word that came to mind. The skinny girl looked defeated and hopeless and scared of what the price of freedom was going to be. In Wren's world, everything had a price, and she was waiting for Molly to tell her what her get-out-of-jail card was going to cost. Molly wondered what kind of future she had.

"Let's just say that I still remember where I came from. No strings, just don't ever steal from me again."

Wren nodded. "That was nice of you and your husband."

Molly gazed out across the bay. She didn't mention that Jack didn't know. She'd have to deal with him later.

"What are you going to do?" Molly asked, turning her attention back to Wren.

"I dunno, find a job, I guess."

"Here? Or going back to Kentucky?"

She shrugged. "No jobs back home. Better chance of finding work down here. Besides, I got no way to get back."

"What kind of job? What kind of work have you done?"

"Waitress. Dancing—that pays better, but I don't like doing it."

Molly started to ask her what kind of dancing, but figured it out before she opened her mouth.

"How old are you, Wren?"

The girl's blue eyes were sad. "Nineteen. I turned nineteen while I was in jail."

A great way to celebrate your nineteenth birthday, Molly thought. This girl was growing up too fast and headed down the wrong path.

"Did you finish high school?" Molly asked.

"Nah. I dropped out to come to Florida with Peabo."

"Your boyfriend? You talked to him?"

"Not yet. I called him when I got out. Not sure where he is."

Molly's heart was breaking. "Where are you going to stay? You can't stay in the park."

"They gave me the address of a shelter. Figured I'd check it out, see if I can stay there."

Kim had given Molly the name of a shelter in Clearwater, which she had passed on to the DA's office. Good, at least she had a safe place to stay, Molly thought. "You have any money?"

Wren shrugged. "A little, not much."

Molly grabbed her wallet. The least she could do was to give the girl some money. She opened it, and thumbed through the bills. Four twenties, a five, and a couple of ones. She pulled out the four twenties and handed them to Wren.

She looked at it and said, "What's that for?"

Molly shook the money and said, "Just take it."

The girl hesitated, then reached out and took the cash. "Thanks."

"Where is the shelter?" Molly asked.

Wren pulled a card out of her pocket and handed it to Molly.

Molly looked at it, recognizing the name. It was the address for the Episcopal shelter in downtown Clearwater.

"Where are you going to look for a job?" she asked Wren.

"Dunno. Figure that out in the morning."

"They have any contacts at the shelter? People you could talk to about work?"

Wren shrugged. "Not sure. I'll find something."

Molly pictured the young girl seated next to her, dancing on a stage and taking her clothes off in front of a bunch of gawking strangers. *God only knows where would that lead to,* she thought. She took one of her business cards out of her purse and wrote her cell phone number on the back of it. She handed it to Wren and said, "Will you call me and let me know when you find something?"

Wren studied the card, then looked up at Molly. "You a nurse?"

Molly nodded. "I work at the hospital in Clearwater."

"What's CCU?"

"Coronary Care Unit, people with heart problems. That's the type of nursing I do."

Wren absorbed the information and got up to leave. "Guess I better be going."

"How are you getting to the shelter? That's a good ways from here," Molly said.

"Walk."

Molly shook her head and got her keys. "I'll drive you. It's too far to walk, especially this time of day."

"You don't have to do that."

"I know, but I want to. We can stop and get something to eat on the way, okay?"

Later that evening, after Jack got home, he and Molly were sitting out under the bimini having a glass of wine.

"Wren came by today. She's out of jail, and came by to get her things," Molly said.

"Out of jail?" He looked at Molly, then shook his head once each direction. "Tell me you didn't?"

She ignored his question. "She looked good. I think the time in jail helped."

"You dropped the charges, didn't you?" He got his answer in Molly's expression.

"Keeping her in jail is doing no good," she said.

"Damn, Molly," Jack huffed. "She breaks into our boat, steals our stuff, and you give her a pass?"

"What's your problem? We got everything back. There was no harm." Her voice was defensive and up a notch. "I told you I'd check at the hospital for an agency to help her, and you agreed."

He drained his glass and stood. "Checking on help for her is one thing. Letting her out of jail is another. She's a thief and a liar. And you turned her loose." He stepped off the boat and onto the dock, walking toward the shore. "I'm going for a walk."

Molly followed after him, not willing to let it rest. "She wants to find a job, Jack. She's staying at the Episcopal shelter in Clearwater. I drove her over there."

Jack kept walking and didn't say anything, Molly keeping step next to him.

"I worry about her, Jack. What chance does she have? She's young, naïve, and has no education. Know what she said when I asked her what kind of work she'd done?"

He shook his head, but he knew Molly wasn't done.

"Waitressing and dancing. You know what kind of dancing I'm talking about—the kind that doesn't involve clothes. She said the money was good, but she didn't like doing it. She's somebody's kid, Jack."

He stopped and shot back, "But not yours or mine, Molly." He shook his head. "That's why I never want kids. She's not our problem."

He started walking again, and they continued for a few minutes, not saying anything. Jack didn't like the way the conversation was headed. He knew Molly well enough to know she was engaged and the wheels were turning.

"I'm going to check at the hospital tomorrow. See if we have anything there she could do. Maybe housekeeping or in dietary," she said.

"That's great. Get her a job where you work. Why not?" he said.

This time Molly jumped in front of Jack, stopping his progress. Her hands were on her hips. "You're being a selfish asshole. I just want to help her. I don't want to see her go back to dancing or whatever else she's involved in. She's a teenager, Jack, a kid without a future. I'm not talking about adopting her, just helping her get on her feet and on the right track. If you can't see that, then I feel sorry for you."

She stormed off, back toward the boat, and he let her go. He headed toward the beach, needing to cool down. He felt sorry for the girl, but he was afraid she would take advantage of Molly's kindness. His first priority was to protect Molly.

Chapter 10

There was still a chill in the air between Jack and Molly since their argument last night. When he'd gotten back to the boat, Molly was in bed and the lights were out. She was on her side of the berth, her back toward his usual spot. He knew she wasn't asleep, but he didn't want to risk rekindling the embers of an argument. He'd climbed in bed and turned facing the other direction, not even saying goodnight, a rarity for them. Neither of them had mentioned it this morning.

It was Friday afternoon. A thunderstorm was passing through, so they were sitting in the cabin of the boat, where Jack was at his laptop, working on a presentation. Molly was across from him, paying bills on her laptop. An odd arrangement, considering Jack's background, but he got enough of financial management at work and was content to let Molly handle their personal finances.

"Are you about done?" she asked, peering over the screen on her laptop.

He glanced at the clock on the bulkhead. "Give me five minutes to finish this section, and I'll close up shop."

When the thunderstorm passed, he saw Molly open a bottle of wine and go up on deck. He finished what he was working on and a few minutes later joined Molly up on deck under the bimini. She had opened a bottle of Sauvignon Blanc, and had put out some cheese and crackers. He had put on some Jimmy Buffett before emerging, and Gypsies in the Palace was playing in the background.

He felt bad about their argument the night before, and wanted to make amends. "I'm sorry about last night. I just don't want to see you hurt."

She moved closer to him, and put her hand on his. "I know, but I have to help her if I can. She reminds me of a time in my life.

"She had an interview today with Chris in housekeeping. I explained her situation, and he understood. He talked to her and offered her a job. She starts next Monday." She held up her right hand. "That's it. It's up to her, now."

He nodded, accepting the olive branch. "Is she still at the shelter?"

"Yes, she's still there. Vicki said they'd help her find a place once she got a job, so hopefully that will happen soon." She squeezed his hand. "I'm sorry, too. I'm just trying to help."

"I know, and I know you mean well. Just be careful."

He took a sip of wine and raised his glass. "You ever get tired of living on the boat?" he asked, changing the subject.

Molly looked at him and wrinkled her nose. "Are you kidding? I love it! Don't tell me you're getting tired of it?"

He laughed and shook his head, glad to have the chill thawed. "No, just wondering about you. It is different, and you've never lived on a boat before."

"Have you heard me complain? I'll let you know if it gets old, but I wouldn't worry about that happening anytime soon."

They essentially had a free place to live. The boat and a slip in Fort Myers had been bequeathed to them by a friend there who had passed away unexpectedly. Jack rented the slip out in Fort Myers, which paid for the slip here in Clearwater, so their housing expenses were minimal. Since both of them were working, they needed two cars, but other than that, their monthly expenses were modest.

They talked about going sailing this weekend or next. They hadn't been out in several months, and it would be good to get out on the boat. Jack nodded west toward the Gulf and said, "We need to go down to Egmont one weekend soon."

Egmont Key, about five hours sail, was a small island at the mouth of Tampa Bay and a state park. It was one of their favorite places to go for a weekend trip.

Molly smiled. "That would be nice. Maybe we could go next weekend?"

He laughed. "Sure. I'm ready for a little sailing trip."

She came over and sat in his lap, putting her arms around his neck. "What would you think about asking Wren to come along?"

After Molly dropped her off at the shelter, Wren went to her room. Her cell phone rang, and it was Peabo. She started not to answer, but she was bored.

"Hello," she said, without much enthusiasm.

"Hey, baby. Whatcha doing?"

"Nothing."

"We can fix that. Why don't I come pick you up? We can get something to eat, come out to the beach, do something."

"I'm kinda tired. Maybe tomorrow."

"What's the matter?"

"What's the matter is I just got out of jail, asshole. And I'm staying in a shelter for homeless girls."

"Jail?"

She explained that after he kicked her out, she got caught breaking into a boat.

"How'd you get caught?"

She shook her head and ended the call. He didn't give a flip that she'd been forced to steal for food money. He was more concerned about the crime.

In a few minutes, he called back. "Look, baby. I'm sorry, okay? Let me come get you. I'll make it up to you, I promise."

She agreed to meet him the next day.

Monday morning, Wren walked into Ms. Vicki's office. Ms. Vicki was the director of the shelter.

Yesterday, Peabo had taken her to the beach, trying to make nice. He'd been good to her, doing whatever she asked and not complaining about anything. She'd had a good time and forgiven him for leaving her. He'd also asked Wren to go to Kentucky with him on Tuesday.

"Vicki?" Wren asked.

The director motioned for Wren to come into her office.

"I was wondering if I could take a few days to go to Kentucky. My mama called, and she's not doing so good.

I thought it'd be a good chance to go see her before I start work."

Vicki looked at her. "How're you planning on getting there?"

"I got enough money for a bus ticket. I already checked. They have a bus that leaves at 5:15 tomorrow afternoon and gets in at 1:30 the next day."

That much was true. She'd checked, and Greyhound had service from Tampa to London, Kentucky. If Vicki asked, she'd say a friend from Harlan was going to pick her up in London. It was only an hour and a half from Harlan.

"When are you planning on coming back?"

"I'll be back Saturday. I want to get back in time enough to get situated before my first day at work."

"That's a lot of riding for a short visit."

"Yes, ma'am. I know, but I really want to see my mama. And once I start work, I probably won't be able to go up there for a while."

Ms. Vicki pondered her request for a few seconds, then said, "Write down the details for me. And call me when you arrive."

She smiled, and said, "Thanks, Ms. Vicki." She turned to leave.

"Wren?"

She stopped in the middle of the doorway, and turned around. "Yes?"

"How are you getting to the bus station?"

"The bus station?" She was confused, then realized Vicki was talking about the station in Tampa.

Ms. Vicki nodded, "The bus station is over in downtown Tampa. That's a good ways from here."

She'd been so busy worrying about the other details, she hadn't thought about that. Finally, she said, "My friend, Molly. The one I told you about who lives on a sailboat in Clearwater Beach? She said she'd take me."

Vicki smiled and nodded. "Okay."

She went back to her room, and wrote down the times and Mama's address in Harlan, along with the phone number just in case. She was a little nervous about giving Molly's name to Ms. Vicki, but figured she wouldn't know how to get in touch with her anyway.

The next morning, she went in to give Ms. Vicki the sheet of paper with the information on it.

"What time is Molly picking you up?" Ms. Vicki asked.

"Around three," Wren said.

"Good. I'd like to meet her."

Wren's mouth fell open. She didn't know what to say. Peabo was picking her up a block from the shelter, and Molly didn't know anything about this.

"Wren?" Ms. Vicki asked. "Everything okay?"

She nodded. "Sure. I just remembered I forgot to pack something."

She got back to her room and sat on her bed. *Now, what was she going to do?* She supposed she could call Molly and ask her to drive her to the Greyhound station. Peabo could pick her up there. But that would mean lying to Molly, and she really didn't want to do that.

At lunch, Wren was getting ready to call Molly and ask her if she'd take her over to the bus station. She'd racked her brain trying to think of alternatives, but had come up with no better options.

"Wren?"

It was Ms. Vicki. *What now?* "Yes, ma'am?"

"I've got to go over to Tampa at two for a meeting. If you want, I can drop you off at the bus station."

Wren was glad she didn't have to lie to Molly. Peabo wasn't too happy about having to go by the bus station to pick her up, but it wasn't too far out of his way.

It was eleven and a half hours of driving, not counting stops. Most of it was boring interstate, except going around Atlanta. Peabo always drove slower going to Kentucky than he did coming to Florida. He was more careful with a carload of pills in the back. Too many people got stopped on I-75, driving too fast or with a headlight out, so he always stayed within five miles-an-hour of the speed limit.

They got to Knoxville around ten that night. They'd lost a little time in Atlanta, which was not unusual, but other than that, they'd made good time.

In Knoxville, they stopped for a break at a truck stop at their exit off I-75. It was mostly two-lane roads the rest of the way to Harlan.

An hour out of Knoxville, they had just turned north on US25E in Tazewell, Tennessee, when they came around a curve and saw flashing blue lights ahead. Traffic was stopped.

"Shit," Peabo said. He was driving and reached over to wake up Shorty, asleep in the front passenger seat. Wren was dozing in the back seat, but sat up when she heard Peabo swear.

They had dumped the empty beer cans at the truck stop, and Shorty had been sleeping since. But a roadblock was not good. And on this stretch of highway, Wren knew there was no other route, other than to turn around and go back the way they'd come.

"Make sure there ain't nothing showing," he said to Wren.

She turned on the light and looked around the back of the SUV. A few wrappers, her pillow and a blanket were in the seat next to her. She turned and peeked over the seat. The duffel bag full of pills seemed to glow, but she knew that was her imagination.

"What's going on up there?" Wren asked. She was nervous.

Peabo shook his head. "Can't tell. Looks like a roadblock. License check or something. Don't see anything other than cops."

They inched closer. Peabo reminded them to stay calm, that they had nothing to worry about. Wren knew his license and registration were in order, so there shouldn't be a problem. Still, she knew they were trapped. If the cops searched their vehicle, they would go to jail for a long time.

A few minutes later, they got closer to the scene. Peabo had let his window down and got his license and papers ready. A state trooper was standing in the middle of the road, checking the drivers ahead. Two cars in front of them, a pickup was motioned to pull over to the right, off the road, where other officers were waiting.

"Be cool," Peabo said.

"License and registration, please," the trooper asked as Peabo pulled up and stopped.

Peabo handed him the requested documents. The trooper glanced inside, then walked behind the vehicle.

Wren held her breath, as she knew he was checking the license plate.

He walked back up to the window and handed Peabo the documents. "Have a nice evening," he said, as he stepped back and waited on the next vehicle.

An hour later, they crossed Martins Fork on US421 as they cruised into Harlan. It was quiet, and nothing much had changed. Peabo turned left, and a mile outside of town, he turned onto a narrow dirt road, flanked by tall trees on each side. They went around a sharp curve, and stopped in front of a metal gate blocking the road. Shorty got out and unlocked it, holding it open while Peabo drove through. Once through, Peabo stopped again, waiting for Shorty, who had locked the gate behind them.

A quarter of mile later, they reached a clearing with a house trailer on it. Peabo had a nice double-wide out there on fifteen wooded acres of land. He paid a local boy to keep an eye on the place while he was away. They parked under a carport in front, got their stuff out and went inside.

The place smelled musty and reeked of cigarette and marijuana smoke. Shorty threw the duffel bag containing the pills down on the kitchen floor. "I'm crashing," he said, heading to his bedroom on the right side of the house. "See ya'll in the morning."

Peabo and Wren went left to the master suite. She was tired, and figured Peabo was, too. She went to the bathroom and got ready for bed. As soon as she finished, Peabo went in.

She threw back the covers, climbed into bed, and laid her head on the pillow. Peabo climbed in beside her, reached over and pulled her close. She realized he was naked, which is how he usually slept, and for a moment, she was afraid he wanted to fool around. Before long, though, he was snoring and she drifted off to sleep.

The next morning at daylight, she opened her eyes and stretched. Peabo was still asleep, snoring, and lying on his side of the bed. Trying not to disturb him, she got up and padded out to the kitchen.

There was no sign of Shorty, and she figured he was also asleep. She fixed a pot of coffee, and when it was done, poured a cup, and took it out on the screened porch behind the house. There was a deer grazing in the yard. She looked up when she heard Wren, but once she realized there was no threat, she went back to eating. Wren sat there in silence, drinking her coffee and watching the deer have breakfast.

It was nice to be back in the hills of Kentucky, but she missed the ocean and the salt air. Harlan was a sleepy little town, and she missed the hustle and bustle of the Tampa area.

She knew Peabo and Shorty would be heading out after breakfast to start peddling the pills. It didn't usually take him long to sell everything. He'd built up a good business, and she knew his customers would be waiting.

After they left, she took a shower and went over to her mother's. Peabo had an old pickup truck that he usually drove around Harlan, so as not to attract too much attention, so she got to drive the Escalade. She pulled into the trailer park where her mother lived, passing mostly older, single-wide trailers.

Peabo had offered to buy Mama a new double-wide, but she refused, insisting on staying in the ratty old trailer she'd lived in for years. Wren tried to talk her into it, but she'd said she didn't want to take the devil's money. Wren had asked her what she meant, and Mama had just looked her in the eyes and shook her head.

She pulled up in front of the trailer. There were flowers planted in front of the porch, and although old, the place looked neat. Mama's ancient Ford was parked out front and Wren could see the trailer door was open. She wasn't surprised; Mama was an early riser.

Wren walked up on the rickety porch, and before she could open the screen door, her mother appeared. She looked older and more frail, wearing her apron as always.

"Well, well. It's my baby," she said, pushing open the screen door. She opened her arms and gave Wren a big hug, kissing her on the cheek. "I was beginning to think you'd forgot about me."

Tears came into Wren's eyes as she looked into the eyes of her mother. "No, Mama. I've just been down in Florida. I got me a job down there, and wanted to come see you."

"A job? Lord, why did you get a job way off down there? Now I won't never see you."

Wren shook her head. "No, Mama. I'll still come see you. Maybe you could come down there and see me. You'd like it. I could take you to the beach, and—"

"That's too far for me to go, you know that, child." Her mother was shaking her head. She'd been as far as London, Kentucky, but that was it.

Wren spent the day with her mother. She offered to take her out to lunch, but Mama insisted on preparing dinner for her only child. Wren had to admit there was nothing better than Mama's cooking. The fried chicken, fresh vegetables, and cornbread tasted wonderful. After eating, they drove out to the cemetery to see her father's grave.

Wren took her home and promised she'd come back tomorrow. Mama insisted she'd fix something better for dinner, and stood on the porch watching Wren leave. Wren drove through town on the way back to Peabo's, which didn't take long. Several stores downtown had closed, but other than that, Harlan looked exactly as it had for years.

A little after five, she stopped and called Ms. Vicki to tell her she'd arrived safely in London, and she'd see her Saturday. When she got back to the double-wide, Peabo and Shorty were counting cash in the living room.

"Hey, baby. You go see Mama?" Peabo asked.

"Yeah, had dinner with her. She's doing good."

He nodded. "We had a good day, didn't we, Shorty?"

The big man was putting rubber bands around bundles of cash and putting it in the bag. He grunted and nodded, then took a swig from his beer on the table.

"We should be done by tomorrow," Peabo said.

"Good, can we go back Friday?" Wren asked.

He shrugged, in a good mood, now that he and Shorty had turned a big part of the pills into cash. "Sure. Ain't no reason to hang around here, anyways."

They left the next morning, arriving back in Tampa Friday evening. Peabo talked her into spending the night with him out at the beach, even making Shorty get his own room for the night. Peabo took her out to eat at LongHorn Steakhouse, and Saturday evening, he dropped her off a block from the shelter.

Wren walked in the front door of the converted house that served as a shelter, pulling her little suitcase, and made it to Ms. Vicki's office.

"Hey, Ms. Vicki," she said, stopping at her office door.

Ms. Vicki looked up from her desk. "Well, hi there, traveling girl. How was your trip?"

Wren nodded. "Good. Mama seemed to perk up seeing me. I'm glad I went to see her. We had a good visit." She yawned. "I'm tired, though. That's a long trip."

Vick laughed. "Yes, it is. Well, glad you're back safe."

"So am I," Wren said, still remembering the traffic stop Tuesday night.

Chapter 11

"How's work going?" Jack asked Wren, trying to make conversation and be civil.

Jack and Molly were having dinner with Wren to celebrate her new job. They had driven over to Clearwater, picked Wren up, and gone to the Blue Dolphin restaurant on McMullen Booth Road. In deference to Wren's staying at the shelter, where no alcohol was allowed, Molly had ordered water to drink instead of wine.

Wren shrugged. "Okay, I guess. The people I work with are pretty cool."

He gave Molly a questioning look, determined to be nice.

Molly picked up the thread. "Are you making some friends there?" she asked Wren in a hopeful tone. She had encouraged the girl to make some new friends, people that may be a good influence.

"I guess. Kinda hard, staying at the shelter and all."

Molly had talked with Vicki, the director of the shelter, yesterday, and they were still trying to find a place for Wren to live. People didn't realize how tough it was to get by on the meager wages earned at the bottom of the food chain.

"Are they making any progress finding you a place to live?" Molly asked. She didn't want Wren to know she'd been talking to Vicki.

"It may take a while."

"Well, at least you've got a safe place to stay," Jack said. They ate dinner, with Wren sharing a few glimpses about her job, after much prodding by Molly.

Wren ordered dessert, and when their waiter brought it, Molly looked at Jack, smiled, and then looked back at Wren. "We've got a surprise for you."

Wren looked up from her ice cream sundae, already half finished. She froze, the spoon almost to her open mouth.

"We're going sailing tomorrow and spending the night on the boat. We'd like you to come with us." Molly had gotten permission from Vicki yesterday. That was the easy part, compared to Jack. He resisted, resulting in yet another argument, but Molly was determined.

The girl's eyes lit up, and she looked at Jack for his approval. She seemed to sense that he was not as excited about the idea as Molly.

He nodded and forced a smile. "That's right. We're going down to a little island south of here and spending the night. Of course, you're going to have to help on the boat."

Wren's smile turned into a frown. "I've never been sailing before. I don't know how."

Jack had to bite his tongue to keep from saying *well, maybe you shouldn't go.*

Molly reassured her. "Neither did I the first time Jack took me out. But, we're going to teach you. It's not that hard. Jack can tell you about the first time he went sailing."

Again, the young girl looked at Jack.

He almost said this wasn't a good idea, but he knew where that would lead. He shrugged, bit his tongue, and chuckled at Molly's suggestion, determined to go forward. "The first time I ever went out on a sailboat, I turned it over in about five minutes."

He saw the look of horror on Wren's face, and was amused. "It was a very tiny boat, much smaller than *Left Behind*. Don't worry, there's no way the three of us could turn her over, even if we tried."

Wren seemed relieved, and started in with all sorts of questions.

Later that night, after they had taken Wren back to the shelter, Jack and Molly were sitting out on the boat having a glass of wine that Molly had promised him on the way across the causeway.

"Thank you," she said, cuddling up next to him. "I know you don't want to do this, but I think it'll be good for her. She's very excited, as I'm sure you noticed."

"For the record, I don't think this is a good idea. You're getting way too invested in this girl and I still don't trust her."

She put her hand on his bare leg and moved it up to his shorts, giving him a gentle squeeze when she got as far as she could. "I'll make it up to you," she said, as she leaned over and kissed his ear.

He could feel his heart rate jump. "You don't play fair."

She nibbled on his earlobe, then whispered. "You complaining?"

Powerless to resist, he finished his wine, and turned to face her. "In that case, we should probably turn in. Got a long day tomorrow," he said.

Early the next morning, they picked Wren up at the shelter and came back to the marina. They had breakfast at the marina restaurant so they wouldn't have to clean up and could leave as soon as they were done. Wren wolfed her pancakes down, eager to get to the boat, and forced Jack to get his last cup of coffee to go.

The weather promised to be postcard perfect, scattered clouds against a deep blue sky and ten-to-twelve knot winds out of the west with temperatures in the low eighties. Molly and Wren were down below, securing everything in the cabin, while Jack readied everything outside.

"I think we're ready," Molly said as the girls surfaced in the companionway. Molly was wearing one of Jack's dress shirts unbuttoned over her green bikini, and her trademark floppy, large-brimmed straw hat. Wren was also wearing a bikini, an orange and white striped one, based on the bottom that showed underneath the cropped t-shirt she was wearing.

She was an attractive girl, Jack thought, and her tan looked good with her blonde hair and blue eyes. He secured the final items on the deck and prepared to depart. He started the diesel, and as it warmed up, Molly explained to Wren what he was doing.

With all the gauges normal, Jack announced they were ready to cast off. After they left the slip, he motored toward the channel leading to the Intracoastal Waterway. The girls came back to the cockpit, where Molly pointed and showed Wren how to read the channel markers.

Jack asked Wren if she wanted to drive. Traffic on the water was light, and he figured it would be a good chance to introduce her to the boat. *Might as well put her to work,* he thought.

She looked at Molly, who nodded, and they stepped behind the wheel, taking the helm. Based on their grins, he knew he'd made the right call and earned a few points with Molly.

He sat down to finish his coffee, relaxing and looking out on the bay toward Clearwater. A powerboat was headed toward them at a good clip, but on the other side of the channel. He turned his gaze toward the Gulf. There were a few cumulus clouds on the far horizon, but nothing more. It should be a nice day.

When he glanced back ahead, he saw the powerboat had closed the gap between them. He looked at the channel markers, and realized the two boats would probably meet at the narrowest part of the tight channel.

He turned around and looked at Molly and Wren. Wren was at the helm, talking to Molly standing next to her. He wondered if they were paying attention to how close they were going to come to the approaching boat. Jack had long since quit worrying about Molly's abilities at the wheel, but she appeared to be distracted.

When he looked back at the other boat, it was closing fast enough to make him uncomfortable. He jumped up, spilling his coffee, and made his way back to the helm, yelling at Molly to watch out for the boat ahead.

She looked out and realized the proximity of the approaching boat. She grabbed the wheel from Wren just as Jack got there. Before he could act, she cut the throttle and turned the boat as close to the edge of the channel as she dared. The speedboat flew past, much too close to the sailboat, the driver oblivious to the danger.

"What the hell were you doing?" Jack screamed, the roar of the powerboat echoing in their ears.

"It was my fault, Jack, I—"

"You weren't at the helm, Molly," he said, glaring at Wren.

"When you're there," he said to the girl, pointing to the wheel, "you're responsible for the boat. You have to pay attention."

Chastised, the girl slunk to the side and sat.

"We're almost to the pass, anyway," Jack said to Molly. "I'll take it."

Molly went and sat next to Wren, trying to console her. The noise of the speedboat faded and the waters in the channel calmed once again. *Not a good start*, he thought.

When they got to Clearwater Pass, Jack turned west, heading toward the Gulf. Molly and Wren went up on top of the cabin, where Molly taught Wren how the sails worked. Before long, they had cleared the pass, and Clearwater Beach was behind them.

He reached down to the lever controlling the throttle and slowed the engine, reducing the forward speed of the boat to a crawl. Molly felt the change, and they prepared to unfurl the sails, Wren at her heels.

They raised the mainsail first, and while it was flapping in the breeze, Jack turned a few degrees to the south while the girls loosed the headsail. It filled rapidly, unfurling on its own, and Jack could feel the boat respond, as he reduced the throttle to idle and put the transmission in neutral.

With the power of the wind against the sails, the boat started to accelerate. He switched the diesel off, leaving nothing but the sound of the water rushing beneath the boat. He smiled, as this was the moment he loved best—they were sailing.

Once he got *Left Behind* settled in a groove, he motioned for Molly and Wren to come back and take the helm. They hesitated, and for a moment, Jack thought they were ignoring him.

"I'm sorry I yelled at you, Wren," he said, hoping to make amends. "That boat wasn't paying attention, and with the speed they were moving, I panicked. I'm not sure he realized how close he was to running over us."

"I'm sorry," Wren said, her confidence gone.

Molly put her arm around her shoulders and hugged her. "It was my fault. I saw the boat earlier, but didn't realize how fast it was going and how close he was going to be."

"We all have to learn, Wren." He motioned her toward him. "Come on back and take the helm. Please. I want you to feel how it is when you're steering a boat under sail. Very different. And I promise not to yell again. God knows, I've made my share of mistakes. At least you didn't turn the boat over." That broke the tension, and they laughed at his reminder of his first sailing trip.

Wren came back and he showed her how to hold the wheel. He explained what a heading was and how to maintain it. He stood there for a while coaching her, then went up front, leaving her and Molly alone. He stretched out on the deck, and relaxed, catching a few rays.

It was the most soothing thing in the world to him. Out on the water, fresh air and sunshine, going from point A to point B, powered by nothing but breeze. Sailing was the closest to getting something for nothing as you could get, he thought.

It was about a five hour sail down to Egmont Key. Wren got lots of sailing in. She was bright, and a quick study, surprising him with a natural aptitude for sailing. Eager to learn, she listened to his instructions, and he only had to tell her something once. He could see she had a passion for it, and wanted to understand how everything worked.

That afternoon, as they approached Egmont, Molly started the diesel and turned into the wind so Jack could drop the sails. He took Wren forward and instructed her on what to do, helping only when necessary. After they got the sails furled, they motored up behind the curve of the tiny island on the east side just south of the Tampa Bay Pilots Association dock. It was not a very protected anchorage, but in good weather and with a west wind, it was acceptable for one night. Three other boats were anchored there when they arrived.

Molly put the boat in neutral and Jack dropped the anchor, watching the line pay out as the boat slowly drifted backwards. He explained to Wren what the scope of the anchor line meant, and when the right marking on the line slipped past, he secured the line on the cleat and motioned to Molly. She engaged the transmission in reverse and revved the engine up, putting pressure on the anchor as the boat stretched the anchor line taut.

Satisfied the anchor was set, Jack signaled to Molly. She reduced the throttle to idle, put the transmission into neutral, and switched the engine off. Jack and Wren went back to the cockpit where they readied the dingy to take ashore. By the time they made it over to the Gulf side of the island, it was almost sunset.

Wren had not stopped talking about sailing. As they set up their chairs on the west side of the tiny island to watch the sun sink into the horizon, she was still chattering away.

It was a beautiful sunset, the huge orange orb disappearing into the blue-gray waters of the Gulf. Wren remarked that it was the most incredible sunset she'd ever seen.

The daylight fading, they piled into the dingy and motored back to *Left Behind*. Once aboard, the girls went below to get ready for dinner and make a salad, while Jack fired up the grill to cook steaks for dinner. He smiled as he heard Jimmy Buffett playing, a tradition for Molly and him on the boat whenever they dropped anchor.

Thirty minutes later, they sat around the cockpit table, a slight breeze blowing, just enough to make it comfortable. They had all donned shirts over their bathing suits and Jack had opened a nice Terra Bella Cabernet Sauvignon to go with dinner. He poured a small glass for Wren, who wrinkled her nose as she watched Jack and Molly clink their glasses together.

"I've never had wine," she said, picking up her glass and touching Jack and Molly's glasses. She took a sip, and made a face. "Yuk," she said. "How do you drink that stuff?"

Molly and Jack both laughed, and Molly said, "Give it a chance. It'll taste better with the steak, but if you don't like it, that's okay. Not everyone likes red wine, especially the first time."

"It's so pretty out here. I feel like I'm dreaming," Wren said, taking in the scenery and the lights of the Sunshine Skyway Bridge twinkling in the distance. "I couldn't wait to get back to Florida. How far did we sail today?"

Jack looked at Molly. "Back?" he said. "From where?"

Wren looked like she'd been caught with her hand in the cookie jar. She sighed and stalled before answering. "I wasn't scheduled to work, okay? It's not like I skipped work or anything." She picked at her food, then said, "I went to Kentucky, okay? No big deal."

Jack shook his head. "The boyfriend?"

Wren nodded without saying a word.

"How did you get away from the shelter?" Molly asked.

She shrugged and looked down. "I told them I had to go see my mama. I did see her, so it wasn't a lie."

"What's going on, Wren?" Molly asked.

Wren fidgeted a bit before responding. "I went to see Mama back home. We left on Tuesday, came back Saturday. No big deal, okay?"

"Peabo drove you back to Kentucky just so you could see your mom? What, a twelve, fourteen hour trip each way? For three days? Don't bullshit us, Wren," Jack said.

"Peabo buys stuff in Tampa and takes it back home to sell."

"What kind of 'stuff?'" Jack said. He was afraid of the answer.

She rearranged the food on her plate while he and Molly waited for an answer. "Pills."

Over dinner, Wren explained. It was a classic pill mill operation, the kind Florida was famous for. Peabo recruited people off the street to get prescriptions, then filled the scripts and took the pills—painkillers—back to Kentucky where he sold them for a handsome profit.

Wren swore she didn't take the pills, but she was in it up to her neck. Molly explained what a huge risk she was taking, even though she claimed not to be involved in the selling.

That night, lying in the forward berth in the dark, Jack felt Molly put her hand on his bare chest. He had almost dozed off with the gentle motion of the boat on the water, combined with the bottle of red wine they'd consumed.

"You asleep?" she whispered.

"Almost."

"What are we going to do, Jack?"

"I don't know, but we've got to get her away from that life. She could end up in prison for a long time if she gets caught. Or worse." He thought about his brother, Ray. They never figured out where the pills came from.

"We should go to the police."

Jack shook his head. "If we do that, she's going to get hurt. We've got to figure out a way to extract her from that guy's clutches first, get her involved in some things."

"Some new friends, people that'll be a positive influence. I think she wants to do the right thing. We've just got to make it easier for her to choose that path."

"I agree. But somebody's writing those prescriptions and somebody's filling them. I want to know who."

Chapter 12

Peabo slowed as he drove up to the gate signifying the entrance to Big Cat Rescue. Big Cat Rescue was a non-profit sanctuary for exotic cats and housed over a hundred lions, tigers, and other cats. Surprisingly, the fifty-five acre facility was located in a heavily populated area north of downtown Tampa. Many people were unaware that such a place was literally in their backyard.

He and Shorty had decided to drive over and check it out. A pudgy young girl stood in front of them, wearing khaki shorts and a green t-shirt with VOLUNTEER blazoned across her chest. She walked up to the SUV as they entered the parking lot.

"May I help you?" she asked, with a mechanical smile on her face.

"Yeah, we wanted to see the lions and stuff," Peabo answered, looking around the small, unsurfaced parking lot.

The girl still wore her orientation face. "Did you have a reservation?"

"No, didn't know you needed one. We just wanted to see them, is all," Peabo said.

"I'm sorry. The only way to see our residents is a guided tour. The general tour starts at three, and you don't need reservations for that one," she said in a cheerful, sing-song voice. Still smiling, as if it were painted on her face, she pointed to a small, one-story building marked TICKETS and GIFT SHOP. "You can get tickets there."

"What time is it?" Peabo asked no one in particular.

The girl consulted her watch, and Shorty looked at his phone. They both answered "1:30."

"We'll come back," Peabo said, already beginning to turn the big Escalade around.

"Residents?" Shorty asked as they drove back out the dirt road they came in on. "What the fuck was that about? I thought we came to see lions and tigers."

Peabo laughed. "It's that tourist crap they teach everybody in Florida. Rat World started it, calling everybody associates or some shit like that. Maybe we should start calling our customers 'cousins' or something."

Shorty laughed and said, "Hell, half of them are." He pulled a cigarette out of the pack. "That girl looked like she had a corn cob stuck up her butt."

Peabo wheeled into the McDonald's parking lot. "We'll get something to eat and go back."

They went in, got some lunch and a six-pack of beer, and came back out to eat in the parking lot.

After they finished, they drove back to Big Cat Rescue, and the same girl greeted them. She was about to launch into her spiel, when she recognized the two. "You're back," she said, not quite as enthusiastic as before. "You can park anywhere over next to the fence," she said, pointing to a tall wooden fence on the other side of the lot.

Peabo parked the SUV and got out, a cigarette dangling from his mouth.

"I'm sorry." It was little miss sunshine again, standing behind the Escalade. "There's no smoking allowed at Big Cat Rescue."

Peabo took another drag, then dropped the cigarette down into the dirt, grinding it out with his foot.

"You can get your tickets for the tour over there," she said, nervously pointing to the ticket office. They started walking in that direction, and she left them to go greet another car that pulled into the parking lot, clearly relieved they weren't going to be trouble.

Peabo noticed a small trailer on the opposite side of the parking lot, marked SECURITY. "Reckon what kind of security they have around here?" he asked Shorty.

"Why would you need security if you've got lions and tigers? Not like somebody's gonna come in and steal them."

Peabo laughed. "Probably a rent-a-cop with a radio, just to keep kids out."

They walked into the ticket office and gift shop. An older man with a young child on each hand was standing at the counter talking to a small, gray-headed woman wearing the same green t-shirt as the girl outside. Peabo stood in line behind them and looked up at the board behind the counter.

"Damn," he swore to Shorty. "This is bad as fucking Rat World." The man turned around and scowled at them before returning his attention to the woman behind the counter. Peabo nodded toward the board and Shorty followed his gaze.

Shorty whistled. "Twenty-nine dollars! I didn't want to buy one, I just wanted to see them."

The old man gathered the two youngsters, gave Peabo another quick look of disapproval, and walked over to the gate where the woman had directed them.

Peabo stepped up to the counter.

"You're here for the three o'clock tour?" the woman asked, with a voice harsher than expected from a sweet little old lady.

Peabo started to say something smart-ass, thought better of it, and asked for two tickets.

At a few minutes before three, another woman walked up to the small group gathered outside the gate, and introduced herself as Gwen. She was to be their tour guide today.

She told them the ground rules and punched in a code at the keypad on the wall. Peabo and Shorty looked at each other, then back at the keypad.

Gwen opened the gate, ushered them inside, and launched into her spiel. A bobcat was perched in a cage over their heads, eyeing them with mild interest.

They walked a few steps, then stopped as Gwen started introducing the residents. Peabo kept looking around, trying to find something bigger than a bobcat.

"I thought you said they had lions?" Shorty asked, in a not-so-soft voice.

Before Peabo could weigh in, Gwen said, "We'll be coming to the big cats in a few minutes."

Peabo shrugged and rolled his eyes. Bored, they continued along, stopping at the cage containing something that looked like an overgrown housecat with long legs and big ears. He looked at the sign on the cage.

Serval

Under the watchful eye of Gwen, Shorty lowered his voice this time and said to Peabo, "I don't give a rat's ass about no serval."

Peabo's attention was also wandering until he heard Gwen say that this was a rare, white serval, and that someone had offered Big Cat Rescue $75,000 for this one.

"Somebody wanted to pay $75,000 for this thing?" he asked Gwen, just to confirm what he thought he'd heard.

"Oh, yes," she replied. "White ones are very rare, but they aren't natural and besides, there's no way we would ever sell one of our residents."

Peabo looked at Shorty, and he returned the look. They were both thinking the same thing.

"Is that why you have all the gates and stuff? To keep people from stealing the animals? I mean, I don't guess they could steal a lion, but one of these little guys, huh?" Peabo said.

Gwen shook her head. "No, we have 24-hour security here. My guess is that we're more worried about people disturbing or harming our residents, or someone getting hurt."

As they walked further down the path, the two became a lot more interested in the tour, asking Gwen so many questions that the other visitors could hardly get in a word.

"How do you take care of these cats? You know, like when the doctor needs to check them or something?" Peabo asked.

Gwen explained how the lockouts in each enclosure functioned, and offered that Dr. Tim, one of their vets, would sedate the animal if necessary.

"Like give him sleeping pills?" Shorty asked.

"He uses an anesthetic, like Ketamine. That's a drug that's also used in humans. It knocks the cat out so he can be examined and any necessary procedures done." She pointed back toward the main building. "We have a complete operating room onsite for procedures that require it."

Peabo nodded and filed that drug name away. He'd have to ask Doc about it. Finally, near the lake at the back of the property, they came to an enclosure with the names Joseph and Nikita on the sign. A full grown lion was lying in the shade not more than eight feet away.

"This is Joseph," Gwyn said. "As you can see, he's a male lion. He shares an enclosure with Nikita, a Siberian tiger. They were raised together and are the best of friends."

"Where's the tiger?" Peabo asked, looking around.

"Oh, Nikita's very shy, and he usually is in the back, sleeping."

"They don't fight?" Shorty asked.

"Oh, no," she said. "Sometimes you see them grooming each other, and playing with each other, but never fighting. They truly are inseparable friends."

Shorty poked Peabo and whispered. "That mean they're queer or something?"

Peabo shook his head and wondered how to explain it. "No, just friends for a long time, like me and you."

Shorty smiled and nodded.

After the tour, when they were driving back to the beach, Shorty said, "Damn, I wish we could get one of those big bastards to guard our place back home. Wouldn't nobody mess with us, then."

Peabo laughed. "Yeah, but first of all, you got to get one. Then you got to feed the damn thing. Not going to happen. We got enough shit to deal with as it is."

Shorty was obsessed with the serval. "Can you believe $75,000 for that overgrown housecat? I bet we could snatch him pretty easy."

"And then what? We don't know nothing about cats," Peabo responded, shaking his head.

"Cat's a cat—feed him some Cat Chow or some shit like that. That'd be a quick 75K."

Shorty was right, $75,000 was a lot, but Peabo figured that a super-sized housecat would be more trouble than they thought. He sure as hell wasn't driving all the way back to Kentucky with a yowling cat in back. "Who you gonna sell him to?" Peabo asked.

"We'll find somebody. Just let me make a few calls, okay?"

Peabo still wasn't keen on the idea, but decided to let Shorty pursue it. As long as it didn't take away from their main business, *what the hell*, he thought. He kept thinking about Joseph, the lion.

Chapter 13

Wren and Peabo walked down the beach, having left Shorty at the Dive Bar, a local hangout on Clearwater Beach. It was late afternoon, and there were still lots of people out, waiting for the sunset and trying to get as much beach time in as possible. She'd called him Sunday after she got back from her sailing trip with Molly and Jack.

That morning on the boat, they'd pressed her for more details about Peabo's business, but she refused to tell them anything else. She knew Peabo would be mad if he knew what she'd told them.

"How's work going?" he asked, as he picked up a football and threw it back to some kids down by the water.

"Okay, I guess. The people are nice there."

"I wish you'd come back to work with me."

"Peabo, I don't—"

"I'm thinking about cutting Shorty loose, and I need you."

Wren was surprised. "You're cutting Shorty loose?" She knew how Peabo had basically raised Shorty, and couldn't believe he'd abandon him.

He shrugged. "I got to do something. You know how he is, he's not too bright, plus he's using way too much product, and I can't afford that."

"You can't do that to Shorty. What'll he do?"

"I can put him in charge of running the sales back home, just keep him out of the trips down here. That's why I need you back, Wren. You're smart, and you're the only other person I can trust. Plus, if you were back, you could help me keep him in line."

She squeezed his hand. "I don't know. I mean, I'm trying to get my life together, you know? That gig in jail was the pits, and I don't want any more of that."

"We could make some good money, way more than what you're making at the hospital."

"Peabo, it's more than the money . . ."

They walked a ways, neither saying anything else. She saw a sailboat out on the water, and pointed. "Did I tell you we went sailing this weekend? It was so much fun—I've never done anything like that."

"Sailing with who?"

"Jack and Molly—you know, the nurse that got me the job? They took me down to an island in Tampa Bay and we spent the night. It was so cool."

"Looks boring to me, you don't go very fast."

She shook her head. "No, it's not, I mean, when you feel the wind moving you along with no motor or anything, that's just . . ."

"Sounds like ya'll are getting pretty tight?"

"They're good people, Peabo. They're just trying to help. You'd like them."

"They probably got something else in mind, nice looking girl like you."

"What're you talking about?"

He shrugged. "Just saying. Maybe they wanna spice up their love life, everybody walking around out on a boat, half-naked. I mean, they may be nice and all, but we just don't fit in with people like that. We're just poor folks from Kentucky. Only reason people like that want to have something to do with us is to use us for something."

She thought about what Peabo said. Neither Molly nor Jack had ever been anything but proper around her, but maybe he was right. She was a nobody. Why would they want her hanging around?

She'd always wanted to marry Peabo, settle down and have kids. But being around Molly and Jack had got her to thinking about a normal life. She didn't want to be driving back and forth between Kentucky and Florida, worrying about getting caught. That traffic stop in Tennessee scared her.

Wren had also known too many other girls back home that had gotten knocked up. Their boyfriends ended up in jail or worse, and left them raising kids on their own. She was determined she wasn't going to fall into that trap.

She didn't depend on Peabo to use birth control—she took her pills religiously. After the first time they'd had unprotected sex, she went to the clinic and got birth control pills and had used them every since.

When she was in jail, her cellmate had talked to her about boys. When Wren told her she was taking birth control pills, she'd laughed.

Don't no pills keep him from giving you something he done caught from another woman, she'd told her, which had gotten her to thinking. When she'd tried to bring it up with Peabo after she got out, he didn't want to talk about it. All he would say is that he didn't fool around with no one and he was waiting on her, which she knew was a lie.

She was pretty sure he cheated on her, but she never caught him at it, and he always denied it. She knew him well enough to know that he didn't go without while she was in jail.

Maybe she belonged with Peabo.

"You tired of walking?" he asked.

She knew what he wanted. "I guess."

"Why don't we go back to the room and watch a little TV?"

"I know what kinda TV you want to watch," she said, laughing.

"If you wasn't so damn sexy . . ."

She let him walk her to the car. "What about Shorty?"

"Ain't worried about him, he can take care of himself while I'm taking care of you," he said as they got into the Escalade.

When they were lying in bed afterwards, he asked her again about going back in the business with him. He wouldn't take no for an answer, so she told him she'd think about it.

She really didn't want to get back into drugs. She hadn't used any since she'd gone to jail, and she wanted to keep it that way. Drugs made her lose control, and that was a feeling she didn't like.

He took her back over to Clearwater before her curfew and let her out a block from the shelter, since he wasn't supposed to know where she stayed. Raine, her roommate, was still up when she walked back into her room at the shelter.

"Have a good time?" she asked.

Wren smiled and said, "Yes, we went out to the beach, had dinner and went for a walk." She started to add *then we went back to his room and fucked like rabbits*, but wasn't sure Raine was ready for that.

Raine had been after her to go to church, so Wren wasn't sure about the girl. She didn't seem like one of those religious nuts, but Wren didn't know. "What did you do?" Wren asked.

"I went downtown for a thing at church."

Wren was confused. "Downtown? I thought you said you went to a church in Tampa?"

"I do," the younger girl said. "But they have a big place here in Clearwater where they have a lot of education sessions. I still want you to come with me some time." Seeing Wren's reaction, she quickly added, "No obligation. Just check it out, okay?"

"Sure, just let me know sometime."

"It's really a great place. They saved me from myself."

Uh-oh, here it comes, thought Wren.

"I was into drugs, big time. Someone talked me into going to Narcono and that helped me kick it. I've been clean now for eight months."

"Wow, that's great. What kind of drugs were you doing?"

Raine laughed. "Pretty much everything, whatever I could get my hands on. I was doing a lot of Oxy—that was my favorite."

Wren thought about Peabo, and the look on her face must have tipped Raine.

"Sorry, did I hit too close to home?" Raine asked.

Wren shrugged. "I know some people who do it."

"Did you ever do it? Or am I prying?"

Wren laughed. "Yeah, I've tried it. Lot of people back home do it, that's why they call it 'hillbilly heroin.' I try to stay away from it, but . . ."

Raine nodded. "It's hard, I know. I still want it sometimes."

"Peabo wants me to go back to him." She'd told Raine a little about Peabo.

The girl shrugged as if she'd heard it before. "You going?"

"Don't know—I need to think about it. He makes good money."

"Yeah? What kinda work does he do?"

"He runs his own business."

"What kind of business?"

"Goes back and forth between Kentucky and Florida."

Raine tilted her head, but didn't press for details, and Wren continued. "He's thinking about firing his best friend and wants me to work with him."

"Is he really going to do that?"

Wren nodded. "I think he might. Shorty—that's his friend—ain't too reliable, and Peabo's having problems with him."

"Just be careful, girlfriend. That's a dangerous 'business,'" she said, emphasizing the word *business*. "Plus, you know how guys are."

She wished she could talk to someone about it, but there was no one, never really had been. She'd always had to make decisions on her own. She thought about talking to Molly. Based on Molly's reaction on the boat, she knew Molly would be totally opposed.

* * *

The next morning, Peabo thought about the previous evening with Wren. It had been good. She'd been getting a little too cozy with that sailboat couple. Wren thought they liked having her around, but he'd gotten her to see the light.

She still hadn't agreed to come back to work with him, but he thought he knew the answer to that. Now was the time to make his move. Shorty was still asleep, so he went to the mall alone.

A couple of hours later, when he got back to the motel, Shorty was awake, sitting up in bed watching cartoons.

"Hey, man, where'd you go?" Shorty said, between bites of a doughnut.

"Just went out to do some thinking, get some breakfast." They were done with business for this trip, so their calendar was open.

"We heading home today?"

"No, I'm going to see Wren tonight, take her to dinner. You're on your own."

"Damn, dude, she's got you whipped. You can't get enough of that, can you?"

Peabo shrugged. "I'm gonna ask her to marry me." He figured he might as well go ahead and tell him.

"Whoa—you're kidding me, right?" Shorty just stared at him. "Damn, you're serious. Why would you go and do that?"

Peabo shook his head. "No big deal, we're not getting married anytime soon, but we need her back in the business."

Shorty frowned. "We did alright last trip without her."

"I know, but I want to expand, you know, get that van we talked about, add some more workers. She'd be a big help."

"You're the boss," Shorty said, finishing his doughnut.

That evening, Peabo picked Wren up on the corner, a block from the shelter. He'd told her to get dressed up and he was taking her to dinner. She was wearing a short blue and white sundress that he'd never seen before, but it looked good on her.

She got in and looked him over. He was wearing his new shorts and a fancy golf shirt that he'd bought at the mall that morning. They set him back sixty bucks, but the nice looking sales girl assured him that he looked good in them. She also gave him her phone number and told him to call her some time.

"You look nice," Wren said, nodding approvingly. "I ain't ever seen you dressed up like that. Where's Shorty?"

"Shorty's on his own. I wanted it to be just you and me." He looked her over, leaned over and gave her a kiss. "That dress looks good on you." He put the Cadillac in gear and pulled away from the curb. "I wanna take you somewhere special tonight, anywhere you want to go."

"Really? Anywhere?"

He nodded.

"I've always wanted to go to that place on the water, you know, over before you get to the Causeway?"

He thought a minute, and then figured she was talking about that restaurant on Gulf to Bay that was always packed. "That big place on the right? The one that looks like a fish house or something?"

She smiled and nodded. "Can we?"

"If that's what you want." He would've just as soon gone back to LongHorn, but he had to keep telling himself that this had to be special to succeed. He felt his pocket to make sure the little box was still there, and smiled. This was going to work.

As expected, Castaways on the Bay was crowded when they arrived. It was a popular local spot, right on the water, and was packed with yuppies. There was a forty-five minute wait for a table, but Peabo didn't want to wait. He'd palmed a twenty on his way to the hostess stand, and as she was writing his name down, he reached over and pointed to the list, casually transferring the twenty to her hand.

"I think we had reservations," he said. "Watson. Party of two."

The twenty disappeared into her hand, and she said, "Oh yes, Mr. Watson, that's right. I'm sorry. Why don't you follow me?" She picked up two menus and Peabo motioned for Wren to follow.

They were seated at a table overlooking the water, not as private as Peabo had hoped for, but at least they didn't have to wait. He tried not to think about how expensive the menu was and was surprised when Wren ordered a glass of white wine.

"I'm going to have to see some ID," their server asked.

Wren looked at Peabo, who was shaking his head. "She didn't bring her purse in," he said.

"Sorry, I'm going to—"

"Never mind. Just bring me one." Peabo took out his wallet and showed the server his license.

"Since when do you drink wine?" he asked when the server walked away. She was clearly enjoying herself, and he was cautious to tread carefully, not wanting to spoil the mood. But he had wanted a beer, and now he was stuck with a freaking glass of wine for his girlfriend.

"I'm trying to learn to like it. Molly and Jack drink it all the time. They say you have to learn to like it."

More Molly talk. Damn, he was getting tired of that bitch. Peabo shook his head and took a deep breath.

Their waiter brought the glass of wine and sat it in front of Peabo. They ordered dinner and he hoped that Wren would down her wine so he could order a beer, but that wasn't going to happen. She nursed her glass of wine through the meal, so he tried to get back in a positive frame of mind.

Dinner wasn't bad, but overpriced, and all he could think about was this evening was costing him a fortune. He was beginning to think the whole plan was a bad idea. Maybe Shorty wasn't so bad after all.

Since Wren had finished her wine with dinner, Peabo ordered a beer with dessert, which improved his outlook. After they finished dessert and he polished off two beers, Peabo reached in his pocket, pulled out the little black box, and handed it to Wren.

She was surprised as she set her fork down and took the box. "What's this?" she asked, grinning from ear to ear.

"A little something for my girl. Just open it."

She carefully opened it and removed the smaller box inside. Her eyes lit up when she flipped the top and saw the solitaire diamond ring. Her mouth was open as she looked up at Peabo, back to the ring, and then up at him again. He grinned at her reaction—it was just what he was hoping for.

"Is this . . ."

Her expectant look told him what he wanted to know. He nodded, and said, "Will you marry me?"

Wren's squeal reverberated throughout the dining room, causing everyone to stop what they were doing and look at the couple. It was the reaction he wanted, but still, he was embarrassed by the attention. In a flash, she was up from her seat, smothering him with kisses and repeating, "Yes! Yes! Yes!"

She put the ring on, held her hand up high for everyone to see. "We're getting married," she announced, and the entire room applauded.

The next afternoon, Molly and Jack sat on the boat, talking about what to do for dinner. When her phone rang, she answered, and silently mouthed *Wren* to Jack as she listened. She wanted to come out and see them.

She ended the call and told Jack that Wren was on her way.

"What's going on?" Jack asked.

Molly shook her head. "She didn't say, but she sounded excited and just wanted to make sure we were going to be here."

An hour later, Wren walked out on the dock. She took her sandals off and stuck out her left hand for Jack to help her board. Molly immediately noticed the ring on her finger.

"Wren? Is that what I think it is?" she asked the girl, and Wren exploded with joy.

"Yes! I'm so excited, that's why I wanted to come tell you." She couldn't stand still.

Jack looked at Molly with a puzzled look. She held up Wren's hand and then he noticed the ring. He looked at Molly, then back at Wren, who was still grinning from ear to ear. Molly could tell he didn't trust himself to speak.

"Peabo asked me to marry him," Wren said, unable to temper the excitement. "Can you believe it?"

"Congratulations," Molly said. She hugged her, and looked over Wren's shoulder at Jack with a baffled look on her face.

"So, when did this happen?" Molly asked.

"Last night. He took me to dinner at Castaways—I've never been there before, it was so good—and after dinner, he took the ring out and asked me to marry him, right there in the restaurant. I still can't believe it!"

Molly glanced at Jack, then looked at Wren, who was admiring the ring. "It's a beautiful ring. Are you sure about this?" She couldn't believe this was happening.

She nodded. "I am, I am. I'd given up on him."

"So . . . what are your plans?"

"We haven't set a date yet, but I'm moving in with him."

"Here? Kentucky?"

"Kentucky, I guess. We haven't got that far."

Molly didn't know what to say. She hated to rain on Wren's parade, but she was worried about the naïve young girl marrying an abusive drug dealer. "So does that mean you're quitting your job at the hospital?"

"Well, yes, I mean, I can't go to Kentucky and work here."

Jack couldn't keep quiet any longer. "Wren, don't quit your job. You're doing so well. He's a drug dealer. What kind of future do you think you've got to look forward to with him?"

She pouted her lips. "This is what I want. It's what I've always wanted."

"If Peabo gets arrested, he's going to prison for a long time. And there's a good chance you'll get sucked into it and be looking at doing time yourself," Jack said.

"I thought you two would be happy for me," Wren said, a frown crossing her face.

"Happy? Happy that you're marrying someone who treats you like shit? He's trouble, Wren. Stay away from him." Molly was determined she wasn't going to let this girl throw her life away.

"But, I love him."

"Listen to me, Wren. He's the only boyfriend you've ever had. He uses you and manipulates you. You deserve better," Molly said.

"You're the ones that use people. What do you care about me? I'm just a pity case, to make you feel better about yourselves."

Molly shook her head. "We care about you, Wren, and don't want to see you get mixed up in this drug business. There's no good ending to that."

"Who's writing the prescriptions, Wren?" Jack asked. "Who's the doctor? Somebody in town is writing scripts for you, and somebody's filling those."

Wren looked at them, then stepped up on the dock and slipped her sandals on. "I should've never said anything," she said as she walked away.

"Wren, please . . ." Molly said. Wren didn't look back.

Chapter 14

Jack couldn't get last night's encounter with Wren out of his mind. A physician in the area was writing illicit prescriptions for Peabo's drug ring, and a pharmacist was filling those prescriptions. Wren was right in the middle of it.

He pushed back away from his desk and looked out the window, where he had a nice view of Tampa Bay. It was another bright, sunny day, with only a few puffy white clouds set against a beautiful blue sky. There was a sailboat off in the distance, and he wondered where it was headed. It was too nice of a day to be stuck inside, looking at numbers on a computer screen, and he wished he was out on the water.

He forced his attention back to the monitor on his desk. Bayview Clinic was processing an incredible number of patients for the number of doctors on staff there. Either they were far and away the most efficient clinic in the Drager system or something was amiss. Jack's inner voice was telling him it didn't add up.

Connie buzzed him. "He's ready for you."

"Okay, I'll be up in a minute." Drager had wanted to meet with him for his monthly update.

As soon as he walked in Drager's office, he knew something was wrong. Drager was aloof, and barely spoke to him.

Once they were comfortable at Drager's conference table, Jack said, "Is everything okay?"

"I had dinner with Winston yesterday evening," he said, letting the words hang in the air. "He's concerned that we don't seem to be making much progress on identifying efficiency measures that we can roll out to the other clinics."

Jack was speechless. Dr. Andrews had gone to Drager and tried to undermine his efforts.

"I'm not convinced that the efficiencies at Bayview are legitimate," Jack said. "There's no way they can be seeing that many patients and—"

"Do you have proof, Jack? If not, I'd suggest you stop right there."

Jack's face flushed with anger. "Not yet, but I need a physician to review a sample of his charts to—"

Drager held up his hand and shook his head. "You were hired to take the best practices at our top performing clinics and implement those throughout the entire organization. Instead, it appears you're on a witch hunt to discredit Winston Andrews.

"I've supported you, Jack, but don't let me down. Focus on the job at hand."

Someone knocked on the office door. The door opened, then Connie stepped inside. "Sorry to interrupt, Dr. Drager, but you've got to leave for your appointment, now, if you're going to be there on time." She stood there waiting on Drager, holding several folders, apparently for his next meeting.

"Thanks, Connie," Drager said. He stood and turned to Jack as he grabbed his jacket. "Sorry to cut it short, Jack, but I think you get the message. Let's get together next week to review your progress."

Jack went back to his office, dumbfounded and angry. He pulled out his cell phone and texted Dr. Marshall, asking her to call him when she got a chance.

A few minutes later, his phone buzzed and he saw it was Dr. Marshall.

"Hey," he answered. "That was quick."

"I had a few minutes in between patients. What's up?"

"You have some time later this afternoon to get together?"

There was a pause, then she said, "How about around six? I should be done with seeing patients then."

"Six it is. I'll see you then."

Traffic was heavy on US 19, and he got to Tina's office at quarter after six. He knew that wouldn't be a problem, since she was probably running late anyway.

He walked in, and Nancy, the receptionist, was still there, in the process of shutting things down for the day.

"She's with the last patient. Should be done in a few minutes," she said to Jack as he walked up to the counter. "You can come on back."

"Thanks, Nancy." He walked through the door and went back to Dr. Marshall's office and sat down. This was the first time he'd had a chance to look at her office. He couldn't help but notice the contrast between her office and Dr. Andrews. Whereas Andrews's had the ultra modern, sleek, contemporary look, Tina's looked like a college student's. Papers, folders, and medical journals were scattered over the desk in no apparent order.

Opened cardboard boxes sat on the floor around the well-worn Shaker style desk. A stack of patient folders were in the seat of an equally worn wooden rocker behind the desk.

Missing were the usual diplomas and certifications that hung on most physicians' walls. A lone picture in a frame sat on the corner of her desk, turned sideways where he could just see it from where he was sitting. He hadn't noticed it in previous visits.

There were two girls in the picture, with a middle-aged man standing between them, holding their hands. All were wearing bathing suits, and they were standing on the gray sand with the ocean behind them. The older girl on the left looked to be around eighteen or so, and the younger girl perhaps a few years younger. Upon further examination, he decided the brunette on the left was Dr. Marshall.

"Sorry I'm late," Tina said, walking in and interrupting his thoughts about the picture. "How are you?" she said as she moved the patient folders and plopped down in the chair. She was wearing her white lab coat with *Dr. Marshall* stitched in blue over the pocket.

He shrugged. "Busy day?"

"Crazy, as usual."

Jack pointed to the picture on her desk. "You and your sister?"

She smiled and nodded. "And my dad. Mom took that at the shore. We used to go there every summer when I was little."

"Where are they now?"

Her smile faded and a look of sadness replaced it. "He and my sister were killed in an auto accident five years ago."

"I'm sorry." He figured that must have been about the time she graduated from medical school, but he didn't ask.

She had a faraway look in her eyes. "He'd picked her up at the train station and they were on their way to the house. A drunk driver ran a stop sign. They never had a chance."

He shook his head. "My God, Tina. That's horrible."

She nodded, and there was a moment of silence as she collected her thoughts. "You wanted to see me?"

It took Jack a moment to shift gears. He cleared his throat and told her about his findings that afternoon.

"The numbers of patients per physician for Bayview are way out of line compared to everyone else. I think so, but I wanted to bounce it off you. Could they be that more efficient?"

Although she said she'd work with him on management reports, he was getting into an area beyond that. He figured it was worth a shot.

She studied the report he'd given her, jotted a few notes on it, and started shaking her head.

"I wish I could see that many patients a day. It's possible, I suppose, but unlikely. They'd all have to be simple cases, which doesn't make sense. Not a normal distribution."

"Would you be willing to look at the charts? Wouldn't that show?"

She winced, then shook her head. "I don't think so, Jack."

"Did Drager talk to you?" he asked, defensively.

"No, why?"

He studied her face to see if she was being honest with him. "Just a bad day."

She stood up and took off her lab coat. "You want to get something to eat?"

He looked at his watch—7:30. Molly had a late meeting at the hospital, so he'd be going home to an empty boat. "Sure, why not."

They went to Ted's Sushi, an unlikely name for a sushi bar, but it was the best in the area. It was located in a nondescript strip mall not far from the clinic. Since it was south of the clinic, and Tina lived on the water in Dunedin, they drove separately, pulling into the parking lot at the same time.

When Ted had come over from Japan years ago as a fledgling sushi chef, no one could pronounce his name, so the Tampa restaurant owner crowned him Ted and the name stuck. Later, when he opened his own sushi restaurant in Clearwater, the obvious choice was simply Ted's.

Rather than sit at the bar, they opted for a small table in the back room, where they could continue their conversation. Tina ordered sake, and they sipped the chilled rice wine as they munched on edamame, waiting on their sushi.

"Why such a bad day?" she asked.

"You said it was unlikely that Bayview could see that many patients. How are they doing it?" he asked, avoiding her question.

She thought for a moment, then said, "Three possibilities: One, the clinician is incredibly efficient, two, the patients are very simple, or three . . . the clinician is not being as thorough as perhaps they should in order to process the volumes." She put an edamame pod in her mouth and watched Jack as she chewed.

"Sounds like your vote is door number three?" he said.

She shook her head, finishing the edamame before speaking. "Leaning, maybe, but I don't have enough information. Andrews is very good—don't forget, he's been doing this a long time."

He nodded, and said, "Fair enough. So, does that mean you'll review the charts for me?"

Their sushi arrived, and after their waiter left, she held up her hand. "I said I'd work with you on management reports, not chart reviews. You're crossing a line here. Maybe you should clear this with Drager."

He shook his head. "I can't." He then proceeded to tell her about his meeting that afternoon with Dr. Drager.

"Are you nuts?" she asked, when he finished. "You've alienated Andrews, and now you're pissing off Drager? Sorry, but I agree with Drager on this."

"I think Andrews is running a pill mill," he said.

"You *think?* Just because his clinic is seeing more patients than the rest of us? That's a huge leap."

He told her about Wren and Peabo.

"That proves nothing. No way am I getting involved in this."

"What if he is? You're telling me you're willing to turn your head the other way and let it continue?"

"Think about this, Jack. What if you're wrong?"

"What if I'm right?"

"Why are you willing to take this kind of risk? If you have something, turn it over to the authorities. Otherwise, back off. You said she was going to marry the guy! It's out of your hands. There's nothing you can do."

All he could think of was his little brother. If someone had gotten involved, then maybe he'd still be alive. He wasn't giving up so easy this time.

"Come on, Tina. I need your help. Drager will never know, I promise."

"You can't promise."

"Drager hired me to improve efficiency across the organization. That's all I'm trying to do, so I don't see why he'd have a problem."

"Maybe, maybe not. But getting physicians to review other physicians is a sensitive area. Add Drager's explicit instructions to you, and that's an area I want to steer clear of."

He looked at her, and it was clear she wasn't going to budge. He'd have to come up with a better argument.

"Why did you leave Fort Myers?" she asked, changing the subject.

Jack twisted in his seat. *Where did that come from?* He'd not talked to anyone about what happened, other than the authorities, and had done his best to build a wall around the past. He wasn't sure how much to tell her.

Sticking to the basics, he told her he'd worked for a for-profit hospital there and wanted to get out of the big-company environment. A friend introduced him to Dr. Drager, and here he was.

She shook her head. "That's all? Why do I feel there's more to the story?"

There was a pregnant pause in the conversation while she waited him out. At last, he said, "I was fired."

Her face registered only mild surprise. "Not unusual in the corporate world. Any particular reason?"

"I stumbled across the cover-up of a cardiac drug—"

"Clearart?" Her eyes opened wide and her mouth dropped open. "That was you?"

He blushed at her recognition of the story and nodded.

"Oh my God! I remember reading about that." She studied Jack and seemed to sense his reluctance to go further. "You don't want to talk about it, do you?"

He looked down, avoiding her eyes, and shook his head.

She reached across the table and put her hand on his arm. "I remember. The pharmacist . . ."

All he could do was nod, and he watched a tear fall from his face onto her hand, rolling down the side. She kept her hand on his arm.

"I'm sorry, Jack," she said in the kindest and gentlest voice. "I didn't mean to pry—I had no idea."

He looked up into her eyes, and all he could see was feeling and compassion. He felt another tear make its way down his cheek, and he nodded, unable to speak for the longest. When he did, the voice sounded distant and strange.

"He was involved only because of me, trying to help. Because of me . . ." He felt her hand tighten its grip on his arm, so much that he looked down at it, then back into her eyes. She was shaking her head, her eyes determined.

"No, Jack. It wasn't your fault."

He started to say something, then felt her fingernails dig into his arm harder.

"Look at me," she demanded. "It was not your fault. There was nothing, nothing you could've done. Sometimes shitty things just happen. I know."

"How could you? You weren't there." He was surprised at the bitterness in his voice.

The sadness in her eyes was almost unbearable. "No, I wasn't. But in my office, when you asked about my sister—and my Dad? What I didn't tell you is that they waited for me. I missed my train, and didn't bother to call, so they waited for my train and didn't leave until it came and went and no Tina. Then they left. Do you realize what I'm saying?"

He shook his head. The fog surrounding his brain was too thick.

"*IF* they'd left after Kim's train came in, *IF* I'd called, they would've left thirty minutes earlier. And the drunk running the Stop sign would've hit someone else's car." Now tears were streaming down her face. "And I'd still have my father and my sister."

He recognized the pain in her eyes, and knew the ache she felt in her heart. He wanted to tell her it wasn't her fault, but realized the hypocrisy of that statement, given what he'd just told her. Logically, talking about her, it rang true, but applied to him it fell short. He couldn't have it both ways.

It was true, he told her. There was no way she was responsible. He repeated her words—for both of them. *Sometimes shitty things just happen.*

Chapter 15

Captain Tony sat at the helm in the back of the Glass Bottom Boat, a tourist boat that operated out of Clearwater Beach Marina. His real name was Doug and he heard his voice over the speakers as he started his spiel for the trip. A total of thirteen people, in addition to him, were on the boat, seated on the benches along either side of the thirty-four foot pontoon boat.

He checked out the passengers as he automatically went through his canned talk. That was the only thing that allowed him to keep his sanity, since going through the motions bored him to tears. Four times a day he did this. He'd wanted to get a recording, but the owner of the boat insisted that paying passengers wanted a connection with the captain, thus the silly uniform, which was hot as hell, and the monotone soliloquy.

By the end of each day, Captain Tony thought he would pull his hair out—what little was left—before the end of the last cruise. If it were not for the libations at the Crow's Nest Lounge every evening, he knew he would be stark raving mad by now.

He looked over the passengers, chatting with each other and enjoying the view as they plowed up the

Intracoastal Waterway. Occasionally, he'd have a hot young girl in a bikini top on the cruise to distract him, but today, there was no such luck. He knew all of them were over at the beach, frolicking around with their friends. Kids that age had better things to do than a stupid cruise on a slow moving pontoon boat.

On the left side of the boat was an older couple, sitting near the front by themselves. He figured them to be on an anniversary trip or maybe considering retiring to this area. Clearwater was a popular haven for the nearly-dead, a category they appeared to fit.

Next on that side was a younger couple with two small kids, both girls, who were clearly excited to be out on a boat. They were probably down for vacation and hitting all the tourist sites. Last on that side was a single spinster by herself, hoping to snag a wealthy old geezer. The cruise was certainly popular with the gray-hair set.

Glancing over to the right side, he saw a young couple up front, probably newlyweds, who were more interested in sucking each other's tonsils out than anything else. The girl was a good twenty pounds overweight, and her husband was ugly enough to give Freddy Krueger nightmares. Captain Tony got the shivers thinking about them procreating.

Behind them on that side were two young boys with an older couple he figured were their grandparents, another popular group of customers.

The grandmother had potential, he decided, the only one on this trip. It never occurred to him how desperate that sounded. She was petite and in good shape, wearing, by beach standards, modest white shorts and a low-cut, tight top that accented her ample bosom. She had short blonde hair, a nice smile, and soft skin, which he'd noticed when he extended his hand to help her during the boarding process, trying not to stare at her chest or at least not be too obvious about it. After all, captains did get a certain amount of leeway. Not bad for a grandma.

They were puttering up the Intercoastal, going to the upper end of Caladesi Island State Park. The expensive, four-color, Glass Bottom Boat brochure spoke of tropical reefs and showed pictures of all kinds of marine life waiting to be seen on the adventure. Captain Tony chuckled when he first saw the pictures, and asked, to no avail, where they'd come from.

In reality, they were going up to float over a sunken drug runner's boat and with any luck, see a sea turtle, maybe a porpoise, and some mullet swimming underneath. Occasionally, they would see a sand shark, which thrilled the passengers even more. The Keys this was not, but tourists kept coming and that meant a job for him and money to burn at the Crow's Nest.

Captain Tony didn't care—he was long past the point of giving a rat's ass about pretty much anything. The passengers had paid, and he'd be paid whether they saw anything or not. There did seem to be a loose correlation between tips and sightings, but he'd long since quit pandering to the passengers. It simply wasn't worth the effort.

He maneuvered the boat around to the north side of the little island, and snagged the buoy to tie up while the passengers crowded around the glass bottom in the middle of the boat. At least the water was clear this morning, so they had no trouble spotting the sunken wreck of a drug running skiff ten feet below them. He had recited the story of it being a modern day pirate's boat—half true, he thought—and with every trip, he'd convinced himself that it really was.

He positioned himself so he had a good view of the grandmother leaning over. While she was intent on seeing what she could through the glass bottom of the boat, Captain Tony was intent on seeing what he could as her top fell open to expose a pair of well equipped and unencumbered breasts. The view didn't distract him from his talk—he'd given it so many times, it was like breathing, totally second nature.

"What kind of fish is that, Captain Tony?" It was one of the boys, and the grandmother looked up just as Tony was glancing over at the fish to see what the hell the little tyke was seeing.

"Those are mullet," he said, "and some mighty fine ones, I might add."

The little girls on the opposite side squealed with delight and pointed as an entire school swam beneath them.

"Delicious eating. One of those would make a great dinner," he said, getting into the role.

"Ugh," the girls said in tandem.

"Look, Nana, a turtle!" It was the other boy, and sure enough, a sea turtle swam underneath as if on cue.

This may turn out pretty good, Captain Tony thought, a little more interested. Grandparents were usually good tippers, especially if the grandkids were excited like those two crumb-snatchers. Maybe the girls' parents would get swept up in the moment, too.

"This is a good day, folks. Conditions are excellent." He decided to go out on a limb. "Just might see a shark here if we keep an eye out."

Everyone was staring down through the glass and Tony resumed studying Nana's boobs. She was leaning over farther, if possible, and he could swear he saw nipples. His thoughts were interrupted by the piercing scream of the eight-year-old girl seated near the front. By the time he'd processed it and shifted his view, another, then another scream emerged.

What the . . . That was when he saw it. The bloated body of a young black man floated face-up underneath the boat, scraping the glass as everyone stared. The adults scurried to cover the children's eyes amidst the screams of almost everyone on board, including Captain Tony.

As he shuffled along the sidewalk in downtown Clearwater clutching a crudely lettered piece of cardboard, Bird kept a watchful eye. Ever since his dunking, he had been more wary. Those two were bad news, and he didn't want any more of them.

He knew his career with them was over, which was fine by him. There were other ways to make a little cash on the streets, ways that didn't risk getting dropped in the bay. Now, he was headed to his favorite corner to panhandle. It was almost lunch, so there'd be lots of people out and about. He had to watch out for the cops, but as long as he didn't bother anyone, they generally left him alone, even though the corner was only a block away from the courthouse.

As he stood on the corner, he watched for black Cadillac Escalades. They were popular with thugs and gangbangers, so there were more of them on the street than he realized. Every time one would approach, he'd step back a few feet until they passed or he determined it wasn't them.

Bird originally thought they may have been working for the Scientologists, or aliens as he called them, but he'd overheard them talking about home in Kentucky. He knew there were lots of Bible-thumpers in Kentucky, so he didn't figure the aliens would bother with that area.

For once, he was glad all the Scientologists were around. They were easy to spot in their dark pants and white shirts. They tended to leave him alone, and he figured he was safe as long as he was in a crowd.

He felt bad about giving Ronnie up, but he was afraid they were going to drown him. He was going to alert Ronnie next time he saw him, but he hadn't seen the short, skinny black guy since. That wasn't unusual on the streets. Sometimes he'd go for weeks not seeing any of the regulars.

Bird figured he'd resume his surveillance on the aliens. He saw two girls walking toward him, and he held up his sign at his waist. "Help for the homeless," he said quietly.

One of the girls, a blonde wearing shorts, looked vaguely familiar. Her friend had on the recognizable Scientology uniform. The blonde reached into her pocket and pulled out a dollar bill and started to hand it to him.

"That just encourages them, you know," the shorter alien girl said. "They can break the cycle if they try." She was speaking alien—Bird recognized it from other encounters he'd had with them. He wondered if the blonde was one of them. She didn't dress like one, but maybe she was a recent arrival.

The blonde handed him the dollar and asked him his name. He was surprised, since most people didn't want to have a conversation with a street person. Most of the time, they would hand him the money and keep walking.

"They call me Bird," he said, again in a quiet voice.

She laughed, and her laugh had an innocent quality to it, almost like a child's. "That's funny. My name is Wren," she said. "How long you been on the street, Bird?"

"Couple of years." He looked at the alien, who clearly didn't approve of this exchange. He thought for a minute the blonde who called herself Wren might be playing with him, but when he looked into her eyes, they were sincere. "Clearwater's a nice place, but you better be careful around here."

Wren smiled. It was a pretty smile—not fake. "Thanks, I will. You, too, Bird." They started to walk away.

"Thanks, Wren."

Later that day, almost dusk, he ran into Megan, the broad that was sitting next to him on his last trip with the Kentucky boys.

"Hey, Bird. How's it going?" she asked.

"Not good. Not good. You?"

She shrugged. "Okay, still doing the prescription thing. Haven't seen you there lately?"

Bird shook his head. "I quit that." That was all he was going to say about it. They were everywhere. For the first time since he'd been in Clearwater, he was thinking maybe he should move on to somewhere else, maybe down to Sarasota. He'd heard Sarasota was nice.

He looked around, expecting the Kentucky thugs to be close by, and started to shuffle off. Megan might be asking for herself, or she might be asking for them. Either way, he didn't care and he didn't want to talk to her anymore.

"You hear about Ronnie?" she said, to his back.

Bird froze in his tracks and turned around, afraid to ask. He stood there, looking at the woman, but not saying a word.

Megan took a drag off the cigarette she was smoking and exhaled. "Found him in the water, up at Caladesi. He was drowned."

"What was he doing up there?" Bird occasionally went over to Clearwater Beach, but Caladesi was out of everyone's territory.

She shook her head. "Don't know. One of them glass bottom boats over at the beach was up there with a bunch of tourists. He floated right under them."

Bird sucked in a breath and started shaking his head again as he turned and walked off as fast as he could. He had a sick feeling he knew what happened to Ronnie.

He decided to walk over to Clearwater Beach. On the way across the causeway, he thought about Ronnie. He felt responsible. He considered telling the cops, but by the time he got over to Clearwater Beach Marina, he'd talked himself out of it. The cops wouldn't believe him, anyway, and would probably end up putting him in jail. Besides, nothing he could do for Ronnie now.

He walked around the marina area for a while, doing a little panhandling. The beach police were harder on that because of all the tourists, so he was careful. He stayed away from the sidewalk under the bridge.

Chapter 16

Late Friday afternoon, Jack and Molly were driving over to Tampa for a Drager Clinic dinner at Big Cat Rescue. Coming across the Courtney Campbell, most of the traffic was heading west, into the setting sun that Jack could see in his rearview mirror.

Every quarter, Drager had a dinner meeting for management, which was mainly a perk for the physicians and their wives. Drager had rented the house at Big Cat Rescue for this quarter's meeting, and this was the first such dinner for Molly and Jack.

Jack took the Veterans north and got off at Exit 9 on Gunn Highway, going west. He made a u-turn at the first opportunity, according to the directions, and drove east on Gunn Highway. He was expecting a large sign marking the entrance, but instead saw only a small, yellow sign marking a non-descript dirt road. Missing the road, he turned into the next drive which led to a convenience store and McDonald's. He went through the parking lot and back out to the intersection to try again.

This time, he turned right onto the one-lane dirt road, went about a quarter of a mile, and came to a gate. A uniformed guard stood at the entrance. Jack stopped and rolled down the window, handing him the invitation.

The guard took a quick glance at it, looked in the car, then waved them in. Jack eased into the unpaved parking lot and squeezed between a large BMW 7 series sedan and a bright red Ferrari.

"We fit right in here, don't we," Molly said, looking at the high-end vehicles that filled the parking lot.

Jack patted the dash of the Mini and said, "Don't worry, girl, we love you just like you are." He shook his head and laughed. "I hate these events—you know that, don't you?"

She grinned. "Me too, but you have to admit, it's kind of nice to rub shoulders with the rich and famous on occasion."

"Whatever."

They got out and followed the lights marking the path to the house. A small crowd was gathered on the porch of the non-descript, one-story building, drinks in hand. Music was flowing from somewhere inside the house. At a tent before the entrance, Jack checked in and acquired name tags for the two of them. They walked up the few steps to the porch, Jack nodding politely and speaking to everyone as they made their way to the bar. At the top of the steps, he almost ran over Doctor Tina Marshall, not recognizing her in a short, red dress.

"Jack?" she said.

He stopped in his tracks, surprised at the transformation. It was quite a change from the shapeless scrubs he last saw her wearing in the clinic. He tightened his grip on Molly's hand.

"Dr. Marshall?" he said.

"I told you, call me Tina." She smiled and held out her free hand, her left one clutching a glass of white wine.

Jack shook her hand and made introductions. He kept thinking back to her picture on the website and how outdated it was. Not only had she dropped a few pounds, she was in good shape. She really needed to update her picture, he thought.

While Tina and Molly chatted, Jack took the opportunity to make a bar run. When he returned with two glasses of wine, both women were standing close together and laughing.

"Sounds like I missed the punch line," he said, handing a glass to Molly.

"Just sharing some hospital humor," Molly said.

"You didn't tell me your wife was a nurse," Tina said. "I would've been nicer."

"Trust me," Jack said, "you were way nicer than some."

As if on cue, Dr. Winston Andrews walked up, nodding to Tina as if it were a secret handshake. He checked Molly out, and spoke to Jack.

"Mr. Davis," Andrews said. Jack introduced him to Molly, and he flashed a lecherous smile. "Could I have a minute with you," he asked, turning his attention back to Jack.

Jack excused himself and followed Dr. Andrews outside. They walked over to an enclosure containing a bobcat, snoozing in the corner. Andrews stopped and turned to face him, stepping closer and invading Jack's personal space.

"I understand you're questioning the number of patients I see?" Andrews said, in a low voice.

Jack was caught off guard, and not sure how to respond.

Andrews continued. "Since you don't have a clinical background, I fail to see how you're qualified to make such a judgment." He paused to take a sip of his drink. "I suggest you proceed very carefully down that path." He turned and walked back to the reception, leaving Jack standing there, flabbergasted.

Jack shook his head and felt his face flush. Once again, he'd been ambushed, and he'd not even responded. He collected himself and rejoined Molly and Tina.

"What was that about?" Tina asked him as he walked up.

"He just wanted to give me some friendly advice," he said, clenching his teeth.

Tina rolled her eyes and looked at Jack. "I can imagine."

"You don't look too receptive," Molly said.

He just shook his head, indicating he didn't want to talk about it. He asked Tina about several of the other doctors present, and she introduced Jack and Molly to some of the other people that Jack had not met. He noticed Dr. Drager and Ivana across the way, working the room, making the rounds, and briefly chatting with each person in attendance.

Jacketed servers circulated with platters of crab cakes, stuffed mushrooms, and grilled shrimp kabobs. He could make a meal from the hors d'oeuvres, he thought, as he sampled something from every tray.

After cocktails, Drager stood at the podium before the microphone and asked everyone to find their assigned seats. Intentionally, no one was seated next to their spouse, presumably to encourage interaction amongst the attendees.

Jack found Molly's placard, situated between Dr. Andrews and a Dr. Winship, who Jack had not met. He seated Molly, introduced himself briefly to Dr. Winship and then found his place at the next table over, surprised to see that he was seated between Dr. Marshall and Winnie Ingram, wife of the radiologist in charge of the diagnostic center.

As soon as everyone was seated, salads were served. After the extended cocktail hour, everyone was more relaxed. Once Winnie found out Jack's role with Drager Clinic and discovered he was not a physician, she shifted her attention to the handsome young doctor seated on her other side. Jack could sense Dr. Marshall's presence next to him and it made him a bit uncomfortable. She was too easy to be around, he thought, thinking back to their dinner at Ted's Sushi.

He took a deep breath and plunged in. "So, Tina," he asked, remembering to call her by her first name. "Is this your first visit here?"

She gave him a warm smile, and took a sip of wine before answering. "You remembered to call me by my first name. I'm impressed."

"I'm slow, but eventually it sinks in."

She laughed. "No, I've been out here a few times. I volunteer and work with Dr. McLaughlin, the head veterinarian."

"Interesting. You like working with animals better than people?"

She nodded. "Sometimes. They complain less. I started out wanting to go to vet school, then changed my mind when I got my undergraduate degree."

"I'll bet it's interesting working with the big cats."

"Fascinating. They are such beautiful creatures."

She told him about some of the cases she'd worked on here, and soon the main course arrived. They'd had a choice of fish or chicken. Jack and Tina both had fish, and he noticed that Winnie had selected the chicken. He wondered if the reason they had no red meat on the menu was because of the surroundings.

Over dinner, with the rest of the table involved in their own conversations, Tina leaned closer and asked, "What was that about outside with Winston?"

Jack chuckled. "Let's just say he was encouraging me to do my job . . . and warning me not to screw with him."

"Maybe you should listen to him."

"I couldn't help but notice—you don't seem to care much for Dr. Andrews."

She took a sip of wine before responding. "Let's just say I think he's a competent physician and leave it at that."

He started to ask what she meant, but she changed the subject and asked him how he liked living on a sailboat. They finished eating without mentioning Winston Andrews again.

After dinner, the founder of the sanctuary took the podium, thanking everyone for their attendance and support. "This evening, I'm pleased to announce the finalists for our annual Top Cat Award. This award is given to the individual in the community who has significantly contributed to Big Cat Rescue in an outstanding manner over the past year. The winner will be announced at our yearly benefit ball, to be held here next month."

She mentioned three names that Jack didn't recognize, and the audience responded with polite applause after each one. When she got to the last name, she paused for effect. "I'm especially honored to name our fourth and last finalist—Dr. Devo Drager."

The ovation was enthusiastic as Dr. Drager stood, and gave a short bow. When the applause finally ebbed, the lights dimmed and a video presentation on the facility played on the large screen behind the podium.

All of the animals there were rescue animals, in the sense they were either mistreated or neglected by their previous owners. People adopted big cats as pets when they were small, but then the animals grew and became a problem. The owners became unwilling or unable to care for them.

After the presentation, Dr. Drager got up and said a few words. He talked about his involvement with Big Cat Rescue and urged those in attendance to consider their support as well.

On the drive home, Jack said to Molly, "I'm glad that's over, though it wasn't as bad as I thought. Interesting place. I would like to go sometime when we could see the animals."

"I enjoyed it. You didn't tell me Dr. Tina was such a hottie," Molly said, pinching his arm. "You seemed to be enjoying yourself."

Jack laughed. "I can assure you she didn't look anything like that when I met her in the office. Besides, you were the hottest one there."

She smiled. "Good recovery. She was nice. I enjoyed talking to her."

"Yeah, she is nice. Sharp lady."

"I better keep an eye on her. Doesn't sound like there's any love lost between her and Dr. Andrews. By the way, what exactly did he say to you? You came back and looked like you were ready to strangle someone."

"He basically told me to butt out. Seems he found out that I'm questioning the number of patients he sees, and he was warning me."

She shook her head. "I'm not surprised. He's pretty full of himself. Modesty is certainly not one of his traits. He did his best to impress me, while pretending not to be looking at my chest."

Jack raised an eyebrow. "Oh, really? Maybe I should keep an eye on him."

Molly laughed. "So not my type, not even under the worst of circumstances. Trust me—you're safe with him around. How was the cougar on your other elbow? Or did you even notice, with Dr. Tina?"

"Winnie? That's Dr. Ingram's wife—he's the radiologist in charge of the diagnostic center. I think she was more taken with the handsome young doctor on her other side. She didn't have a whole lot to say to me, but she seemed nice enough. Obviously comes from big money. Once she realized I was just the hired help, she dropped me like a bad habit. I don't think I had a big enough bank account to impress her."

They compared notes about the other people they met, and were still talking when they arrived back at the boat.

People were milling about the marina, the Pirate Ship unloading across the way. Summers were the busy time for Clearwater Beach, and this weekend was no exception.

"How about a nightcap? I don't feel like I got to spend any time with you this evening," Jack said, as they stepped aboard their boat.

"Sure, a Baileys would be nice, thank you." Molly sat down in the cockpit while Jack went below to get a couple of glasses of Baileys.

He set the glasses down on the table, and sat next to Molly. They raised their glasses, touching them and not saying a word, none necessary. It was a comfortable silence as they watched the tourists.

"What's the weather supposed to do?" she asked, breaking the silence.

"They're watching an area out in the Gulf. Sky was red this morning when I ran." He was referring to the old sailor's adage, *red sky at morning, sailor take warning*, still one of the most accurate predictors around. Living on a boat on the coast of Florida made one pay close attention to the weather, especially in June, which was the first month of hurricane season.

"What do you think—anything to it?"

"We're definitely going to get some rain out of it. Anything else is anyone's guess at this point. We'll keep an eye on it. Who knows?"

Chapter 17

It was Friday, and Wren was sitting up front in the Escalade. Peabo was driving to the Waffle House in Clearwater Beach to pick up the runners for the morning. Seven managed to show. Shorty loaded them into the big SUV, and drove across the causeway to Clearwater. They were headed to the clinic to get prescriptions.

Peabo had eight hundred Oxys in the back, a good week's work so far. He was already thinking about buying a van for the next trip to Florida. That way, he could double the number of people they could run at one time, thereby doubling their haul and their profit in the same amount of trips to the clinic and the pharmacy.

Wren had the day off at the hospital, and Peabo had talked her into working with him. She was wearing shorts and a thin, loose fitting top with no bra. She had a nice body and took advantage of it when meeting with Doc. He was well compensated for his role in their business, but this was insurance, Peabo had told her.

They got to the clinic, parked, and Shorty went through his routine even though a couple of the people had worked for them before. Wren went with the first group into the clinic. Peabo and Shorty stayed in the SUV, claiming they needed to stay out of sight in case anyone was watching. She knew they wanted to keep an eye on the runners coming and going.

She didn't have to do anything, other than give Doc a good look and let him cop a cheap feel. It was no different than when she had danced, she told herself. But now she felt like a toy.

She sat on the edge of the exam table. Doc had his clipboard and the little Asian nurse was standing next to him looking bored.

He pretended to flip through the chart, then turned to the nurse. "Could you get Ms. Lawson's last MRI? I think I left it on my desk."

He always made up an excuse for the nurse to leave the exam room. As soon as she walked out and closed the door, he said, "We probably need to check you again." He moved closer and waited for her to pull up her shirt, exposing her breasts. She wasn't that big up top, but they were full and perky, and she knew that men liked them.

When she didn't comply, he cleared his throat and told her she'd have to pull up her shirt so he could examine her. She closed her eyes, and pulled up her top, feeling the cool air on her naked chest.

She opened her eyes in time to see him lick his lips at the sight and set his clipboard down on the exam table next to her. As he felt his way around both of her boobs, he paused to rub her nipples with his thumbs. They were sensitive, and she hated that they got stiff, but with the cool air and him touching her, she couldn't help it.

Closing her eyes, she convinced herself that he was doing a legitimate breast exam. She could feel his wedding band on her right boob, and she wondered what Doc's wife would say if she could see him now. It occurred to her that he probably fondled a lot of tits in his job and Mrs. Doc didn't care. When he'd finished and removed his hands, she opened her eyes to see him standing in front of her staring at her chest.

"I don't feel any abnormalities," he said, a little hoarse and breathing heavy. "And they look perfectly fine. I'll check you again when you come back next month, just to be sure."

I bet you will, she thought. *Just like you do every time.*

There was a soft knock on the door. Wren pulled her shirt down, and Doc grabbed his clipboard, pretending to write out the prescription he'd written earlier.

"Take these as needed, and continue to do your exercises," he said, handing her the prescription as the nurse opened the door and walked in with the MRI. He took the report and placed it in the chart, barely looking at it.

"See you next month," Wren said, hopping down from the exam table and walking out.

She got back in the Escalade and waited for the rest of the group to get back.

"Everything okay?" Peabo asked.

She nodded and sat there quietly. She wondered why Peabo didn't care that another man touched her, especially now that they were engaged. Most men were jealous about stuff like that. She'd asked him about it the first time it happened, and all he said was that it was business, like actors kissing in movies even though they were married to other people. Besides, he told her, Doc was a real doctor.

"Does Megan let him touch her?" Megan was the only woman in their group of runners today. A heavy-set woman, she had worked for Peabo before.

He snorted and looked at her. "Is that what this is about?"

She didn't answer and stared at him, waiting for an answer to her question.

"I don't know what he does with her, and don't care. He's a damn doctor, okay? What difference does it make?" He lit a cigarette.

"You don't care if another man plays with your wife's boobs?"

"You ain't my wife yet," he said, in a huff. "Why? Did he do anything else?"

She shook her head, and the others returned to the SUV. Peabo told them to get in, and yelled at them for taking so long.

Peabo drove to the pharmacy, and when they got there, Wren went in with the first group. At least with the pharmacist, she didn't have to do anything like she did with Doc. The pharmacist on their payroll, Kirby, was the only one they dealt with there. Peabo would make sure he was working on days they came.

She waited for the slight, middle-aged man to walk over. As soon as he came up to the counter, she handed him her prescription along with two others for Peabo and Shorty. A hundred dollar bill was folded out of sight between two of the prescriptions.

Kirby smiled knowingly, took the scripts and said it would be a few minutes. He went behind the counter and pretended to read them, although he knew what they were without looking. He glanced around to make sure no one was watching, and Wren knew he was palming the money.

The pharmacist wasn't supposed to fill Schedule II prescriptions for people not present, but for appearance's sake, she claimed they were for her brothers. Like other such restrictions, all it accomplished was a more circumventive process.

Five minutes later, she paid cash for the three prescriptions and walked back out to the car. Just outside the pharmacy, she ran into Jack Davis. Surprised to see him there, she barely acknowledged him and kept walking, telling Megan to keep her mouth shut. She hoped Peabo hadn't seen him talking to her.

Jack was headed over to Bayview Pharmacy, his first visit there. He had made the rounds to all of the clinics, and was now starting to visit the remaining facilities of the Drager Empire, as he called it.

Bayview Pharmacy was the largest of the ancillary businesses, and located only a few blocks from the clinic with the same name. It was a very profitable business, and while the clinic couldn't insist that patients get their prescriptions filled there, most did as a matter of convenience.

He found a parking spot and when he was almost to the front door, he looked up and saw Wren Lawson walking out with two other people. She hadn't spotted him yet, so he stopped and said, "Hi, Wren, how are you?"

The girl looked up and recognized Jack, smiling at first, then looking confused. She stared out toward the parking lot behind Jack, then looked back at him and shook her head, not speaking. He turned to see who or what she was looking at in the parking lot, but saw only dozens of vehicles parked out there, none conspicuous.

"Are you okay?" he asked the girl, now walking past him. He noticed she had a bag from the pharmacy in her hand. She glanced at him, shaking her head almost imperceptibly. She kept walking, acting as if she didn't recognize him. He overheard the short, heavy-set woman with her say, "Who's that? Somebody you know?" Then he heard Wren tell her, "No, just shut up and keep walking."

He walked inside the pharmacy, stopped, and looked out through the door. Wren and the two people with her got into a black, Cadillac Escalade parked near the back of the parking lot, facing the building. Strange, he thought. Wren acted like she didn't want to acknowledge she knew him.

He went to the prescription counter and asked for Lee Kirby, the manager of the pharmacy. The clerk turned around and spoke to an older man with gray hair, standing behind the raised platform containing the drugs and the business end of the pharmacy. He nodded, finished what he was doing, and stepped down to the counter.

"I'm Lee," he said. "What could I do for you?"

Jack stuck out his hand and introduced himself. Lee motioned to the door to the right of the counter and told him to come back. He explained to the pharmacist why he'd stopped by, and mentioned that he'd like to get an overview of the business.

Lee took him over to an unoccupied computer screen and typed in his password. He explained to Jack that everything was computerized, including most of the prescriptions, which were sent electronically from the physicians' offices.

"Most?" Jack asked.

Lee laughed, and said there were a few that still insisted on handwriting prescriptions.

"Do all of our physicians do it electronically?"

"Most of them," Lee answered, shaking his head. "Andrews still insists on doing his by hand. We keep trying to change that, but so far, not much success."

Lee showed him how prescriptions came up, and how they accessed the information by patient.

"Can you access the entire day's worth of patients?"

"Sure," Lee responded. He tapped a couple of keys, and a color-coded list of names popped up on the screen, along with status, doctor's name, and drug name. He explained that red signified that refills had expired and the prescription was no longer valid. Yellow signified that the script was for a Schedule II drug. Green indicated the prescription had been filled that day, whereas no color indicated that it had not been yet picked up.

Jack looked down the list of names and saw Wren Lawson's name in yellow. Beside her name were Dr. Winston Andrews and OxyContin. "How much OxyContin do we sell a month?"

Lee shrugged. "Don't know for sure—I could look it up, but it's a boatload. Hey, our clinics are in the pain management business, so that's not surprising."

Lee finished his tour of the system, then took Jack over to the counter to observe the pharmacists busy filling prescriptions.

* * *

When Wren got in the Escalade, she handed the bag to Shorty, who never bothered checking her haul. She was relieved that neither Peabo nor Shorty had noticed her encounter with Jack. Still, she was unnerved that she'd run into him.

When all of the runners had turned in their drugs, they drove back out to the beach. Two of them had decided to stay in Clearwater, and the others wanted to ride back. When they got across the causeway, Peabo pulled into the marina parking lot and let everyone out.

She, Shorty, and Peabo walked down to the restaurant to get a bite to eat.

"Good days work," Peabo said, taking a bite of his burger. The three of them were sitting out on the deck, enjoying the sunshine. "Good week. Glad you're back," he said to Wren.

She finished chewing her French fry and said, "They're moving me to a new job at the hospital Monday," Wren said.

Shorty grunted, and looked at Peabo, who processed the information.

"A new job? What's that mean?" Peabo asked.

She shrugged. "They're moving me over to Environmental Services, or something like that. Fancy word for cleaning rooms and stuff. I work days, so that will be good."

Peabo wrinkled his brow. "How you gonna work in my business if you're doing that every day?"

"I work four days a week. I need a real job, Peabo."

Shorty looked from one to the other, but kept his mouth shut, except to shovel in food. He looked pretty uncomfortable for a three-hundred pound man with a plate of food in front of him.

Peabo finished his beer and belched. "I thought you were coming back in the business with me. That's a real job, making real money."

She didn't feel like arguing, and she knew that's where this discussion was headed.

"I'll help when I can, like today. I'm just tired, Peabo. Plus that week in jail scared me. I don't want to do that again."

The reality is she wanted a real life, like Jack and Molly. She didn't like doing something illegal, not that she had any moral objections. The money was good, but she sure as hell didn't want to spend any more time locked up. That was a wake-up call, and one she didn't want to repeat.

Peabo shook his head slowly, but held his tongue. "I thought you wanted to go back to Kentucky? How you going to do that if you're working at the hospital? Where you gonna stay down here?"

"You know there ain't no jobs for me up there. They said at the shelter they'd help me find someplace to live."

"I don't like it."

Shorty gulped down the rest of his lunch, got up and said he was going to smoke.

She reached over and put her hand on Peabo's arm. "If we had a place here, then ya'll would have somewhere to stay when you come down." She was hoping he'd offer to help pay for a place.

Peabo seemed to think about that angle, considering the possibilities, then shook his head. "No, you need to be with me. I ain't leaving you down here while I go back to Kentucky."

She started to say *it didn't stop you before*, but bit her tongue. "We could try it for a while until we get married."

"We'll see," he said, and went back to his dinner.

She knew he wasn't wild about the idea, but maybe he was thinking about it. So far, he'd been reluctant to talk with her about setting a wedding date. She almost wished he'd back out.

Chapter 18

That afternoon, when Molly got home, Jack told her about seeing Wren at Bayview Pharmacy. "She recognized me and started to speak. Then, she looked out at the parking lot and her entire demeanor changed. Have you talked to her lately?" he asked.

Molly acknowledged she hadn't heard from her since the night she came over and told them she was getting married. "Did you recognize who she was with?"

Jack shook his head. "I've never seen either of them. One was a heavy-set older woman, short, and the other was a young guy, looked to be about Wren's age, maybe a little older."

Molly asked if he was sure they were together, and he told her about watching all three of them get into the Escalade. "They all had bags—prescriptions—from the pharmacy."

She shrugged, and said, "Maybe they were friends from the shelter or something. Who knows?"

"She was getting painkillers," he said. He explained that he saw Wren's prescription for OxyContin on the computer screen in the pharmacy. He also told her that

Winston Andrews was listed as her doctor. "I'll bet they all had pain meds."

"That's where Peabo's getting his scripts? At your clinic?"

He nodded as he reached for his phone. "What do you want to do for dinner? I'm going to call Tina and ask her if she can join us."

"How about Rockaway? I've been craving a grouper sandwich and some she-crab soup."

Rockaway Grill was a couple of blocks up from the marina, on the beach, and a favorite hangout for locals and tourists. It was nothing fancy, but the food was good and the view of the sunset magnificent. It was their favorite place close by.

Tina said she'd meet them at the marina in thirty minutes. Jack and Molly walked up to the parking lot just as she was pulling in.

She parked and walked over to them, giving them each hugs.

"We thought we'd walk over to Rockaway," Molly said.

"Sure, one of my favorite spots on the beach," Tina said.

They walked past the crowds gathering at Pier 60 for the daily sunset festivities. There were jugglers, magicians, contortionists—the usual street performers. They had to walk around an especially large crowd gathered around a girl juggling batons with fire burning on each end.

"Reminds me of Key West," Jack said as they dodged the tourists.

"A little. Not the same, though," Molly responded.

Key West was one of their favorite destinations, and they'd sailed to the island several times from Fort Myers, an overnight trip. Sunset at Mallory Square was not to be missed. Clearwater Beach, with a great venue, had tried to copy the format, but it was hard to duplicate the eccentric appeal that only Key West could offer.

"Haven't made it there, yet," Tina said, "but it's on my list."

They arrived at Rockaway, and as usual, the line of people waiting for a table was out the door. As locals, they knew the secret, and when they approached the hostess, they told her they just wanted to go to the bar. There were a limited number of tables there, available on a first-come, first-served basis. They didn't mind eating in the bar and Jack couldn't remember the last time they'd waited on a table here.

They found a table next to the wall across from the bar, and Jack sat with his back facing the water, where the large golden orb was getting close to the flat horizon of the Gulf of Mexico. They ordered drinks, and Tina said, "Thanks for inviting me. I was looking at leftovers tonight at the Marshall bar and grill."

"Glad you could join us, but I have to confess to an ulterior motive," Jack said. Over dinner, he told her about what he'd discovered that afternoon.

Tina listened attentively and didn't interrupt. "Maybe it's legitimate? Winston writes a lot of scripts," she said when he finished.

Molly shook her head. "No way. If she's having chronic pain, then she's doing a great job of disguising it."

"I checked this afternoon when I got back to the office. His clinic writes the most scripts for oxycodone by a huge margin," Jack said. "And I'm talking per doctor."

"We know Wren's boyfriend is running pills to Kentucky, but she wouldn't tell us where they were coming from," Molly said. "Now we know."

Tina shook her head. "You've got one person with a prescription. That proves nothing."

"Look at a sample of charts. I told you before, he'll never know," he said.

Tina frowned. "Winston's not stupid. If he's involved, I guarantee his charts are airtight. The fact that he prescribes a lot of oxycodone doesn't mean anything by itself."

"Come on, Tina. Do you really believe what you're saying?" Jack asked.

She shrugged. "Doesn't matter what I believe, if there's no proof."

He was getting frustrated. For some reason, Tina Marshall was unwilling to get involved too deeply. "Why are you so afraid of him?"

The waitress appeared with the check, and Tina handed her cash, telling her to keep the change.

On the way back to the marina, Molly suggested walking out on the pier. Tina still hadn't answered his question, in fact, she hadn't said much since leaving the restaurant.

About halfway out Pier 60 was a tiny bait shop that blocked admittance to the far end of the pier. There was a nominal charge to go through, but the threesome stopped just short, looking out at the water. A few fishermen passed by with their gear, heading out to the end of the pier. Tina put her elbows on the railing and looked out over the open waters of the Gulf.

"When I first came to work here, Winston asked me out for dinner. I thought it was a nice gesture, and naive me, assumed it was strictly business. I was staying at the Westin, right across the bay. He insisted on picking me up, claiming that since I was new to the area, he'd be glad to drive."

Molly took his hand and squeezed.

Tina took a deep breath and exhaled before continuing. "He took me to Bern's for a nice, intimate dinner and a wonderful bottle of wine. Afterwards, when he took me back to the hotel, he insisted on walking me to my room.

"As soon as I unlocked the door, he pushed me inside up against the wall and tried to force himself on me. I was so shocked, I didn't react at first. When I felt his hand under my dress, I snapped out of it and brought my knee up right into his groin as hard as I could. Needless to say, that cooled him off.

"At first, he claimed I led him on, then he apologized and blamed it on too much wine. He begged me not to tell Devo. Like a fool, I agreed, but told him if he ever so much as looked twice at me again, I'd kill him."

Jack shook his head. "That asshole. Sorry, I didn't mean to open up an old wound."

"Believe me, I understand," Molly said. "Sometime—maybe after more wine—I'll have to tell you about my ex-husband, also a doctor. Sounds like he and Andrews are related."

Jack was shocked. As far as he knew, she'd never told anyone that story. He clenched his fist as he thought about it. In Boston, she'd been married to an abusive doctor who had convinced her that she was at fault and not worthy of him. Publicly, he played the part of the doting husband, while privately making Molly's life a living hell. After he raped her and threatened to kill her, she left in the middle of the night and drove to Florida, determined to escape.

Jack said, "I don't understand. Why would you be reluctant to go after Andrews? From what you've just told us, you should welcome the opportunity to hang him."

She looked at Molly and Jack with a sadness in her eyes and shook her head. "I'm sorry, I just can't. You don't understand—I can't take the risk."

"At least talk to Wren. We can't let him get away with this, Tina." Jack was frustrated. They had a witness that could prove Andrews was prescribing OxyContin—a witness that was tied into a known drug ring. It was a sure bet that others were getting their drugs there as well.

"Easy for you to say," Tina said.

"Maybe we should take it to the police," Molly said.

"No," Tina said. "Please—"

"Why—"

"It's getting late," Molly said, interrupting him. "We should be going." Her eyes signaled to Jack to let it go.

He didn't understand. Tina didn't want to press Andrews, but she didn't want them to involve the cops?

Tina stood and put her hand on Molly's. "I'm sorry. I wish I could help."

"Don't worry. We'll figure something out," Molly said.

They walked across the street in silence, Tina taking his arm and Molly's on the way to her car.

"We still have stories to share," she said as they walked up to a late model BMW parked out by itself at the far end of the parking lot. "But not tonight. Maybe some evening soon, when none of us have to work the next day."

"That'd be nice," Molly said.

Jack didn't respond, still trying to figure out what was going on with Tina. At her car, he mumbled, "Thanks for dinner."

She turned to face him at the car. "I'm sorry, Jack."

Before he could respond, she leaned up and hugged him, then pulled away and hugged Molly.

"Thanks for understanding," she said.

He felt the comment was directed toward Molly, not him.

She took out her car keys, pressed the button, and he heard the locks activate. "Good night," she said, getting into her car and shutting the door.

He stood there with Molly as Tina pulled out of the parking lot. "Can you tell me what's going on?"

"I don't know," Molly said, as they walked to the boat. "There's some reason she doesn't want to tangle with Andrews, and she's not ready to tell us. You realize how hard it was for her to share that story about him, don't you?"

Jack nodded. "I do, especially knowing your story. But I don't understand why she won't help."

She shook her head. "There's something else, and she'll tell us when she's ready."

"What are we going to do, now? I need a physician to look at the charts before I can take it to Drager."

"What about one of the other physicians?"

"No, I'm not sure I can trust any of them. I've thought about trying to hire someone, but that gets more complicated. And, it would take significantly longer."

"Don't give up on Tina. She's wrestling with a ghost. I think she may still come through."

"I hope you're right. I'm going to see Drager in the morning."

Chapter 19

While running the next morning, Jack tried to figure out how to approach Drager. He didn't want to give details, since he really didn't have any proof. But he had to do something, and he'd hit a wall with Tina.

He walked into the boss's office after Connie had squeezed him in for a few minutes in Drager's busy schedule.

Drager's desk was swamped, so Jack didn't waste time with small talk. "Yesterday, I met with Lee Kirby at Bayview Pharmacy. He runs a tight ship, and I was impressed. But, I got to thinking. We dispense and sell an awful lot of pain medications. How do we prevent happening to us what happened with Walgreens over in Orlando?"

Jack was referring to the headlines last month. Walgreens, the largest retail pharmacy operator in the country, had agreed to pay $80 million dollars to settle charges they were over- dispensing painkillers.

Drager studied him for a moment, then asked, "Do you have any specific concerns?"

Jack shook his head. "No, just worried about something like that happening to us." He tried to be casual about it. "That's my job, you know."

Drager nodded and folded his hands together under his chin. "I understand. Believe me, it's something I worry about as well. The potential for abuse is enormous, and I've witnessed a lot of people get caught up in it. The truth is that it's hard to prevent. That was one reason I brought you on board. I think if we copy our best practices to all our operations, we go a long way toward preventing something like that from happening to us."

He left Drager's office frustrated and feeling helpless. He was convinced Andrews was involved, and he couldn't sit back and let it continue. There had to be a way.

Peabo called Wren and arranged to pick her up at the front door of the hospital at 3:30, when she got off.

They pulled up in front of the hospital and parked next to the curb. When he saw Wren walking down the sidewalk toward them, he turned to Shorty.

"Here she comes, get in the back."

"Fuck, man, why can't she get in the back? You know I hate riding in the back."

Peabo gave him a hard look. "You wanna walk?"

Shorty mumbled, but opened the front passenger door as Wren walked up. He left the door open, muttered a "hello" and got in the back seat.

Wren got in and Peabo leaned over to give her a hug and kiss.

"Hey, baby. Glad to see you," he said, before giving her a deep kiss and letting his hand linger on her chest.

He pulled away, started the SUV, and pulled out into the street, heading east.

"You look like a doctor or something," he said. Wren was wearing green scrubs.

She shook her head. "Just an orderly. Doing shit work is all."

"I wanna take you somewhere nice to eat. To celebrate." They drove for a few minutes and he pulled into the LongHorn Steakhouse restaurant.

During dinner, he was most attentive to Wren, ignoring Shorty. It was dark when they left the restaurant, and he drove straight through downtown Clearwater, headed to the Two Palms, where he had gotten a room earlier.

"Where are you going?" Wren asked, as they started across the causeway toward the beach.

"I thought we'd go out to the beach for a while," Peabo said, his hand in Wren's lap.

He turned into the motel parking lot, pulled up in front of the room, and left the car running.

"Shorty wanted to go out for a while, so I thought we could have a beer and relax." He got out, came around to Wren's side of the Escalade, and opened her door.

"Don't stay out too late partying, Shorty. And be careful," he said as a sullen Shorty got out of the back seat and walked around to get in the driver's side.

Shorty knew better than to challenge Peabo in front of Wren, so he mumbled a "sure," and started to get behind the wheel of the Escalade.

"How am I gonna get back to the shelter? You know I have to be back by ten," Wren said, still sitting in the vehicle. Shorty got in behind the steering wheel, but didn't close his door yet.

Fuck, Peabo thought. Wren was starting to be a pain in the ass.

He forced a smile on his face. "Shorty will be back in time." He leaned across Wren so he could see Shorty. "Be back by nine-thirty."

Shorty opened his mouth to say something, but saw the glare from Peabo and closed it. "Whatever," he mumbled.

"Nine-thirty." Peabo repeated it so there would be no misunderstanding.

"Yeah, yeah, I got it. Nine-thirty." Shorty was still grumbling as he slammed the door.

Chapter 20

The next day at work, Molly's phone rang. It was Chris, the housekeeping manager at the hospital.

"You wouldn't happen to know where Wren is, would you?" he asked.

Shit, Molly thought. "No, and please don't tell me she didn't show up this morning."

"A no-show and no-call."

She knew what was next. Wren was still on probation at the hospital, and not showing up for work was grounds for immediate dismissal.

"Unless she's got a very good excuse, you know I have no choice but to terminate her," he said.

Molly exhaled. "I know. I'm sorry, Chris. I appreciate you giving her a chance. Let me try to get in touch with her. I'm sure she's got a good reason."

"It's a shame," he said. "She was smart, and a good worker. But you know I can't allow this. Rules are rules."

"I understand. Let me try to get in touch with her and I'll call you." As soon as Chris hung up, she took out her cell phone and called Wren. No answer. Damn, she wished she could get the girl to see how Peabo was using her. She'd hoped Wren was getting her act together, but now she wasn't sure.

She called Vicki, the director of the shelter. Vicki said that Wren had not come in last night by curfew, but she did call this morning and said she was with her boyfriend and wouldn't be back.

Molly put her phone down and shook her head. At least Wren wasn't hurt. She dreaded calling Chris back and waited until lunch to call, hoping he'd be away from his phone.

At 12:30, she called Chris. She was in luck—her call went to voice mail. Relieved, she left a message saying she'd be in meetings all afternoon and would call him in the morning. She wasn't sure she'd have a better answer in the morning, but she'd stall as long as she could.

"This is a surprise," Molly said to Jack, as she took off her shoes and stepped onto the boat. "You never get home before me." He was at the cockpit table, under the bimini, working on his laptop. Jimmy Buffet was playing in the background.

He laughed. "I needed to work on financial statements, so I left the office early. Too many interruptions."

She came over and leaned down to give him a peck. He pulled her close and gave her a long, passionate kiss.

"Wow," she said, as she stepped back. "You must have really missed me. I needed that."

"Why? What's the matter?"

"Wren was a no-show today at work. I'm going below to change, then I'll fill you in. Can I get you anything?"

"How about a beer on your way back?"

She laughed. "Guess that answers my question about dinner."

In a few minutes, she came back up, wearing shorts and a halter top, carrying two bottles. She sat across from him, putting his beer on the table next to the computer.

Jack took a swig, then closed his laptop. "Tell me about your day. It doesn't sound good."

"Chris called this morning. Wren didn't show up for work today and didn't call in."

Jack shook his head. "She okay?"

"I called Vicki at the shelter. Wren called her this morning and said she was with her boyfriend and not coming back. You were right—I should've stayed out of it." She took a long drink from her beer.

"No, you were right. That asshole is taking advantage of her, and she doesn't deserve that. Nobody does."

She shrugged. "I don't know what else to do. I put Chris off until in the morning, but I'm out of options."

"We're not giving up."

Molly shook her head. "You want something to eat? I didn't eat anything all day long. How about some nachos?"

Out in the cockpit, they had some nachos and talked about how to find Wren. The truth was they didn't know where to start. By the time they'd finished eating, it was getting dark. They cleaned up and prepared to go below for the evening, still trying to figure out some way to find the girl.

As they grabbed the last few items outside, they looked up and saw Wren walking down the dock toward them in the shadows.

"Wren, where have you been?" Molly asked.

She stopped at the boat and in a meek voice asked if she could come aboard.

"Take off your shoes," Molly said.

Wren slipped her sandals off and stepped down in the boat, head down.

"I'm sorry, Molly," she said, still looking down at her feet. "I know I screwed up."

"Maybe. How about telling me what happened? The truth, please."

The girl stood, shifting her weight from one foot to the other as if unsure whether to sit.

"Sit down. You hungry?" Molly asked.

Wren nodded and sat. When she finally looked up at Molly in the pale light, Molly gasped when she saw a bruise around her right eye.

"My God, Wren! What happened?" Molly said.

Jack strained to see, and when he made out the bruise on the young girl's face, Molly saw his anger rise.

A single tear ran down Wren's face, soon followed by another, then another.

Molly put her arms around the girl and held her close. She looked up at Jack and gave him a slight shake of her head. He nodded and went down below.

Molly could feel the thin girl sobbing on her shoulder, knowing it would come out in due time. She was feeling mixed emotions; compassion toward Wren and anger at the monster she knew who was responsible for this.

"I ... so ... stupid," Wren said, between sobs. "I believed him. I thought things would be different this time. Now I fucked up everything. I didn't know where else to go."

Molly patted the girl's head as Wren started crying again, her chest heaving with sobs. Molly didn't say a word, knowing that now was not the time. Wren just needed a friend to listen.

When the crying subsided, Molly handed her a napkin. She took Wren's shoulders and forced her to look Molly in the eyes. "It's going to be okay, Wren. We'll get things sorted out."

Wren looked at her with pleading eyes, hanging on to every word. "I'm sorry I let you down," she said, still sniffling.

Jack walked back up on the deck, carrying a glass of water and a fresh batch of hot nachos covered with cheese and beans. He set them down on the small table and sat on the other side.

"Thank you," Wren said, in a small, contrite voice, as she reached for the food.

Molly looked at Jack and could tell he was itching to confirm what they knew had happened. She gave him an almost imperceptible head shake, conveying that now was not the time and pleading with him to be patient. He gave her a slight nod, sat back, and folded his arms.

"Peabo picked me up after work yesterday," Wren said, between bites. "He took me out to eat, then after dark, we went back to his room. We fooled around, and then, when I told him it was time to go back to the shelter, he told me I didn't need to go, that I could just stay with him."

Molly noticed that she'd finished the entire plate of nachos and wondered if she'd eaten anything since last night.

Wren took a deep drink of water, set the glass down and continued.

"I told him I was going back to the shelter, and if he wouldn't take me, then I'd walk. I went to open the door and that's when he kicked it shut and pushed me out of the way. I tried to get past him, and he hit me. He told me I wasn't going nowhere, that he needed me.

"He got out some pills and held them out for me to take. I slapped his hand away and knocked them on the floor. Then he got really mad. Started kicking me, grabbed my hair, made me get down on the floor and lick them up off the carpet."

Jack's hands and jaw were clenched and Molly could only imagine what he was thinking.

Wren told them the next morning, when she woke up, Peabo was still asleep, but he had tied her to the bed. She held up her wrists and Molly could see the marks. Jack's grimace was even more foreboding.

Peabo woke up and told her they had work to do. Wren didn't know what to do. She knew she couldn't go back to the shelter or to work, so she convinced him she'd cooperate and wouldn't cause any trouble. They went out that morning, picked up runners, and drove over to the clinic.

After the morning's haul, they got some lunch, and came back over to the beach to pick up the afternoon shift. When they went to the pharmacy, she found a back entrance and escaped.

"How did you get here?" Molly asked.

"Walked. I was afraid to try and catch a ride, afraid he'd see me." She looked over at Jack with pleading eyes. "I didn't know where to go, so I came here."

"You're staying here tonight," Jack said, glancing at Molly. "Nothing we can do tonight, but you're safe here—I promise. We'll figure it out tomorrow."

Bird stood in the shadows, watching. He was in the parking lot at the Clearwater Beach Marina, his first trip back since his encounter with Boss. He had been over here since yesterday evening, flying signs—the term street people used for panhandling.

He'd done good on the beach. Money was better over here, more tourists and fewer aliens, but the cops were tougher.

That afternoon, he ran into Petey, one of the regulars.

The scrawny boy with a buzz cut turned and smiled when he saw him. "Birdman, what's up? Haven't seen you in while."

"Been busy. You still going over to the clinic?"

Petey nodded. "It was exciting today."

"Yeah? What happened?"

"Boss's girlfriend bailed. Man, he was pissed."

"Girlfriend?"

"Some blonde chick named Wren." Petey wiped his mouth with his hand. "She rode over with us and went into the pharmacy to pick up some pills. We came back out to the car, and she didn't come out."

"Didn't come out? Where'd she go?"

Petey shrugged. "Don't know, man. Boss went apeshit. Screamed at Shorty to go find her. He comes out a few minutes later, says she's gone, don't know where. Boss screamed and cussed all the way back over here. Everyone got out as soon as the car slowed down."

Bird had walked back over to the marina, puzzled. He couldn't believe that Wren, the blonde girl he'd met downtown, was Boss's girlfriend. He was doing a little nighttime flying when he saw Wren across the parking lot.

She was by herself, and his first thought was to look for Boss and Shorty. He glanced around the crowd, but didn't see them.

Her head was down, and she looked sad. He watched as she walked down to the docks, and punched in the code for the gate. After she passed through, he moved closer to see where she was going. He was surprised to see her walk out to a sailboat, where she was greeted by a couple sitting out on the back of it.

Later that evening, Jack and Molly were lying in their berth. It had been an emotionally draining night, and everyone had turned in early. The lights were out, but they were both still awake.

Molly knew the wheels were turning in Jack's head. And she also knew he wouldn't let the young girl go back to Peabo. She saw the look of anger in his face when he saw the bruises, and she was afraid of what he might do.

"We've got to turn this over to the police in the morning. We need to let them deal with it," Molly said.

"I agree. Either that, or I'm going to kill that asshole."

Chapter 21

The next morning, the three of them were in the cockpit, having coffee. Wren's face looked worse in the light of day than it did last night.

Jack picked up his coffee cup and sat back. "It's time you told us everything, Wren."

A tear rolled down Wren's cheek as she looked at Molly. "He'll kill me if I tell anyone."

Molly focused her attention on the shaking girl. "Wren, he's not going to hurt you again, I promise. He'll have to get through both of us," she said, looking at Jack and then back at Wren. "But you have to tell us what's going on. That's the only way we can help you," Molly said.

The girl was still sniffling, but nodded her head. She proceeded to tell them how Peabo recruited people off the street and take them to a doctor's office to get prescriptions. Then, he'd take them to a pharmacy down the street, get the scripts filled, and take the pills back to Kentucky where he'd sell them on the street for a profit.

That was what she was doing that day when Jack ran into her outside the pharmacy.

"So he's a drug dealer and you're helping him," Jack said.

Wren shook her head. "No, I mean, yes, I did yesterday because I had to. But, no, I don't sell drugs."

"What did you do?" Jack asked.

She told him that she helped recruit street people and she also went in to see the doctor and get prescriptions written for Peabo, Shorty, and herself.

"Where is this doctor's office?" Molly asked.

Wren shook her head. "I don't know exactly—somewhere in Clearwater—before you get to that nice restaurant on the water. Bay Clinic, or something like that."

"Castaways?" Jack asked. "Is that the restaurant you're talking about?"

Wren nodded. "The clinic was right down the street from the pharmacy where I saw you, maybe a block or two."

Jack looked at Molly, then back at Wren. "That has to be Bayview. What was the doctor's name?" Jack asked.

Again, Wren shook her head. "We always just called him 'Doc.' I didn't know his name."

Jack exhaled, exasperated. "You went in to see a doctor, let him examine you, and you didn't even know his name? Was he from another country? What'd he look like?"

Wren shook her head. "He was an older, tall, white man. Not a foreigner."

He caught a hard look from Molly and shook his head. He lowered his voice and asked in a more gentle tone, "Did you see his name on the prescription?"

The girl looked up at him, her eyes red from crying, and said, "There were a lot of names on it. It was a big clinic with lots of doctors, but we always saw the same man every time."

"Is there anything about the place you remember, anything at all?" Molly asked.

Wren thought a minute, then said, "It was a big building—maybe five or six floors. The receptionist was a big, black woman. She had a nametag that said *Tabitha*."

Jack cocked his head and stared at the girl. "What did you just say?"

"It was a big building—"

"No, the last part. What did you say?" he asked.

"The receptionist?"

Jack nodded.

"She was a big, black woman named Tabitha."

He looked at Molly. "It's got to be Bayview." He turned to Wren and said, "Would you recognize the building if we took you there?"

Wren wiped her face with her arm and nodded. "Sure."

He got up and said. "I've got a better idea. I'll be right back." He went below, got Molly's iPad and came back up on deck. With his forefinger, he tapped out a website address, clicked on a couple of tabs and turned the device around so Wren could see it. He'd pulled up the picture of one of Andrews's associates at Bayview.

Wren immediately shook her head. "I told you, he wasn't a foreigner."

Jack took the iPad, clicked a few more times, then showed it to Wren.

Her eyes got big, and she looked up at Jack and nodded. "That's Doc! That's him!"

Molly leaned over and looked at the picture of Winston Andrews, M.D. on the screen.

"Are you sure?" Jack asked.

Wren arched her eyebrows and nodded. "I think I'd recognize the bastard that played with my boobs."

"What are you talking about?" Molly asked, suddenly animated.

Wren explained her visits to see Dr. Andrews and what took place in the exam room. "All he did was look and feel, nothing else. But I knew he was getting his rocks off."

Jack wanted to make absolutely sure, so they got in his car and drove out to Bayview Clinic. As soon as they pulled into the parking lot of the closed place, Wren nodded and said, "Yep, that's it."

When they left, he drove by the pharmacy, where Wren confirmed that was where they took the prescriptions to have them filled.

"Which pharmacist did you see?" Jack asked.

"His name was Kirby. He was the only one we were supposed to work with. I'd slip a hundred-dollar bill in between the prescriptions, and we always paid cash for the drugs."

Jack described Lee Kirby, and Wren confirmed he was the pharmacist they used. He remembered Kirby saying that Andrews didn't transmit his prescriptions electronically.

"What're we going to do?" Molly asked.

He shook his head. "Damned if I know."

"You think Drager knows?"

He shrugged. "Right now, I'm not sure of anything, other than the fact we have to be very careful until we sort out what's going on."

They got back to the boat, and Jack went straight to the safe to take out his pistol. He checked to make sure it was loaded, put the gun in the holster, and fastened the holster to his belt. It was a holster designed to fit inside the waistband, but it was still bulky and uncomfortable. He pulled his shirt over the exposed grip and turned to Molly, who nodded.

"Are you going to start wearing that all the time, now?" she asked when they went back up on deck and sat at the cockpit table.

"Pretty much. I know you don't approve, but like I said, until I figure out where everyone stands, I'm going to be prepared."

Wren was sniffling now, the tears let loose. Molly moved over and put her arm around the girl, holding her close. Jack could see the sadness and fury in Molly's eyes.

After a few minutes, Wren continued talking, telling them all she could about Peabo's business. Jack had heard of prescription drug abuse, Florida was well-known as the Mecca for it, but never had he seen the consequences up close. Just last week, a small pharmacy in Tampa had been busted for filling prescriptions for narcotic painkillers. And now, his employer was involved. What he didn't know was where Drager stood.

"I'm sorry I'm so much trouble," Wren said. "I didn't mean to get you involved in my problems."

Molly shook her head. "It's okay, Wren. We'll help you."

"What are you going to do?" Wren asked.

"I don't know yet, but we'll figure it out. In the meantime, you're going to have to stay with us. You'll be safe here. We have security here at the marina," Molly said.

Jack couldn't help but chuckle. "Yeah, for what it's worth." He nodded toward the girl. "She didn't seem to have much trouble getting around it."

Molly shot him a warning look, and he kept quiet. He didn't say so, but he was worried that Peabo knew where the boat was, and this was the first place he'd come looking for Wren.

"Why don't you take a shower and get cleaned up, Wren," Molly said. They went down below, and when they came back up top, they were both holding towels and toiletries.

"I'm going with her," Molly said.

"I'll walk you up there," Jack said as he followed them down the dock. "I know there are lots of people around, but I'm not taking any chances." He patted his hip.

When they got back, Wren went down below to get dressed.

When she was out of hearing range, Jack turned to Molly and said, "So, now what? Any ideas?"

"I think we should take her back to the shelter. I know Vicki, the director, and I'm going to see if they'll give her a second chance, considering the circumstances. They're equipped to handle things like this, and it'll give us a little time to sort things out. Plus, we can't leave Wren alone here at the boat while we're at work."

"Makes sense."

"I'm going to go see Chris in the morning, see if I can talk him into giving Wren another chance."

"You think she's ready?"

"I think she needs to get back into a normal routine as quickly as possible. My guess is that'll help her recover."

"Don't you think we need to get the police involved?" he asked.

"Yes, but we need to get her situated first. She's pretty fragile, and I want to make sure she's taken care of."

"I'm going to call Tony in Fort Myers, get his advice," Jack said. Lieutenant Anthony Budzinski, was a friend of theirs with the Fort Myers Police Department. They trusted him, and knew he would give them good advice.

"Good idea," Molly said.

Wren was adamant about not involving the police. Part of it was fear, and part of it was mistrust. She was afraid she'd be arrested, and was not anxious to take that risk.

Jack had talked to Tony, and he had given him the name of someone at the Clearwater Police Department. But, according to Tony, without Wren's cooperation that wouldn't lead to much. And Wren was not willing to cooperate.

In a way, Molly understood, remembering what she and Jack had gone through in Fort Myers. They had stumbled onto a counterfeit drug conspiracy, but justice was elusive and not as easy to come by as in the movies. Money and fear carried considerable weight.

They decided to give it a rest, and get Wren over to the shelter. Molly had talked with Vicki, and she had agreed to take Wren back.

"Does Peabo know about the shelter?" Molly asked Wren as they were sitting out on the boat.

Wren shook her head. "He knows I stayed at a shelter, but I don't think he knows where it is."

"You sure? How did he take you back that first night?"

"I made him drop me off a couple of blocks from there and I walked. And I made sure he didn't follow me, just like they told me."

"Does he know about the boat?" Jack asked.

Wren lowered her head, and Molly looked at Jack, who was shaking his head. This was not the answer Molly would've preferred.

"He might. I talked about the boat—I'm sorry, I was just so excited about it. I don't remember if I told him the name or not, but he knows where we're parked."

"We need to get you back to the shelter, Wren," Molly said. "I think you'd be safer there, and they can help you."

"But I can't—"

Molly held up her hand. "I've already talked with Vicki. She said you were welcome back, and that you'd be safe there. They're used to dealing with . . . situations like yours."

"You know Vicki?" Wren had a betrayed look on her face.

Molly nodded. "Yes, I do. I'm sorry I didn't tell you, but I didn't want you to think I was interfering."

Wren seemed to consider it, and said, "That's okay."

Molly could tell by the expression on her face that she meant it. "Let's go below and see if we can find a few things for you to wear for a couple of days until we can go shopping."

A half hour later, the girls emerged with Wren carrying a small duffel bag. Jack insisted that he accompany them to the shelter, and Molly knew why.

After dropping Wren off at the shelter, they headed back across the causeway to the beach.

"You worried about this?" she asked Jack.

He shrugged. "Will you buy 'concerned?' I just think we need to be careful. I'd say we can expect a visit from the dickhead boyfriend within the next couple of days, and we need to be prepared."

"What do you mean?"

"Just more vigilant. I'm going to have a chat with Don and let him know what's going on, so he can pass it along to whoever he needs to." As the marina manager, Don kept a tight rein on everything in his domain. "I wish you'd reconsider letting me get you a gun."

Molly shook her head. They'd discussed this before, and although she'd agreed to take the concealed weapons class with Jack and had her permit, she had no plans to carry a handgun. "You know how I feel about that."

"I know, but it doesn't keep me from trying. Just please be a little more cautious, okay? This guy's trouble."

"I will. You think Wren's going to be okay?" she asked, changing the subject.

He nodded. "She's tough, and I think they know how to deal with that kind of stuff there at the shelter. You think you're going to be able to get her job back?"

Molly shrugged. "I spent the better part of the morning trying to persuade Chris, but I don't know. I'd say it's fifty-fifty."

Jack reached over and grabbed her hand. "I don't know, you can be very persuasive."

Molly had to laugh. "Yes, but you're easy. And ... I can use methods with you that I can't use with him, unless—"

Now he laughed. "I don't think so. You'd better not be using any of your wily tricks with anyone else but me."

"Not to worry, love, not to worry."

Chapter 22

Jack was tired the next morning at the office, having slept only a couple of hours. Chris had called Molly last night and said he was willing to give Wren another chance if she showed up promptly for work this morning. He made it clear that there would be no more exceptions, but they were relieved that Wren got her job back. Wren was ecstatic when Molly called and told her the good news.

That evening, when he got home, he and Molly went to Rockaway for dinner, but decided to bring it back to the boat so they could talk. She set the cockpit table while he went down below for utensils and a couple of cold beers. He put her beer down, took a long sip from his, and sat next to her.

"What if I told you that a prominent local clinic is a prescription mill?" he said.

She took a sip from her beer and nodded. "So, it's true?"

"No doubt about it. Everything she told us fits."

Jagged lightning jumped from cloud to cloud out over the Gulf. He could barely hear the thunder, but knew it was moving their way.

"Do you think Drager's in on it?" she asked.

Jack chuckled. "That was my first question. And I still don't know. Part of me thinks there's no way, but the other half thinks this is too big for just one doctor and a pharmacist to be the only ones involved."

"I'd agree. Any idea how many pills the pharmacy's pushing?"

"More than a million a year for OxyContin alone, but I just got into it today. I'm almost afraid to dig deeper." He'd also found out that OxyContin was the most widely prescribed and abused opioid. Every year, more people died from prescription opioid overdoses than from heroin and cocaine overdoses combined.

The breeze picked up and the temperature dropped. He heard another thunderclap, and this time it was louder. The thunderstorm was fast approaching. "We probably need to take this inside," he said.

They grabbed the food and their beers and took everything down below to the small table inside. Just as they got in and he'd closed the companionway door, rain started pelting the boat. Through the hatch at the top of the cabin, he saw a flash of lightning, followed by thunder, only a few seconds later. That was close, he thought.

Molly sat there, shaking her head. "Well, that answers your question about how efficient Dr. Andrews is and how he's putting up the numbers he's doing."

"No kidding. So . . . what do we do? The way I see it, we've got two choices: One, we take it directly to the authorities, or two, I take it to Drager. If we take it to the authorities and he's not involved, then he's going to be pissed we bypassed him and I'm probably out of a job."

Molly completed his thought. "But if you take it to Drager and he's involved, we're also screwed and we've tipped off the bad guys. I think this is what is termed a conundrum. I'm leaning toward taking it to the police."

He shook his head. "We do that, and Wren goes down with them. If she's not willing to testify against Peabo, then there's nothing they can do about the abuse. Can you imagine what he'll do to her if she goes to the cops?"

Molly pondered that for a while. They finished eating and Jack brought out two more beers. "Neither is a particularly good choice—more like choosing between the lesser of evils. I think I'll take my chances with Drager."

She nodded in agreement. "Do you have any indication that he's involved?"

He shook his head. "Nada. Zero. Without any basis for suspicion, I'm inclined to give him the benefit of the doubt."

The next day in the office, he called Connie and told her he needed to meet with Dr. Drager. He heard her tapping on the computer keyboard, and she asked if Friday would work. He told her it was important, and she squeezed him in for late that afternoon.

When he got to Drager's office, Connie had already left for the day, so Jack walked to the doctor's open door and peeked in. Drager was working on his computer, saw Jack and motioned him in. Jack had commissioned his pitch to memory, and had nothing with him but what was in his head.

"Jack, good to see you. I apologize for the late hour, but this was one of those days, and Connie said you needed to see me. Have a seat." He pointed toward the conference table. "What's on your mind?"

Jack took a deep breath and plunged into his story. "I have information that shows a prescription drug ring is operating out of Bayview Clinic and the pharmacy."

"What kind of information?"

Without naming names, he told him he'd talked to a patient that was involved and had gotten prescriptions with others for OxyContin. Those prescriptions were filled by Bayview Pharmacy. The pills were subsequently taken out of state and sold on the street.

"Who told you this?" Drager asked.

This was the critical point in the revelation. He was hesitant to give out Wren's name, but he knew that Drager would want specifics.

"I'm not at liberty to say."

Drager exploded. "You walk in here and accuse my company of writing and filling illegal prescriptions, yet you won't tell me the name of the person who gave you the information? How reliable is it? How do you know this person is telling the truth? Have you spoken to Winston?"

"Dr. Drager, I realize how serious this is. I wouldn't be bringing it to you if I didn't think there was substance to it. The person that gave me the information is scared for her life. My choices were to take it directly to the authorities, or discuss it with you. I chose the latter."

Drager was still leaning forward over the table, but appeared to calm down a bit. "And you're convinced?"

Jack explained how he'd checked the numbers and gave Drager the facts relating to the pharmacy. "I don't know yet the extent of Dr. Andrews's involvement—that will take some time to go through the medical records. But, I know for a fact that Bayview Pharmacy is prescribing an inordinate amount of OxyContin, and the timeframes match the dates that the person gave us."

"Do you think anyone else is involved?"

Jack shook his head. "The only people I know, at this point, are Dr. Andrews and Kirby, the pharmacist. I'm not saying no one else is involved, but I have no indications of anyone else."

"Who else is aware of this? Anyone?"

"Only you. That's why I wanted to see you ASAP." He wasn't about to give Molly's name, knowing he could claim Drager was asking about others within Drager, LLC.

"I still find this hard to believe," Drager said, clasping his hands together in front of him, shaking his head in disbelief.

"We've got to report it to the authorities, in this case the DEA. There'll be an investigation." *And lots of bad publicity,* Jack thought.

"I'd like for you to finish your internal review, first."

"Dr. Drager, we—"

Drager held up his hand, "I want you to find out what you can first. I'm not suggesting we delay things, but I need to know the extent of this . . . disaster before we bring them in." He leaned over and looked at Jack. "You realize that once they come in, we lose all control over everything."

Jack nodded. He didn't like postponing notifying the authorities, but had to admit Drager had a point. It was going to be a circus, and Drager wanted to have some idea of the magnitude of the problem. They could certainly justify taking a few days to do that.

Drager asked for a week. This sounded reasonable to Jack, so they agreed to meet next Monday to discuss the results and map out their strategy.

"Can you finish your review without anyone else knowing?" Drager asked as Jack was about to leave.

Jack thought about it, and nodded. "I think so. Most of what I need is on the computer, so no one else needs to know." He held up his hand. "On second thought, I'd like to discuss it with Dr. Marshall."

"Why?" Drager asked.

"I need a doctor's eyes, and you don't have the time. I trust her, and she can be discreet." He didn't mention that he'd already talked to Tina Marshall about his suspicions.

Drager thought about it for a moment, then said, "Okay, but I'd like to keep this as close as possible. No one else. I'm sure you understand."

"Sure, no problem."

"Drager gave me permission to talk to you," Jack said. He and Tina were in her office.

"He agreed?" she asked, obviously surprised.

Jack nodded. "I've got a week to finish an internal review for him, so we don't have much time."

"What's your plan?"

He pulled out a list of medical record numbers. "This is a random list of patients from Bayview—all Dr. Andrews's patients. I'd like for you to review the charts and see if you note anything suspicious or missing. I've arranged for you to have access to them on your clinic computer."

She looked at the list. "A week? That's a lot of—"
"I know. But this is important. Please."
"I'll do my best."
"Thank you. We'll treat you to dinner, okay?"
She laughed. "And a nice bottle of wine, too."

Friday night, Tina called. "Can you and Molly come over tomorrow evening? I should be finished by then."
"Great. How about you come over to the boat, and I'll prepare dinner?"
"You're on. Seven sound good?"
"Perfect."
"And Jack? Don't forget the wine."

He decided to grill shrimp. It was simple, and delicious. That afternoon, he walked down to the seafood market and picked up a couple of pounds of jumbo shrimp. He peeled and deveined them, put them in a plastic container, then poured in half a bottle of Italian dressing and half a bottle of poppy seed dressing. He covered it, and placed it in the refrigerator to marinate for a couple of hours.

Tina arrived a few minutes before seven, just as he was getting the grill ready. She was carrying a bottle of wine.

"Come aboard. Molly's down below preparing a salad. What are you doing with wine? I thought that was my job?" he said.

She laughed and took off her shoes before stepping aboard. "My mother taught me never to go to anyone's house without bringing something," she said, walking over to him and giving him a hug.

Molly stuck her head out of the companionway. "I thought I heard you. Come on down, you can help me with the salad."

Over dinner, Tina updated them on her findings.

"Pretty conclusive, I'd say. There's no way he's doing what should be done from a prudent medical point of view. They're basically herding people through and cranking out prescriptions—a classic pill mill operation. Several of the MRI's I looked at didn't even match the patient."

Jack shook his head. "What do you mean, didn't match the patient?"

Molly answered. "There was an MRI in the patient's record, but it was someone else's MRI."

"Exactly," Tina said. "Or, in some cases the same MRI was used for multiple patients. There was a similar problem for labs and other tests."

"But that sounds dumb," Jack said. "Why would he think he could get away with it?"

"Because, you'd have to do a detailed review to catch it. Someone doing a cursory chart review would see an MRI, lab test, and so forth, and not check to see that they actually matched the patient. If Winston took the time to do everything by the book, there's no way he'd be able to see the volume of patients he does."

After dinner, Tina went through the detail, showing them on her computer what she'd found.

"This is great. Will you email me this, so I can include it in my report to Drager?" Jack asked.

Tina shook her head.

"What?" He couldn't believe it.

"My name can't be on it," she said.

"You've got to be kidding me! I told you Drager said you could work with me."

Tina closed her laptop. "I know, and I did. But I'm not putting anything in writing with my name on it until Drager tells me to do so."

He looked at Molly for help, but got a blank look in return. *Unbelievable,* he thought. He tried to control his temper.

"You're telling me Monday I can report to Drager that you reviewed the charts, and I can relay your findings, but you won't give me anything in writing unless he tells you directly?"

She nodded. "I'm sorry, but I have my reasons."

Chapter 23

Monday morning, Jack got off the elevator and walked over to Drager's office. He was still upset that Tina had bailed on him. He'd spent all day yesterday working on his report, but knew it didn't have the credibility it would have had he been able to include something in writing from her. Molly tried to persuade him that he had the information, and all Drager had to do was call Tina directly.

Connie was at her desk, and he noticed Drager's office door was closed. "Hi, Connie, how are you?" he said to the petite, middle-aged brunette behind the desk. "How's your son?" He'd remembered that Connie's son had surgery recently.

"He's doing fine, Jack, thanks for asking. His doctor said he'll be as good as new in no time. Could I get you some coffee? Dr. Drager will be a few minutes." She looked around, and lowered her voice. "Dr. Andrews is in with him."

He tried to smile and act like he knew, but his stomach just did a flip. "Thanks. And yes, I'd love some coffee, please." It paid to be on good terms with the boss's assistant, a lesson Jack had learned long ago.

He was shocked that Andrews was there, and his mind was racing. Of course, there was no guarantee that Andrews being there was related to his appointment, but Jack didn't believe it was a coincidence. He was still trying to sort out the possibilities when Connie returned with a steaming mug of coffee and handed it to him.

"Thanks, Connie. Glad to hear Jeff is doing well. I know you were worried about him."

"Boys," she commented, as she shook her head. "No offense, but males can be a pain sometimes."

Jack laughed. "I'm sure Molly would agree with you on that."

He sat in a chair across from Connie's desk and picked up the Tampa Tribune to read while he was waiting. He didn't need to go over the information in the report he had with him, as he had almost memorized the entire thing. He couldn't concentrate on the newspaper.

Connie's phone buzzed and she picked it up. Jack heard her response, and he figured it was Drager. She hung up the phone and said, "He's ready for you now."

He stood and walked to the door, thanking Connie as he passed. The two doctors, sitting at the conference table, were laughing as Jack walked in. He closed the door behind him.

"I'll have to remember that one, Devo," Andrews said. He stood, and extended his hand. "Good morning, Jack." His upper lip curled into a faint hint of a smile.

That was the first time Jack had heard Andrews refer to him by his given name. "Dr. Andrews," Jack said, as he shook his hand.

Drager remained seated, motioning for Jack to take a chair. "I asked Winston to join us. I didn't think you'd mind."

"Of course not," Jack said, smiling. *Would it have made any difference?*

"After we met last week, I decided to call Winston and ask him what was going on." Drager said, settling in his chair at the head of the table.

Jack nodded, waiting for Drager to continue. He'd love to know what was going on.

"After we discussed it, he's been looking at it all week, including this past weekend, trying to get answers," Drager said. He turned to Winston. "Why don't you fill Jack in on what you've discovered?"

Dr. Andrews smiled at Jack and cleared his throat. "First, let me say how appreciative I am to you, Jack, for bringing this to our attention. Devo knows I've been after him for some time to bring in an experienced financial person, and it is already paying dividends."

This should be good, Jack thought.

"I spent all weekend with my administrator going through the data, trying to determine what happened. There is clearly a problem, as you've pointed out, specifically the extraordinary amount of OxyContin prescribed."

Jack was puzzled. *Andrews was admitting he had a problem?* This was unexpected.

"We went through the charts with a magnifying glass, and . . ." he paused, "and we've pinned it down to one physician—Dr. Patel."

Jack sat up. *Dr. Patel? Rohit Patel?* Now he was really confused. From the records Jack had pulled, all of the patients were Dr. Andrews's patients, not Patel's. And, Wren had positively indentified Andrews, although he hadn't shared that piece of information with Drager.

As if reading his mind, Dr. Andrews continued. "As you pointed out to Devo, the patients are listed as mine, at least on the computer. I knew that wasn't true, so we pulled the detailed records. Upon further review, we found questionable prescriptions related to office visits that had actually been performed and signed off by Dr. Patel."

Jack interrupted, "How could that be? I checked, and those patients were shown on the system as your patients."

Andrews nodded, and gave Jack a patronizing look. "I agree, and it would appear that way to someone with no clinical background."

He went on to say that, since Dr. Patel was the newest doctor at the clinic, he had been passing patients along to Patel in order to help him build up his practice. This was common to give a new doctor an established book of patients. That would explain why the patients were originally listed as Andrews's patients, not Patel's. "Where I made a mistake was in not formally transferring these patients over to Patel on a timely basis."

"Have you talked to Dr. Patel?" Drager asked.

"Well, I've tried to call him several times this weekend, but so far have not been able to get in touch with him," Andrews said.

Jack was stunned. He couldn't believe that Andrews had outmaneuvered him on this. He was about to mention Wren, but decided not to at this point, since it might put her further at risk. He needed time to regroup.

"So, how should we proceed? Jack?" Drager asked, as he and Andrews looked at him, waiting for a response.

Jack cleared his throat and tried to maintain his composure. "I'm not sure I understand. We've got two problems here: First, a physician on our staff has been writing excess scripts for painkillers, and second, *our* pharmacy has been dispensing this stuff like candy. Assuming Dr. Patel has been writing these scripts—" he paused to look directly at Dr. Andrews, "there is still the huge issue of *our* pharmacist dispensing these drugs."

The two doctors passed a knowing glance, then Drager spoke. "From what Winston has showed me, Kirby was merely filling what he thought were legitimate prescriptions. Granted, his antennae should have detected a problem, but it didn't. Clearly, you need to implement tighter controls on our pharmacy system. This directly relates to your primary directive of implementing efficiency measures throughout our system. If you have any proof of wrongdoing on Kirby's, then his employment will be terminated."

Drager held his hands out, palms up. "Without Patel, I'm not sure what else we can do. Until we talk to him, I'd say we've resolved the issue."

Jack opened his mouth to object, but Drager continued. "Of course, we expect you to immediately implement improved controls to prevent this from happening again. I can assure you that Dr. Andrews is committed to complete cooperation on that."

Unbelievable. And they were serious, Jack thought. *Did Drager not understand the gravity of the situation?* He spent the next thirty minutes arguing with the physicians. He pointed out the severity of what had happened, repeatedly telling them that a criminal act had been committed. Andrews didn't dispute that Patel had acted inappropriately.

"You're missing the point," Jack said.

"And what exactly is your point, Mr. Davis?" Andrews said. "I've acknowledged that Dr. Patel was wrong, but you seem to be implying something else."

He started to say *you're covering up a criminal act, and I'll not have any part in that.* He looked at Drager and realized the outcome had been decided. Drager was backing Andrews, and that was that.

As soon as Jack walked out of Drager's office, he left the building and called Molly. "Un-fucking believable," he said, as soon as she answered. He told her about the meeting with Drager and Andrews, pacing outside the building as he talked.

"They're setting Patel up as the fall guy. Andrews sat right there and lied through his teeth. And on top of that, Drager blamed me for not implementing better controls at the pharmacy."

"What about Wren?" Molly asked.

"I haven't given anyone her name, so they don't know who gave me the information. I just had to get out of there before I blew a gasket."

"You talked to Tina, yet?"

"No, she's next on my call list. Right now, I'm so pissed I can't think straight."

"I've got to run, but settle down and don't do anything foolish. We'll talk about it this evening."

"Later," he said, ending that call and calling Tina's number. She didn't answer, so he left her a message asking her to call him as soon as possible.

Chapter 24

Wren's phone buzzed again. She looked at the number. It was Peabo, for the third time since she'd been at work. She put the phone back in her pocket without answering and went about her job.

Molly had called last night to tell her the good news that Chris was giving her a second chance, and cautioned her that this was it—no more breaks.

When Wren got back to the shelter yesterday, she'd decided she was done with Peabo. She talked to Vicki for several hours, and the reality had flooded over her. She realized that he had no intention of marrying her and was only manipulating and using her. All of that made her angry, at him and at herself. He could screw Shorty for all she cared, but she was done with Peabo Watson.

She finished her shift, glad for the opportunity and glad to have the distraction of being around other, normal people. Outside the hospital, she turned and walked toward the shelter, only a few blocks away. A homeless man, a familiar sight in this neighborhood, shuffled along the opposite side of the street with his head down and hands in his pockets.

Halfway home, she looked up and saw Shorty standing in the middle of the sidewalk, blocking her path. She froze, looking around to see if anyone else was on the street. No one was in sight. She turned around to go back to the hospital, took one step, then stopped. Peabo stood there on the sidewalk. He was too close for her to run.

"If you touch me, I'll scream," she said, almost spitting the words out. She was determined not to let him ever touch her again.

He held up both his hands and didn't move, indicating he was harmless. "I don't think that'd be a good move," he said, in a calm voice. "Not if you want to see your friend Molly again."

Her breath caught in her throat as she tried to stay cool. "What do you mean?" Her voice didn't sound as confident as before.

"What I mean is, Molly is tied up at the moment over at a room on the beach. If you don't come with me, she may have an accident, know what I'm saying?"

"You're lying. That's bullshit, and I'm not listening to you." She turned back toward Shorty and started walking, but her hands were shaking.

"You might want to see this, first," Peabo said, behind her.

She stopped and turned back around. He hadn't moved, but was standing there, holding up his phone. Wren was too far away to see what was on it, but now she was afraid—afraid Peabo wasn't lying.

She took a couple of steps toward him as though she was approaching a poisonous snake, careful to keep her distance. When she got closer, her hand came up to her mouth. It was Molly. She was tied up, but Wren recognized the red hair and the face. It was Molly.

Wren sat in the back seat of the Escalade, shaking. She had no idea where Peabo was taking her, but maybe there was a chance to save Molly. She didn't care about herself, but she was determined to do everything possible to save Molly, regardless of the cost. Peabo had made it very clear that the only way to save Molly was for Wren to not cause any trouble.

Bird shuffled along in the shadows, appearing to have no interest in what was happening across the street. His hands were shaking as he recognized the girl, Wren, from downtown. He had started to cross the street to speak to her when he saw the two thugs from Kentucky on the sidewalk.

The only thing he heard was something about a room at the beach. That night they almost drowned him, he remembered them talking about the motel where they stayed. It was clear she didn't want to go with them until they showed her something on Boss's phone. Wren's shoulders slumped, and Bird saw her walk away with them.

He watched from a safe distance as they went around the corner and got into the black Escalade. They drove away, headed toward the beach.

Bird was scared and his hands were shaking, but he felt sorry for the girl. He remembered how sweet she was. She had a nice smile and a genuineness about her that was hard to fake. He figured he knew where they were headed, so he turned and started walking toward the beach. It was a long way and he wasn't sure what he could do, but he couldn't do anything here.

Peabo pulled into the parking lot of the Two Palms Motel and parked. Wren walked between the two men to the motel room, where Shorty unlocked the door and they entered. The room was empty.

"Where's Molly?" she asked, as Shorty closed the door behind him.

Peabo just looked at her with those beady eyes and a sick grin crossed his face. "I ask the questions here. Sit," he said, pointing to the chair beside the bed. He pulled his leather belt off, doubled it up and laid it on the bed.

She sat in the chair, her mind racing, wondering where this was going. Shorty stood in front of the door, his arms crossed and legs apart, standing guard.

Peabo walked over to her, took her chin in his hand and tilted her face toward his. "Here's how this is going to work. I'm going to ask you some questions and you're going to give me answers. Simple, right?"

He pinched her chin and moved her head up and down. "But, there's a catch, and you need to listen carefully. I've already talked to your friend, Molly, so at this point, you don't know what I know and what I don't. Understand?" Again, he moved her head up and down.

He picked up the belt and popped it in his open hand right in front of her face, startling her, and she jumped. "You tell me everything, and tell me the truth—you don't get hit. First time you lie to me or I feel like you're holding back—" He smacked the belt against his hand once again. "You'll have to be punished. Are we clear?"

This time, he didn't have to move her head up and down. She did it on her own.

She told him everything he wanted to know. It was clear he was trying to find out how much Jack and Molly knew about the business. She regretted telling them, but there was nothing she could do about it now. They were all going to die and she was helpless to stop it.

He'd only hit her once, but that was enough. She'd told him she didn't give them Doc's name, which was true. But somehow, Peabo knew they had Doc's name, and he hit her, hard, right across the chest. Her boob ached from the blow, but she figured that was just a taste of what was yet to come.

When he'd finished, he told Shorty to tie her up. As Shorty was putting the rope around her wrists, pulling her arms behind the back of the chair, she said, "Where's Molly? You said you'd let her go if I told you everything."

Peabo laughed and looked at Shorty. "Can you believe this bitch? I told you she had a mouth on her. Put something in that hole, would you."

Shorty stuffed a washcloth in her mouth and duct-taped it in place, forcing her to breathe through her nose. When he'd finished, Peabo walked over to her, pulled his phone out, and pulled up the picture he'd showed Wren. He held it up so Wren could see it.

"I just put her face on another picture so as to get you to come along without making a fuss," he said, grinning. "But don't worry, I'll have her soon enough."

Peabo stood back and snapped a picture of Wren tied to the chair. "This time, the picture will be real."

After he shoved the phone back in his pocket, he stepped forward, grabbed a handful of her shirt and ripped it open. She could feel the cool air of the motel room on her breast, and she wanted to close her eyes, but she made herself stare at Peabo and Shorty. Peabo continued what he started, until he'd ripped her shirt completely off, leaving her sitting there naked from the waist up in front of the two men. Then, he reached out and squeezed her bruised boob so hard it brought tears to her eyes.

"I wanted Shorty here to get a peek at what's in store for him later," Peabo said, licking his lips and grinning. "I'm done with you, but I suspect he may want a few turns. I told him I've had better, but you ain't half bad. I'm anxious to sample the redhead—I ain't never had one of them."

She stared at him with all the contempt she could muster. *It would be over her dead body,* she thought, hoping that he wouldn't be able to kidnap Molly.

"Why don't you untie me, and I'll take care of both of you," she said. Maybe if she could stall for time, Molly could avoid capture. She was willing to do anything to save Molly, even humiliate herself with these two.

Peabo stepped back, and laughed. "You wouldn't be trying to sidetrack us, would you?" He turned to Shorty. "See, I told you she was a smart one."

Turning back to Wren, Peabo shook his head. "Got things to do, and they don't include you at the moment."

They left, and she heard them locking the door to the room. As she heard the car start and leave, she started looking around the room, trying to figure out some way to escape.

Chapter 25

The next day, Jack was sitting out under the bimini, working on his computer. He'd decided to work from home to reduce the distractions. He heard footsteps on the dock, but didn't pay any attention until he heard a male voice say, "Jack? Jack Davis?" The hair on the back of his neck stood up.

He looked up to see two men standing next to the boat. He didn't recognize either of them. One was huge, probably a good six-four and close to three hundred pounds. He had close cropped brown hair and a dull look on his face. The other, who looked small in comparison, was bigger than he appeared at first glance. His eyes were sharp and focused, and Jack figured him for the brains.

"Who's asking?" Jack felt for the pistol on the seat beside him, where the pair couldn't see.

Brains looked around, then spoke, and Jack recognized the voice as the one who had first called his name. "We need to talk."

Jack put his hand around the grip of the pistol. He glanced around the marina, but no one was close. The usual crowds were up near the restaurant and the other buildings onshore, but they seemed far away, too far. The other docks were deserted. He tightened his grip, and said, "So, talk. I'm listening."

"Not out here. Somewhere private."

Jack put the pistol up on the table, his hand still on it, but where the two could see it. The big one started to reach into his pocket, but Brains put out his hand to stop him.

Jack kept his eyes on them. "This is as private as it's going to get. You must be Peabo."

The shorter one nodded. "That's right." He looked around again, and continued. "Just want to deliver a message. Two, actually."

Jack nodded, but didn't say anything.

Peabo said, "Wren's with me. She don't need you or your little redhead anymore, so just forget about her."

Jack's hand tightened around the grip of the gun at the reference to Molly.

"Second, you best forget everything she told you. You're messing with stuff you don't know anything about. Leave it be."

"Where's Wren?" Jack asked.

Peabo shook his head. "Don't concern you."

Jack thought about the bruise around the young girl's eye and said, "That's where you're wrong. When she tells me herself, then I'll believe it."

The big man took half a step back and looked at his boss, as if awaiting instructions. Peabo never took his eyes off Jack, but gave a slight shake of his head.

"You're making a big mistake, Davis," Peabo said.

"I want to know Wren's okay. Then I'll consider letting things go. Otherwise, I'm going to the police."

"How do I know you're not going to them anyway?"

Jack thought about it a minute, knowing he might be negotiating for Wren's life. "Look, all I want is to see that Wren's okay and she's free to do whatever she wants. Bring her here and let her go, and I'll drop everything."

Peabo considered his request. "You back off, everything's cool. You don't . . ." He made a slashing motion across his throat with his hand. "They might find another body in the water. We'll be back in an hour." He turned and walked back toward the main dock, the hulk following him, occasionally looking back over his shoulder at Jack.

Jack laid the pistol back down on the seat next to him and took a deep breath. He'd been expecting this, but it still shook him up. The reference to the body in the water scared him. When he'd gone up to the marina office to ask Don to keep an eye out, the man had told him a dead body had been found up at Caladesi Island, apparently a street person. The Pinellas County Sheriff's office thought it was drug related.

He stuck the pistol into the holster he was wearing and pulled his shirt down over it. He locked the boat and hurried down the dock toward the gate. Throngs of people milled about the marina area, and he couldn't see his two visitors anywhere. He walked out to the parking area and looked for Molly's car. It wasn't in its usual spot.

Just as he pulled out his cell phone to call her, he saw the white Nissan Altima pull into her space. He disconnected the call and walked over to greet her, checking out the surroundings as he did.

"Well, you must have really missed me," she said, getting out of the car.

"You don't know," he said, taking the bag from her hand and kissing her.

She stopped and studied him. "What's the matter?"

On the way to the boat, he told her about the visitors. When they got there, they sat where he could see anyone coming down the dock. He took the pistol out of its holster and placed it on the seat next to him.

"You're serious," she said, glancing at the gun.

"Even more so, now. I'm worried about Wren."

Molly raised her eyebrows, and had a questioning look on her face.

"They should be back in an hour—hopefully with Wren."

"Are you nuts? After what you've just told me?"

"Look, I just want to get Wren back. Safe. If they do that, then we'll go from there." He motioned toward shore. "They're not going to do anything foolish with all these people around."

Molly leaned toward him. "Jack, listen to me. These people don't screw around. Call the police so they can be here waiting for them."

Jack shook his head. "No time. They said they'd be back in an hour." He looked at his watch. "That's only forty-five minutes. Not enough time to do anything."

She considered it, then shook her head. "I don't like this—at all."

Jack reasoned with her, saying the worst that could happen is they'd not show, in which case she could call the cops. If they did bring Wren, then everything would be fine, and they could still call the cops afterward. "What could go wrong?" he asked.

"Too many things—I just can't name them right now. I still don't like this."

Thirty minutes later, Jack saw three figures coming down the dock. "Showtime," he said, and Molly moved over next to him, so they were facing the dock.

Peabo, the hulk, and a frightened Wren between them stopped and stood there next to the boat.

"Wren, you okay?" Molly asked.

Wren nodded, glanced at Peabo, then looked back at Jack and Molly.

"Wren, do you want to come aboard and talk?" Jack asked, choosing his words carefully.

Once again, she looked at Peabo, then back at Molly, shaking her head. "I want to stay with Peabo," she said, in a timid voice.

Peabo held up his hands. "Satisfied?"

"This is bullshit! You—"

"Hey, asshole. You heard her. She's free to go with you if she wants, but she said she didn't want to. Now, I expect you to hold up your end of the bargain. Otherwise . . ." He looked down at the water. "Remember what I said." The three of them turned and walked back toward the main dock, the big guy watching to make sure they didn't follow.

"Jack!" Molly said.

He looked at Molly's desperate face, her face mirroring how he felt. "Shit," he said, slamming his hand on the table, spilling the wine. He'd not seen this one coming. Molly urged him to call the police.

"For what? So they come, and get here in time to stop them? What exactly do you think Wren's going to tell them?"

"Jack, she's scared, can't you—"

"Of course she's scared! I repeat, what do you think she's going to tell them? He outmaneuvered us, Molly."

The realization slowly fell over Molly and engulfed them with a sense of gloom.

"He's holding Wren as insurance," Jack said. "That's his trump card. As long as we don't pursue the Bayview thing, Wren will be okay. He knows we won't go to the authorities."

Molly nodded. "Okay, but how do we know she's alright?"

Jack shrugged. "Our problem. So we have to keep pressing him to make sure she's not hurt. In the end, though, he can't afford to harm her, unless . . ."

"Unless what?"

"Unless he's willing to give up his business here in Clearwater." He didn't think Peabo was willing to do that, but who knew?

"What's to prevent us from going to the police?"

Jack shook his head. "If we do, Wren dies. You heard his threat, and I told you what he said about 'another body in the water.' This guy's serious, Molly. He killed that homeless guy and he won't hesitate to kill Wren."

"What do we do?"

"We've got to figure out a way to get Wren out."

Chapter 26

Peabo's phone buzzed. He picked it up and looked at the caller-ID. Although it was a disposable phone, he never programmed any numbers in it in case it fell into the wrong hands. It was a 727 area code, and unless it was a wrong number, there was only one 727 number that had his cell number.

"Yeah," he answered, waiting for the voice on the other side. It was not a wrong number. He listened intently for a few minutes, then said, "Okay, the usual place and time."

He pressed END and slammed the phone down on the console.

Shorty looked at him and said, "What's the matter?"

Peabo shook his head. "Got a little problem. Doc needs to chat. Looks like somebody's interfering in our business."

At two-thirty, Peabo drove over to their pre-arranged meeting place at the International Plaza in Tampa, on the lower level outside Nordstrom's. It was a busy spot, with lots of people coming and going, and the kind of shopping mall where a Cadillac Escalade and a late model Jaguar would not be out of place.

He knew it was serious. Doc never called unless it was. They never discussed anything on phones, even the disposable ones. They were too easily tapped, which was why Peabo had set up a pre-arranged meeting spot and time. All Doc said was that someone was about to screw their arrangement up, which meant that the business was in jeopardy.

They got there right at three, and circled the parking lot, looking for a green Jag. Peabo thought he spotted it, and Doc flashed his brake lights as they drove behind. He found a parking spot the next row over and parked. He left Shorty in the Escalade and walked over to the Jag, opened the passenger door, and got in.

"We've got a problem," Andrews said, not wasting any time.

"Yeah, I figured that much. What's going on?"

Doc was jumpy, which was not a good sign. He proceeded to tell Peabo about how the new CFO had been digging around and stumbled onto their business.

"How do you know he's on to it?" Peabo asked. "I thought you had everything documented and our asses covered?"

"I do, I do. But this asshole is relentless. He claims he has a patient that's told him everything."

Peabo perked up at that tidbit. "Did he say who?"

Doc shook his head. "He wouldn't tell us. He did let it slip that it was a female."

Wren. Had to be, he thought. He wondered how much she'd spilled. He thought he'd found out everything, but maybe he needed to question her again. "What about that other doc, the Indian? I thought his name was on everything?"

"It is. But I'm telling you, it's about to hit the fan. And I'm not going down alone."

Peabo stared at the doctor with cold, dark eyes. *Did you just threaten me, you spoiled little bastard?*

Doc seemed to read his mind, and backtracked. "What I meant was we needed to do something, you know, clean this up before anything goes down."

Peabo grinned. Doc was more perceptive than he thought.

"Get rid of the Indian," Peabo said.

"What?" Doc looked shocked. "We can't just—"

"Easy, Doc, listen to me. Just send him back to fucking India, or wherever it was he came from. That was the plan if anything ever came up, remember?"

Doc looked relieved. "Oh, yes, right." Then another worried look fell across his face. "What if he won't go?"

What a pussy, Peabo thought. *And he's a doctor?*

"Convince him. Tell him he's going to spend the rest of his life being somebody's bitch in federal prison. Then give him the money and make sure he gets on a plane with a one-way ticket. Take him to the airport if you have to, but get him the hell out of here—like this afternoon."

Doc nodded, and seemed to process the information. Peabo thought for a minute that he was going to ask him for the money for the plane ticket, but he correctly interpreted Peabo's look as one meaning that conversation was over.

Peabo started to open the door, then turned to Doc. "Hey, Doc? What's Ketamine?" Peabo asked.

"Ketamine?" Doc asked. "Why are you asking about that?"

"What is it?"

"It's an anesthetic, more often used in veterinary settings, typically injected. We use it occasionally in pain management, but it has some rather severe side-effects."

"Like what?"

"It's a dissociative drug—"

"English, Doc, English."

"It can produce hallucinations, and cause amnesia—make the person—"

"Yeah, yeah, I know what that means. Like roofies. So is this something you can write a script for?"

"Yes, but you still didn't tell me why you wanted to know?"

Doc was starting to be a pain in the ass. "Give me a script for some," Peabo said.

Doc shrugged. "I don't carry a prescription pad around with me."

"Call it in for me. I'll pick it up this afternoon."

"About that—I think we need to lay low for a while, you know, until things settle down."

"We're almost finished for this trip, anyway, so no problem. We'll be back in a few weeks."

"That may be too soon."

Peabo shook his head. "You don't understand, Doc, this is a business. We can't just shut down for a few months until you get comfortable."

"Yes, but—"

Peabo held up his hand. "We're done, just be cool and we'll be back in a couple of weeks. Things will have settled by then. Make sure this Indian doc is gone and don't forget that prescription. I'll get Shorty to bring you a little package."

Andrews licked his lips and nodded.

Peabo opened the door, started to get out, and then turned to Doc. "What's this guy's name?"

Doc looked confused, and said, "Patel, Rohit—"

"No, no, not the Indian. I'm talking about the guy snooping around. What did you call him? CFO?"

"Oh, Davis. Jack Davis."

"Jack Davis? Lives on a boat?"

Doc nodded. "Yes, why, do you know him?"

Shit, he thought. This could be more trouble than he realized. He knew that Davis worked for Drager, but not his position. "I'll be in touch," he said, as he got out of Doc's car.

Peabo walked back to the Escalade, got in, and slammed the door, not saying a word. He just sat there, shaking his head and frowning.

"Everything okay, Boss?" Shorty asked.

"Unbelievable. A place the size of Tampa, and . . ." He slammed his fist against the dash. "Doc's getting nervous. Their top financial guy is poking around and you'll never guess who it is?"

Shorty just sat there with a blank look on his face.

"Our friend, Jack Davis."

The big man grunted. "Anything we need to do?"

"First things first. Let Doc get rid of the Indian first. Then we'll deal with Doc. In the meantime, I gotta figure out what we need to do about Davis," Peabo said, starting the SUV and leaving the shopping center. Running a business could be a pain in the ass, he thought.

Chapter 27

"What's bothering you? I know something is going on up there in that head of yours," Molly asked Jack. They were sitting out on the boat after work.

He started to answer *nothing*, but thought better of it. She knew him too well, which was both a blessing and a curse. "It all seems too convenient, know what I mean?"

"What?"

"Andrews blames it on Patel, then can't find him? Drager didn't say he'd tried to call him—just Andrews. Don't you think that's a little strange?"

"Maybe Patel did screw up, and then disappeared. He wouldn't be the first."

"I know, but it's just too neat. Andrews is claiming that Patel did all of the questionable procedures, so Patel is the only one that can dispute it. We need to talk to Tina."

She slapped his arm, laughing. "But you better keep your paws off Dr. Tina. I saw the way you were ogling her at the management dinner."

He shook his head. "Not true—I was just surprised to see her dressed up. You have nothing to worry about."

"Good. Keep it that way."

He called Tina and asked if they could meet with her. She told them to come over to her place, which worked out good. Jack wasn't comfortable hanging around the marina, and with thunderstorms rolling in off the Gulf, it wasn't any fun cooped up on the boat.

Jack and Molly stopped at Ted's and picked up some sushi for dinner. Tina's condo, which neither of them had been to before, was on the Gulf in Dunedin, a city just north of Clearwater. They made their way out Curlew Road, headed toward Honeymoon Island and turned into the gated complex. Tina had given him the code, and they parked in the visitors' area next to her building.

They took the elevator to the ninth floor, where Tina opened the door to her unit, ushering them inside. It was typical of Florida condos, with tile floors, and a wall of glass facing the water. She told him to make himself comfortable while she and Molly got a few things out of the kitchen.

The condo was comfortable, not overdone, like a place where a real person lived. She had not gone overboard on the decorating, with a minimum of knick-knacks and wall hangings. What was there was authentic and reflected its owner, not some decorator's taste.

Tina walked up behind him and set a tray containing three plates, a bottle of sake, and three tiny cups on the table in front of the couch. Jack was looking out the wall-length sliding glass doors at the remains of the day, the sun dropping into the calm waters of the Gulf of Mexico behind the clouds.

"Nice view," he commented.

"Thanks. I figured if you live on the coast, you might as well enjoy the view. I figured we'd eat over here—more comfortable."

Molly set down the bag from Ted's, and Tina poured sake in each of the cups, handing one to him and one to Molly. She raised hers, and said, "Thanks for making my day," then drained the cup and set it down.

"Sorry, I don't usually slam shots, but after what you told me earlier . . ."

He and Molly chuckled and drained theirs, too.

"Certainly called for," Molly said.

They opened the sushi and passed it around, while Jack filled in the blanks. Tina mainly listened, occasionally interrupting to clarify something he said, and Molly adding to his comments. By the time they were half done eating, he'd finished telling her everything he knew about the meeting with Drager and Andrews, and Wren's appearance.

"Do you think Drager's in on it?" Tina asked.

Jack shrugged. "Not sure. I don't think so, but I wouldn't bet against it. No doubt that Andrews is dirty, but how do we prove it? I do know he's awful tight with Drager, and Drager refuses to believe Andrews is rotten."

As they finished the food, they discussed what to do. Molly wanted to turn it over to the authorities. Jack convinced them that without more concrete evidence, Andrews would wiggle out of it. He'd already convinced Drager, and was several steps ahead of them.

They had two big cards, according to Jack. First was Wren. She had gone through the entire process, knew all the players, and could positively identify Andrews. She was their strongest asset, and one who Andrews would have a hard time ignoring.

He also felt that Kirby, the pharmacist, was in play. While he could hide behind the fact that all he'd done was fill legal prescriptions, according to Wren, he had more to hide. Jack wanted to pay him a little visit to see what he could turn up.

He believed that if they increased the pressure, they could flush Andrews out or at least force his hand. Drager was an unknown, but his participation didn't appear to have any impact either way. Jack wanted to believe that he wasn't involved and simply protecting his friend Winston, but he couldn't be sure. He did know, after his meeting with Drager and Andrews, that any indictment of Andrews needed to be ironclad.

"What about Patel?" Molly asked. "Has he surfaced yet?"

Tina shook her head. "And I don't think he will. Something's fishy with that. I know Rohit, and he's as straight as an arrow. He's as by-the-book as any physician I've ever known. That's total bullshit what Winston said.

"New docs rotate through all the clinics when they first come on board. When Rohit started, I was the first stop for him. He was a good doctor, very conscientious, always by the book. Anyway, after he left my clinic, we stayed in touch. I had dinner with him a few weeks ago."

Seeing his questioning look, she explained. "Not like that, Jack—strictly professional—nothing else. He kind of looked at me as his mentor."

Jack smiled, embarrassed. "None of my business, but thanks for clarifying."

"He was obsessive about his documentation, crossing every *t* and dotting every *i*. I've never seen anyone more compulsive about it," Tina said.

"That's interesting. I guess you know everyone's saying Patel was fudging on the documentation?" Molly said.

Tina nodded. "Yes, and that's why I'm so surprised."

"Do you have any way of getting in touch with him?" Jack asked.

She shook her head. "No, I don't know much about his personal life. He didn't talk about it in any detail, so I have no idea where he is."

"Do you think he did it?" Molly asked.

She was quick to shake her head. "No way. My bullshit detector is pretty good, and it's pinging away."

"What do you think about Dr. Andrews's explanation, saying he passed along patients to Patel?" Jack asked.

She explained that older doctors do sometimes push patients to the new doctors. However, it was typically done completely above board, with a visible trail. A patient's physician of record was important, especially in a private setting, and was usually well-documented and recorded.

The other aspect of what Andrews said was equally suspect—that Patel signed Andrews's name on prescriptions for patients where he'd done an evaluation.

"We don't write prescriptions for patients based on other doctor's evaluations, especially when it comes to Schedule II drugs. In recent years, everyone's cracked down on that. It's not normal practice, and Winston knows that."

But without Patel, there was no way to corroborate or refute any of Andrews's allegations. It smacked of being too convenient.

"Why can't we have the cops pick up Wren's boyfriend, Peabo? We know he's dirty," Tina asked, trying another option out with the group.

Jack shook his head, and told Tina about their visitors at the boat. "They've got Wren. We put the cops on to him, there's a good chance she's going to get hurt. I don't want to take that risk right now."

"Maybe Patel will surface," Molly said.

"Maybe, but I'm not counting on it. We've got to get more on Andrews," Jack said.

The next day at work, Connie called Jack and told him Drager wanted to see him, pronto. He walked upstairs to Drager's office, and Drager asked him to shut the door when he walked in.

"We've found Rohit," Drager said, motioning for Jack to have a seat at the conference table. "Or, to be more accurate, I guess I should say we've found out where he's gone."

Jack cocked his head and waited for Dr. Drager to continue.

"He's gone back to India. He left this weekend, and based on what we know, he bought a one-way ticket," Drager said.

Apparently Dr. Patel had left the country Sunday, taking a flight from Tampa to Mumbai, going through Amsterdam. No one had any contact information, and with a population of over twenty million people, Rohit Patel was not likely to be found if he didn't want to be.

Although India and the United States had an extradition treaty, the reality of the situation was that Rohit Patel would likely never be heard from again.

Jack shook his head. All they had left was Andrews and Wren. Wren was with Peabo, so they were down to Andrews.

"This clearly confirms Patel was guilty. Why else would he flee the country without a word to anyone? Maybe our problem is solved, no?" Drager spread his hands and looked at Jack.

When Jack didn't respond, Drager continued, "Look, I know what you're thinking. Winston is certainly guilty of questionable . . . procedures. I discussed that with him and made it clear that's unacceptable. Any more improprieties and he will be terminated, friend or not. You have my word."

Jack stroked his chin and waited for the other shoe to fall, the one he knew was coming.

"But . . . we've identified the problem and taken steps to correct it. Without Patel, I'm not sure where any good would be served by involving the authorities."

Jack started to speak, but Drager held his hand up.

"I know we made mistakes, but we can't go back and undo what's been done. We have to look forward."

"This is bullshit," Jack said.

Molly pointed to the headline of the Tampa Tribune lying on the table in front of them. *Local Doctor Disappears.* "I assume you're talking about this." They were having their usual glass of wine after work.

The article said that Dr. Rohit Patel, employed by Drager Clinics, had disappeared this past weekend.

Unnamed sources said he bought a one-way ticket to India. Since he left his car and furnished condo behind, there was the strong implication of wrongdoing on Patel's part. No specifics were mentioned.

Jack nodded. "I mean, those were Andrews's patients. He claims he passed them along to Patel and Patel committed the fraud, then skipped the country. Right."

"Doesn't the documentation point to Patel? Why did he leave the country?" Molly asked.

"Thanks—you sound like Drager. That was his point, and one that I don't have a good answer to. The best I can come up with is that Andrews had something on Patel and called it in. Unfortunately, I have zero proof, so I'm back to square one. All we have left is Wren and Andrews. She's back with Peabo, so now Andrews has no reason to be concerned."

"What about Kirby, the pharmacist?" Molly asked.

They didn't have anything on Kirby, and Kirby knew it. Besides, Andrews and Peabo would cover him, so again, where was the proof? Lots of orders for OxyContin, but as Kirby pointed out—they were in the pain management business, so that wasn't surprising. Now that everyone was on alert, it would be even harder to find a chink anywhere.

Jack heard someone walking on the dock, looked up, and was surprised to see Tina standing there.

"Mind if I join you?" she asked.

"Hi, Tina. Of course, step aboard. Can I get you a glass?" Molly said.

Tina slipped off her sandals and stepped aboard. "That'd be nice. Thanks." Molly went down below to get another glass, and Tina sat next to where Molly was sitting.

She looked at the Tribune on the table. "I read the paper this morning. That's total crap."

Jack nodded as Molly appeared with another glass and a bottle of wine.

"Thanks," she said to Molly. She took a sip of wine and looked at him. "What do you need me to do?"

Chapter 28

"This is Tabitha, may I help you?"

"Hi, Tabitha. Jack Davis. I need to talk to Dr. Andrews. Is he there today?" He'd looked at the schedule and knew Andrews was supposed to be off, but he wanted to verify it.

"No, I'm sorry, Mr. Davis. He's off today. He should be home, though. As far as I know, he didn't have any appointments planned."

"Thanks, Tabitha." He hung up the phone, and headed to Dr. Andrews's house.

On the way, he called Dr. Andrews, but got no answer. He hoped he wasn't making the trip for nothing. While out for his run this morning, he'd decided to confront Andrews, one-on-one.

Yesterday, Tina had given him additional information regarding Andrews's charts. Not only that, she said she'd be willing to put it in writing. He'd been dying to find out what had changed her mind, but didn't want to pry. There'd be time to talk about that later.

Jack wasn't sure what he was going to say to the arrogant doctor. He'd put a small digital recorder in his pocket and intended to record the conversation, hoping

Andrews would slip and say something incriminating. While he knew that wouldn't be admissible in court, he could at least take it to Drager.

He was going to lean on Andrews, and planned on telling him that he'd talked to two patients who were willing to testify. He was also going to say that he knew Peabo was behind the ring, and suggest that Peabo was willing to throw Andrews under the bus. It was a gamble, but if Andrews thought the evidence was mounting, maybe he'd make a mistake.

Andrews lived on Davis Islands, a quaint little area just south of downtown Tampa that was also home to Tampa General Hospital. Two bridges connected the two small islands to the mainland, even though the area was sometimes referred to as Davis Island.

It was the dream of Florida native and real estate developer David Paul Davis, who went by the initials D.P. He built the islands during the Florida real estate boom in the 1920's. Davis was from Green Cove Springs, just south of Jacksonville, and the thought crossed Jack's mind that maybe they were distant relatives. He doubted it, since he had never heard any stories growing up that would indicate such, and Davis was a rather common surname.

In 1926, as the boom was slowing, Davis set sail for Paris on the ocean liner *Majestic* with his mistress. At some point during the voyage, he fell overboard and vanished at sea, with different stories explaining how he ended up in the water.

Davis Islands was also home to an airport and the Davis Island Yacht Club. The area contained an eclectic mix of retail shops, surprisingly modest homes, and multimillion dollar mansions. Dr. Andrews's home, located on the bay on the west side of the island, was clearly in the latter category.

Although he'd been over to Davis Islands before, he'd never been to Dr. Andrews's house. He glanced down at his phone for directions, made the last turn, and slowed as he neared the address shown.

Wrought iron gates guarded the drive, but they were open. Jack pulled in and saw the doctor's dark green Jaguar parked in the circular drive in front of the house. The grounds were well groomed and the large, two-story house imposing, with a three-car garage at a right angle to the house, facing the driveway.

He parked behind the shiny sedan, got out and walked to the front door, hearing the crunch of the gravel drive beneath his feet. He rang the doorbell several times, but there was no answer, although he could hear the chime ringing in the house. He banged on the door with his fist, and when there was still no response, he tried the doorknob. To his surprise, it wasn't locked.

Opening the door, he stuck his head in and yelled, "Dr. Andrews? Hello? Anyone home?" He repeated his greeting, and hearing no answer, stepped inside. The two-story foyer was impressive, with a circular staircase leading up to the second floor and a large, crystal chandelier hanging overhead. The house was quiet.

He walked past the staircase to the rear of the house, again, calling out the doctor's name. His footsteps on the tile floor echoed in the silence. He passed a huge kitchen on the left. A television screen was on and tuned to CNN, but the volume was off. There were no signs of anyone, not even a coffee cup next to the coffee pot. The placemats on the bar were in position, as if waiting to be used.

Past the kitchen, the house opened up into a large, informal living area that seemed to stretch across the width of the house. The back wall was solid glass with a magnificent view of Tampa Bay. There was a small study on the right. He peeked in the door, calling Dr. Andrews's name. There was a desk there with papers scattered on top—out of character messy for Andrews, he thought, shaking his head.

He continued to the living area. Between the glass and the bay was a large pool that matched the width of the house, enclosed by a screened cage. The glass doors were open, and he could hear water running. In the corner of the pool was a rock feature, water cascading down the irregular face and into the pool.

Jack was beginning to think no one was home. He stepped out into the pool area, and saw a man in a t-shirt and shorts floating face down on the surface of the pool, near the steps at the shallow end. At first, he thought the person might be swimming, then realized in shock that the body wasn't moving.

Jack yelled for Dr. Andrews, ran over, kicked his shoes off and waded into the pool. He struggled to pull the lifeless body out of the water, up on the pool deck. He turned the man over and recognized Dr. Winston Andrews.

He put his ear next to Andrews's nose and mouth, hoping to feel even a faint breath of air against his cheek. Nothing. He looked at the doctor's chest to see if it was moving, but again, nothing. Last, he put his fingers on the carotid artery, hoping for a faint pulse, but knowing the answer as he held his breath. There was nothing.

As a teenager, Jack had worked as a lifeguard on the beach in Jacksonville. He knew the protocol was to call 911, then start CPR. But working on the beach, he'd pulled several people out of the water, bloated and pale just like Dr. Andrews, and he knew it was too late. The man was dead.

He pulled his phone out to call 911, and the tiny voice recorder fell out of his pocket. Remembering why he came there, and knowing Dr. Andrews was beyond help in this life, he decided to take a quick look around first.

He walked back to the study and over to the desk. It occurred to him that he shouldn't touch anything, and saw a pen lying on the desk. He picked it up and used it to poke around. There were bank statements, bills, and underneath a folder, a small clear plastic baggy containing what looked like a tablespoon of white powder.

Jack wasn't sure, but he was willing to bet it was cocaine. He wiped the pen off with his shirt, put it back where he found it, and walked out to the pool.

He called 911, and in a calm voice, described the situation to the dispatcher. Though the dispatcher wanted him to remain on the phone until someone arrived, he assured her there was no urgency and he would be waiting. After giving her his personal information, he disconnected the call and sat by the pool, waiting for the police to arrive.

Now what, he thought. So much for confronting Dr. Andrews. A huge piece of the puzzle was gone, and he was at a dead-end, with nowhere to turn for answers.

Jack decided it would be better to wait for the police outside the front door. He retraced his steps back to the foyer, calling Dr. Drager as he walked. Drager was stunned, wondering aloud what happened. Jack went outside and sat on the top step, still talking to Drager. In a few minutes, a police car pulled in the drive.

"Gotta go. The police just pulled up. I'll call you later," he told Drager as he ended the call. He pulled his wallet out and removed his driver's license, figuring the cops would want to start there.

The two police officers eyed Jack carefully as they walked up to the steps.

"You the one who called?" the shorter one asked.

Jack nodded, told them his name and held out his license as proof. They looked at it, and asked him a few questions. Satisfied he was who he said, they followed him into the house. Jack led them out to the pool, explaining what he'd found a short time ago.

Soon, the house was crawling with people. Detectives, crime scene technicians, and representatives from the medical examiner's office were on scene. He watched as they made it to the study. After a few minutes, one of the detectives came out and motioned to one of the crime scene technicians.

"Expecting something, Mr. Davis?" Jack jumped. He'd been watching the activity at the door of the study and didn't hear the detective walk up behind him.

"No, just wondering why all of the attention to the study."

"How'd you know it was a study? I thought you said you'd never been out to Dr. Andrews's house before."

He hesitated, trying to remember if the door was open when he walked by. "I walked past it on my way to the pool."

The detective, a thick, middle-aged black man, nodded, still staring at him. "Did you go in?"

Jack looked away as if he were trying to recall. "No, I just stuck my head inside the door, looking for Dr. Andrews."

"What did you see in there?"

"A desk with a bunch of papers on top. No sign of Dr. Andrews, so I walked out to the pool."

The detective in the study stuck his head out and motioned for the one questioning Jack.

"I've got a few more questions for you, Mr. Davis. Excuse me a minute," he said, as he walked over to the study.

Jack was relieved to be out of the spotlight. Both of the detectives emerged from the study, came over and questioned him at length. After another forty-five minutes, they seemed satisfied with his answers and told him he was free to go.

On the way home, he called Drager and gave him an update, although there wasn't much he could add. Andrews was dead and Jack didn't know why or how. After he finished with Drager, he called Tina with the news. She didn't seem as surprised as Drager.

"Any idea what happened?" she asked. Drager had asked the same thing.

"No, not really. The police took my statement, and there's a bunch of people at the house, but nobody commented on what happened. He was dead when I got there, and I'm not sure how long he'd been in the water. Long enough for me to know it was too late for CPR."

"Sad. As you know, he was not one of my favorite people. How are you doing? That must have been quite a shock," she said.

"Certainly not something I see every day, but nothing gory about it. I honestly can't say that I'm sorry. Guess that bothers me more than anything."

"It shouldn't." Her voice was dispassionate. "He was not a nice person."

When he got to the marina, Molly was home. He filled her in on the events of the afternoon, and they talked well into the night about what to do.

The next morning, Drager called and asked him to come to his office as soon as possible. Jack wasn't surprised, and drove straight to the Rocky Point office when he left Clearwater Beach.

Connie was on the phone, but motioned him into the doctor's office. Drager sat there shaking his head as Jack made himself comfortable. Dispensing with niceties, Drager said, "Thanks for coming down. I didn't want to discuss this over the phone."

Jack looked at his boss with a curious look as Drager continued.

"They discovered cocaine in Winston's body and in his house."

Jack tried to act surprised. "What . . . are you sure?"

Drager nodded. "I'd heard rumors, but I refused to believe it. A classic case of denial, I'm afraid. Why were you over at his house?"

He wasn't going to get into details with Drager at this point and had rehearsed his answer to the question on the way to Drager's office. "I wanted to go over some of the chart reviews with him. I had some questions about Dr. Patel's record-keeping. I figured with him at home, it would be more convenient."

Drager shook his head, mumbling to himself, "Such a shame. He really was an incredible doctor." He stared out the window for a moment, then looked at Jack. "Anyway, I wanted to tell you the news before it gets out. I'm not sure what, if anything, we can do, but I wanted you to be prepared."

"I'm sorry, Dr. Drager. I know he was your friend."

On his way back to his office, he called Molly and told her the latest.

"Now what do we do?" she asked.

"I'm not sure. We still have the pharmacist's name, but not sure how to proceed. We'll talk later."

"Maybe you should call Tony," she said, referring to their detective friend in Fort Myers.

"Maybe. Later," he said, and disconnected the call.

Driving back across the bay on the Courtney Campbell, he decided to stop by Bayview Pharmacy. No time like the present, he thought.

He walked in and asked for Kirby.

"Hello, Jack. I didn't realize you were coming. What could I do for you?" Kirby said, walking up to the counter.

Jack asked if they could go somewhere private. The pharmacist said he needed a smoke, and asked if Jack minded going outside.

"I'll get right to the point, Lee," he said once they got outside and Kirby lit his cigarette. "Dr. Andrews is dead."

He watched the pharmacist for a reaction, and could tell he was surprised by the news.

"I found him in his pool. It's coming out about the cocaine, too."

Now Lee had a puzzled look on his face. "Cocaine?"

"You're going to tell me you didn't know he had a cocaine habit?"

The pharmacist stared at Jack. "Andrews was doing coke?"

He had him off guard, and went for the kill. "I also know all about the deal you and Andrews had going with prescriptions. I've got two patients who can identify you, Andrews, and Peabo. It's coming out, Lee. You can cooperate or you can stonewall."

The older man's eyes narrowed and he took another drag from his cigarette. "I don't know what you're talking about." He looked at his watch, dropped the cigarette and ground it out with his foot on the sidewalk. "I've got to get back to work." He turned and walked away, leaving Jack standing there alone.

"Where do we go from here?" Tina asked. She, Jack and Molly were on the sailboat at the marina. Jack had told them the surprising news that Andrews had a cocaine habit.

"Explains why Andrews was doing the prescriptions," Tina said, "financing his drug habit."

"I know, but I didn't see that one coming," Jack said.

"Not that uncommon," Molly said. "He was functional. I worked with a neurosurgeon in Boston—same deal. He was one of the best at the hospital, yet he was regularly using cocaine and had been for some time.

He overdosed, or got a hold of some ultra-pure stuff, and they found him dead on the floor of his condo."

"How did Drager know about the cocaine?" Tina asked.

"Drager knew the next morning. That's when he told me," Jack said. "Maybe he's got a source in the police department?"

"That would explain knowing about the cocaine in the house, but you said Drager specifically mentioned they found it in Winston's body. That doesn't make sense. The tox screens usually take a couple of days."

Jack and Molly looked at each other, then at Tina.

"Do you think Drager's involved in this?" Molly asked

"We're speculating. Let's look at what we've got at this point," Jack said. "Patel's gone and Andrews is dead, so they're obviously out. Wren and Peabo know, but we can't get to her. Kirby's involved, but he's not talking."

Tina and Molly looked at Jack.

"Yeah, since I was in the vicinity, I dropped by to see Kirby. I surprised him with the news about Andrews's death, but he didn't know about anything about Andrews using coke."

"Maybe he wasn't," Tina said.

Jack nodded. "Someone could've planted it."

"Andrews is gone. How do we get Wren away from Peabo?" Molly asked.

"We've got to find some way to press Peabo," Jack said. "Maybe we make him a deal."

"What kind of a deal?" Molly said. "We don't have anything on Peabo."

"What if we had something Peabo wanted?"

Chapter 29

Jack sat in his car, waiting for the black Escalade to show. He remembered Wren saying that Peabo always made sure that Lee Kirby was working whenever they came to get scripts filled, so he had called Bayview Pharmacy and asked if the pharmacist was working. The clerk said she thought so, but would check. In a few minutes, Kirby picked up and said, "Lee Kirby, can I help you?" Jack hung up. By nine-thirty, he pulled into the parking lot and had been waiting there since.

He watched as a lawn maintenance guy with headphones strapped on his head handled a gas trimmer on the opposite edge of the parking lot. He slumped down in his seat and pulled the Bucs cap down lower over his head as he saw the Cadillac SUV pull into the parking lot. It parked on the next to the last row, and backed in so it would be facing the pharmacy. Three people soon got out and headed toward the front door of the pharmacy. Wren wasn't in the group.

Jack pulled his cap down lower, got out of his car and took the long way to the pharmacy so anyone in the Escalade couldn't get a good look at him. He walked in and went straight to the pharmacy counter, where he saw

Lee Kirby talking to one of the people Jack had seen step out of Peabo's SUV.

Jack pulled his cap off and Kirby looked up, surprised to see Jack standing there.

Jack leaned over the counter and said in a low voice, "Call Peabo and tell him to send Shorty in here—now. Go to your office, and I'll meet you both there when I see him come in. Otherwise, I'm calling the cops."

Kirby looked confused and scared. When he hesitated, Jack repeated the instructions and walked a few aisles over where he could watch the pharmacist. Kirby's eyes followed Jack, then he took out his cell phone and made a call. Jack nodded, and made his way to the front of the store where Kirby could no longer see him.

He slipped out the side door and walked back to his car, just in time to see Shorty getting out of the Escalade and scanning the parking lot. When he got to the Mini, Jack took the pistol and put it in his holster, pulling his shirt over the handle to conceal it. He watched as Shorty checked his belt, tugged his shirttail down, and lumbered toward the pharmacy entrance.

Jack walked toward the Cadillac from behind. As he approached the Escalade, he glanced around the parking lot to see if anyone was watching. The lawn guy, in another world, was still working the trimmer on the other side of the parking lot. He was making a lot of racket but paying no attention to anything other than what was in front of him.

Jack saw what had to be Peabo's elbow on the open window of the driver's door of the SUV. He pulled the pistol out, walked up to the window and pointed the gun toward Peabo, close enough to get his attention, but far enough away to eliminate Peabo grabbing for it.

"Don't do anything stupid, Peabo," Jack said, holding the gun steady. "Keep your hands on the wheel where I can see them." He took a quick glance in the back, but there were only two guys sitting there. Keeping his eyes on Peabo, he said to the pair in the back seat, "Stay where you are and do exactly as I tell you and you won't get hurt."

Peabo swiveled his head toward Jack and his eyes got wide as he saw the black barrel of the pistol pointed toward him only a few feet away. "What the hell are you doing?"

"Just doing a little business. Where's Wren?"

"She took the day off."

Shit, Jack thought. *Now what?* He'd planned on Wren being with Peabo. He risked a quick look around the parking lot. No one around—yet, but he knew that wouldn't last long.

"Why don't you point that thing somewhere else? You ain't got the balls to shoot me," Peabo said, gaining back a little of his cockiness.

Jack locked eyes with the thug, and his hand was surprisingly steady. "You want to take that chance? I'm holding a loaded forty caliber SIG pointed at your face.

"Listen to me carefully. Peabo, I want you to put your hands behind your seat, very slowly. If I even think you're going for the gun I know you have, I won't hesitate to pull the trigger."

"You're making a big mistake, Davis," Peabo spat the words out.

"Just do it." He kept his eyes on Peabo's as Peabo put his hands behind the seat. "You, the guy in the back. Take these." Jack reached into his pocket with his left hand and pulled out a handful of thick plastic electrical ties. He reached underneath his gun hand and handed them to the outstretched arm from the back seat.

"Tie his wrists together—tight." Jack waited, then saw Peabo's shoulders get pulled back as the runner in the back seat pulled Peabo's arms together.

"Done," the shaky voice said from the back seat.

"Good, now both of you get out and walk away from here as fast as you can." The back door opened, and the two runners emerged from the car, looking around and walking toward the street as fast as they could.

Jack walked around and looked in the open door. Peabo's wrists were tied together, but Jack reached in and checked. He nodded; the runner had done a good job. Jack put the pistol back in the holster and covered it once again with his shirt. He closed the vehicle door and stepped back to the window next to Peabo.

"What the fuck you want?" Peabo said.

"I want the girl," Jack said. "And I don't have time to make you tell me where she is, so I'm taking a little insurance."

He walked around to the back of the SUV and opened the tailgate. The black duffel bag was inside, just as Wren had said it would be. He opened it, quickly verified the contents, then zipped it back up and slung it over his shoulder. He was surprised at how heavy it was.

He walked back to Peabo's window, reached in, took the keys out of the ignition, and flung them as far across the parking lot as he could.

Peabo's dark eyes glared at him. "You don't know what you're getting into."

Patting the bag, Jack said, "As soon as I get Wren back, you'll get this."

Quickly, he walked back to his car and left. As he was pulling out of the parking lot, he saw Shorty coming out the pharmacy door. Damn, that was close, he thought.

His hands were shaking as he drove back to Clearwater Beach. It had been easier than he thought. That was the first time he'd ever pointed a gun at anyone. Peabo was right; he didn't have the balls to shoot him, not like that. Thank goodness Peabo decided not to chance it.

He got back to the marina parking lot, opened the hatch on the Mini, and looked around. Nothing seemed suspicious, so he hefted the bag over his shoulder and locked the car. He tried to look casual as he walked toward the boat, another boater carrying an overnight bag.

When he got onboard, down below in the cabin, he unzipped the bag and looked inside. It was loaded with Ziploc bags, all full of pills, numerous green plastic pill bottles, and stacks of money.

He picked one up of the green containers and examined it under the light. The label was from Bayview Pharmacy, on Thornton Street. The patient was a Megan Roberts, and the prescription was for OxyContin, 30 mg. The doctor was Andrews. He opened it and shook out the small, round, brown pills. He dumped the pills back into the bottle, closed it, and threw it back in the bag. He grabbed another and looked at the label. Everything was the same, except for the patient name.

Then he picked up one of the clear plastic bags and held it up. It was full of the small brown pills. Peabo's haul for the week, he thought.

He turned his attention to the money, and the smiling face of Benjamin Franklin looking at him. Quite a few faces, it turned out. He was surprised to see so much money. He picked up a bundle rubber-banded together and counted one hundred bills. Ten thousand dollars and that was just one stack.

He counted ninety-two bundles, along with lots of loose bills, most of them bearing Franklin's face. He had to be looking at almost a million dollars in cash.

Jack sat back, stunned. *A million dollars in cash? How in the world?* He'd just stolen a million dollars from a drug dealer.

Wren had told him that in a good week, Peabo usually made somewhere around a hundred thousand dollars. Jack did the math in his head and confirmed that amount, based on the information Wren had given him. *So what was Peabo doing with this kind of money?*

Something didn't add up. He'd stumbled into something way bigger than he realized.

He knew he couldn't keep this on the boat. Rummaging through the change jar sitting on the chart table, he scrounged up four quarters and three one-dollar bills. He grabbed the duffel bag and headed toward the marina, hoping he didn't run across anyone he knew.

Thankfully, nobody else was there in the locker room. He walked up to the change machine, inserted a dollar bill and watched as the machine spit it back out, almost as quick as it went in. "Shit," he said out loud. He stuck another bill in and heard the familiar click of coins in the tray underneath.

He took the coins and walked over to the row of lockers. After stuffing the cash bag into the small locker, he deposited the quarters and turned the key, removing it. He tested the door to make sure it was locked, then stuck the key in his pocket and walked out.

He checked his phone, surprised that Peabo hadn't called yet. He went outside and stood, throngs of tourists milling around. Peabo wouldn't be foolish enough to try anything here with this many people around.

Molly was at work, so she was safe, but he needed to call her and tell her to stay put. He took out his phone and punched in her number, but the call went straight to voice mail. He left her a message telling her not to leave the hospital under any circumstances and to wait for his call. It was still two hours before her normal shift ended, so he hung up the phone.

Something was wrong, and he felt it in his gut. Peabo should've called by now or shown up. He knew the thug wasn't going to walk away from this kind of money.

He called Wren, thinking maybe she could help, but no answer. Too much time had passed, and he was starting to worry. He decided to call Molly's nursing unit. Cecilia, a nurse Jack had met before, answered.

"Cecilia, hey, it's Jack Davis. How are you?"

"Good, Jack. Haven't seen you in a while."

"I know, busy with work. You know how that goes. Listen, I've been trying to call Molly on her cell and she didn't answer. I figured she got tied up there on the floor, but I really need to talk to her."

"Oh, she went across the street to get a sandwich at Larry's about . . . an hour ago. In fact, she should've been back by now. I'm surprised—she never takes this long."

Jack's heart sank to his stomach. "Thanks, Ceil. Would you please tell her to call me as soon as she gets back?"

"Sure. Nice talking to you, Jack."

He disconnected the call and stood there.

His hands were shaking as he pressed Molly's number. After a couple of rings, a man answered. "Wondered what was taking you so long."

Jack almost dropped the phone. It was Peabo Watson.

Chapter 30

"Hey asshole," the voice on the phone said. "Cat got your tongue?"

Jack took a deep breath and tried his best to remain calm. "What are you doing with this phone?"

Peabo laughed. "Whadda ya think? I told you you were making a mistake."

"How'd you get her phone?"

"Don't fuck with me, Davis." Peabo's voice had an edge on it. "I've got her and her phone. You don't believe me, then call where she works."

Jack's mind was racing. "Look, I'll give you the bag back, okay? Just let her go."

Peabo laughed again. "You ain't so cocky now, are you, Mister Big Shot?"

There was a silence on the phone, and Jack was afraid Peabo had hung up on him.

"Listen carefully. Be out at the far end of the marina parking lot at seven o'clock with the bag. Any sign of cops or that anyone is with you, game over. Got it?"

He swallowed, tasting bile in his mouth. "I'll be there. Where's Molly? Let me talk to her. Hello? Hello!" The line went dead. Shit. They had Molly.

Maybe not. Maybe Peabo just had her phone. After all, he hadn't talked to her. His phone, still his hand, chimed. He stared at the screen. It was a text message from Molly's phone. His finger was shaking as he pressed it.

He gasped as he saw the picture. It was Molly.

She had a gag in her mouth, and there was a bruise on her cheek. A man's hand held a fistful of red hair, and her eyes stared defiantly into the camera. She was alive, at least for now.

He sat there and realized he'd just wasted five minutes. Not a lot of time left. He looked at his watch—three hours till Peabo got here.

Peabo wasn't about to let Molly go before getting the money, and Jack wasn't inclined to give up the money before getting Molly. The only difference, and it was a huge difference, is what Peabo had was infinitely more valuable than what Jack had. And both parties knew it.

He called Tina Marshall on her cell phone and asked her to come to the boat as soon as she could. When she asked what was going on, all he would say is that it was extremely important and he'd explain when she got there.

After he hung up, he reached down and felt the pistol in its holster. He started to put it back in the safe, then hesitated. When he took the class for his concealed weapons permit, the instructor told them not to carry a gun if they weren't prepared to use it. Jack left it in the holster, knowing he wouldn't hesitate to use it if he had the chance.

He walked up to the marina to get the duffel bag out of the locker. No need to worry about Peabo showing up here now. Walking back through the breezeway with the bag over his shoulder, he noticed two bundles of the free Tampa weekly newspaper Tampa Beat outside the back door of the gift shop. He looked around, saw no one, picked up the bundles, and walked out to the boat.

On the boat, he set the bundles down on the floor of the main cabin, then went back to the aft cabin. He rummaged through the wardrobe, found what he was looking for and went back to the main salon where he started preparing for the exchange.

He was about halfway done, when he heard Tina's voice out on the dock. "Jack? You in there?"

He went up the steps to the cockpit and stuck his head out. Dusk was settling in and the temperature had dropped some. "Hey, come on down," he said.

"Jack, what's going on?" she said, standing next to the companionway. She was still wearing scrubs and tennis shoes. "Where's Molly?"

He stuck his hand out to assist her. "Not out here. Come on down below." He took her hand and led her down the steps into the cabin.

She froze at the sight. Stacks of hundred dollar bills were piled on the settee. Shreds of the Tampa Beat littered the cabin, with rubber bands around cut-up bundles of paper, stacked over on the other side of the small table. It looked like a tornado had come through the cabin of the boat. "What in the hell—"

Jack held up his hand. "They've got Molly. And Wren, too."

Tina looked totally confused. "Who . . . what?"

He proceeded to explain what had happened and what he planned to do. When he finished, she was shaking her head. "Jack, we've got to call the police."

He shook his head. "No. No time, and besides, I'm not taking the risk."

"How much money is here?"

Jack shrugged. "Close to a million dollars."

"A *million* dollars? This is way out of control. I'm calling the police." She pulled out her cell phone, and he snatched it out of her hand.

"What do you think you're doing? Give me my phone." She held her hand out.

He held up his hand. "Tina, please. Just hear me out first, okay?"

She nodded, but he didn't give up her phone.

"They will be in the parking lot here at the marina in an hour. He wants me out there—alone. There's not enough time for the police to set anything up. It would take me longer than that to explain it to them. Think about it."

He pleaded. "They've got Molly and Wren, Tina. I've got to get them back."

"You're an idiot. You actually think he's going to let them go when you give him the bag?"

He shook his head. "I've got to get them back. It's my only chance. I'm going. You can either help me or not."

He looked at her and held her phone out. "Please don't call before I meet them." She took the phone and watched as he started cutting and assembling more bundles of newsprint.

She watched him for a few minutes, holding her phone. "He'll kill you, Jack, even if Molly and Wren manage to get away."

He shrugged. "I don't care—I just want them safe."

She set her phone down and pulled up her sleeves.

By the time they were done, they had almost eighty bundles of newsprint that were close to the same size and shape as the bundles of hundred dollar bills. He took the duffel bag he'd stolen from Peabo and dumped out all of the money and pills on the floor of the sailboat. Then, he placed all of the worthless bundles into the bag while Tina started placing bundles of money into a similar sized bag he'd found in the aft cabin.

When they were finished, they had two duffel bags roughly the same size and weight. Peabo's bag contained bundles of newsprint, covered with fifteen or twenty bundles of hundred dollar bills, along with Ziploc bags and green pill bottles containing OxyContin. The other bag contained nothing but money, in the neighborhood of three-quarters of a million dollars, by Jack's best guess.

"You really think he's going to buy this?" Tina asked, as they sat down topside, catching some fresh air.

"I do. You unzip the bag, look inside, take out a couple of bundles—everything looks fine. Drugs are there just like he left them. He's not going to stop and count the whole thing."

"But, what if he does?"

Jack pointed at her. "That's where you come in. You're the ace in the hole. If Molly and Wren aren't there, then I tell him he doesn't have the whole package. Either way, he has to produce the girls to get the money. Trust me, he wants the money more than anything."

He looked at his watch. "He'll be here soon. Hand me your phone."

She handed him her iPhone and he punched away. "You don't have the Find My iPhone app?" he asked.

She shook her head.

"It's a poor man's way of tracking an iPhone. What's your Apple ID and password? I'll set it up on your phone so you can track mine," he said.

She gave him the information and he entered it into her phone. He installed the app and linked his phone to her account. Starting the app, he handed it back to her and showed her how to use it to track his phone.

"That's pretty cool," she said, looking at the green dot on the map of the screen of her phone showing the location of Jack's iPhone.

"It's relatively accurate and reliable," he said.

"Oh, that inspires a lot of confidence—relatively?" she said, looking up from the phone.

He shrugged. "Best I could come up with, given the time we have. Besides, he doesn't know you or your car, so that's in our favor. Just don't follow too close."

"I really think we should call—"

Jack held up his hand. "No, not an option. Only if everything goes to hell, okay?"

She hesitated, then nodded in agreement.

They went back down below, and he picked up the pistol, first releasing the magazine, and then racking the slide to eject the bullet in the chamber. He racked it again and flipped the catch up with his thumb, locking the slide open.

"You know what to do with one of these?" he asked, holding it out toward her, pointed toward the floor.

She didn't say a word and just held her hand out. She took the pistol with one hand and the magazine in the other. Without looking, she popped the magazine in, racked the slide, which chambered a bullet, then with her thumb released the slide.

"Weapon is now hot," she said, then repeated the same process Jack had just done. She handed the weapon, now cold again, back to him.

Jack stood there with his mouth open. Not only did the lady know what to do with one, she was obviously familiar with this particular model.

Tina laughed. "Surprised? My dad was a cop. A SIG was his service weapon. He taught my sister and me how to handle one of these when we were teenagers. I can put all thirteen rounds within a three-inch circle at thirty feet."

"Okay," he said. "Better than I can do. You need to go ahead and get to your car. I'll come along in fifteen minutes."

Tina looked at him and gave him a quick hug. "Be careful," she said. She took the bag with most of the money, slung it over her shoulder and left for her car.

He gave Tina fifteen minutes to get to her car and went back over his plan one more time. It wasn't perfect, but Jack felt it was the best they could do under the circumstances.

He hefted the bag containing the drugs and part of the money over his shoulder. It felt about the same as the original bag. He walked up the steps and out onto the dock and headed toward the marina parking lot. It was the longest walk of his life.

Past the main dock, on the parking lot side of the building, he ran into Don, the marina manager.

"Hey, Jack. You okay?" the burly man said, blocking his path.

Jack scanned the parking lot. No black Escalade yet. But he had to get rid of Don, and fast.

"Hey, Don. Yeah, I'm fine. Kind of in a hurry, though." He went to walk around him toward the far end of the parking lot.

Don turned and walked next to him. "Okay, I'll just walk with you. Wanted to ask you a quick question." Don stopped, looked back at the other side of the parking lot where Jack's car was parked, then toward the far end of the lot. "Where're you headed? Your car's back over there," he said, pointing back behind Jack.

Jack stopped and grabbed Don's shoulders. "Look, Don. I don't mean to be rude, but I really need to be alone right now, okay? No offense. I'll give you a call later." He kept scanning the parking lot, hoping not to see a black Escalade while Don was standing there.

Looking confused and a little angry, Don just shook his head and walked back toward the marina, saying, "Whatever."

Jack exhaled and kept walking. About halfway to the end of the lot, he heard a car and turned in time to see a black Cadillac Escalade pull down to the end of the lot and stop. As he got closer, the driver's window came down and Peabo's face filled the frame, a cigarette dangling from his mouth.

"Right on time. I like that."

"Where's Molly?" Jack answered.

"Somewhere safe, where we're going."

Shorty emerged from the other side of the vehicle, and stood there, his hand in his pocket. Jack had no doubt it was wrapped firmly around a gun. He looked around, hoping against hope that someone would come to his rescue, but there was no one near.

The huge man frisked him, took Jack's cell phone out of his pocket, and held it up for Peabo to see. "Just this, Boss."

Peabo nodded. "Let him keep it. He'll need it. Hop in, Davis. We're going to take a little ride."

Shorty opened the rear door of the SUV.

"I want to see Molly first," Jack said, planting his feet and tightening his grip on the bag.

"You'll see her soon enough. Just get in the Escalade and we'll drive there."

Jack shook his head as he talked. "No, I'm not getting in the Escalade until I see—"

"Look, asshole," Peabo interrupted. "I'm not here to negotiate. You either get in the car, with the bag, or we leave. You got three seconds to decide. One. Two—"

Shit, Jack thought. He didn't like this setup, but at least Tina had his back.

He slid into the seat with the bag still over his shoulder. No one else was in the vehicle. Shorty climbed in, closed the door, and held his hand out.

"Gotta make sure everything's there," Peabo said, turned around facing them.

Jack handed the bag to Shorty and held his breath.

Shorty unzipped the duffel bag, spread the sides, and looked inside. He picked up one of the cash bundles, and held it up to examine. Like a bank teller, he thumbed through the stack, checking the bills. He put it back in the bag and reached in to grab another without looking.

Jack could swear his heart stopped as a strange expression fell over the big man's face. Shorty pulled out a plastic bag full of OxyContin, held it up to see the contents, and smiled. He verified another bundle of cash, then nodded to himself.

"Everything's here, including the pills," he said to Peabo.

Jack had to remind himself to breathe again. "You've got the money, now, tell me where Molly is."

Peabo started the car and told Shorty to check some more.

"C'mon, man, I told you it's here," Shorty said, rolling his eyes.

"I know, but I want to make sure," Peabo said. "I don't trust this wiseass. Check it."

Shorty shook his head and reached deep into the bag. Jack watched as he moved his hand around the bag. He wasn't sure what the big guy was doing, but he knew if he pulled out a stack of newsprint with a rubber band around it, things were going to go bad real soon.

"At least let me talk to her. I want to know she's okay." Jack hoped his nervousness didn't betray him, and that the continuous questions would divert them.

Shorty got a strange expression on his face, and his hand in the bag stopped moving. He looked over at Jack and slowly pulled out two bundles.

Jack's heart stopped as he saw the tips of the bundles emerge, and for a brief second, he thought one of them was a bogus bundle. Shorty grinned and held up two bundles of hundreds. He thumbed through them, and put them both back into the bag. Jack was afraid he was going to dig for more, but Shorty zipped the duffel bag up and placed it on the seat next to him, opposite Jack.

He didn't say a word to his boss.

"Well, did you check?" Peabo said, in a tone of voice that indicated he was tired of waiting for Shorty to comment.

"Yeah, and everything's there—just like it's supposed to be." Shorty rolled his eyes and shook his head again. Once more, Jack remembered to breathe.

Peabo put the car in gear and they left the parking lot, heading east over the causeway toward Clearwater. Jack glanced in the mirror and hoped it was a blue BMW that he saw pull out behind them.

Chapter 31

They drove through Clearwater and were almost to the bay and Courtney Campbell Causeway. Jack tried to figure out where they were going. He could feel the phone in his pocket, and he hoped that Tina wasn't too far behind. He wanted to check, but was afraid to risk it and alert Peabo to the fact that something was up.

He was looking out the window, when he felt a huge arm press against his neck, pinning him against the side of the vehicle. He reached up to try and move it and felt a prick on his leg. Jack looked down as he saw Shorty plunging a syringe into his thigh.

"Just to calm you down," the big man said.

He tried to swat Shorty's hand away, but with the big man's forearm pressed hard against his neck, he couldn't get much leverage. It didn't matter, because in a few seconds he was unconscious.

He woke up lying in the back seat of the Escalade, his face next to the leather seat. It was dark outside and he saw Shorty in the passenger seat, which meant that Peabo was still driving. His head hurt, and he was groggy from whatever they'd injected him with. His hands were tied behind his back and he had duct tape across his mouth, making it difficult to breathe.

He had no idea where they were and didn't know how long he'd been out. He could feel his phone in his pocket, and he remembered. He prayed the tracking function was working and Tina was nearby. Shorty turned and looked at him.

"He's awake," the big man said.

"Good. We're almost there," Peabo said.

Jack felt the car slow, then come to a stop. He heard thunder in the distance, but no other cars. The road was bumpy, not paved, he thought. There were not a lot of lights around and it was quiet.

He was still dazed, but he knew he was in trouble. Shorty got out, and shut the door. Jack tried to sit up with his hands next to the door, but it was awkward. He could see Peabo behind the wheel, staring ahead. No one else was in the car.

He could feel the door handle next to his hands. If he opened it, he'd just fall out on his back. A few minutes later, Jack heard a gunshot and jumped. He had to get out of the car. Just as he was about to pull the handle up to open the door, Shorty pulled it open and pushed him back down on the seat.

"Going somewhere?" Shorty asked. Peabo turned around to see what was going on. He laughed as Shorty got back in the SUV and closed the door. The handle of a pistol stuck out above Shorty's waistband. Peabo drove forward a short distance, then parked.

They dragged Jack out of the vehicle and propped him up against the door of the Escalade. In the dim light, Jack could make out a wooden fence and a few buildings, but still had no clue where they were. There was no sign of Molly or Wren.

"Let's take a little walk, Davis," Peabo said, grabbing Jack's shoulder and pushing him toward a small building. Shorty picked up a small cage the size of a dog carrier and followed them.

"Where's Molly?" Jack asked. His tongue was still thick from whatever they'd given him, and his words were muffled behind the duct tape over his mouth.

Peabo ignored him and switched on a flashlight, illuminating an eight foot tall closed wooden gate in front of them. The light shone on a keypad next to the gate, and Shorty reached out from behind him to punch in a series of numbers. When the last number was punched, a green light came on, and he heard the click of a mechanical lock.

Jack almost tripped as he was shoved through the gate. He stumbled and followed the beam of light pointed toward the ground in front of him.

Once inside the inner gate, they locked it behind them and Peabo said, "Shorty, go get your damn critter and meet me in back by the lake."

Shorty headed off to the right, taking the cage with him. Peabo pushed Jack, and they walked forward, in the dark. Peabo switched the flashlight on for a few seconds at a time indicating the path to take.

There were trees all around, and Jack heard noises on either side. They were strange sounds, not recognizable. He strained to make out the source. He could make out the outline of what appeared to be wire fences on each side, and he was startled when several times he saw the reflections of eyes looking at him.

They walked for perhaps ten minutes down this forest trail, when Peabo clamped his hands down on Jack's shoulder. "That's far enough."

Peabo clicked the flashlight on and pointed it toward the sign on the fence in front of Jack.

Joseph, African lion

Jack shook his head, confused. All of a sudden it dawned on him. He knew where he was, and a knot formed in the pit of his stomach.

Peabo laughed. "You figured it out, didn't you?"

Jack looked back into the hollow eyes of Peabo. Peabo shoved him backwards, and Jack stumbled, falling on his back. Before he could react, Peabo had tied his feet together.

"Just so you don't go anywhere while I go lock the kitty up," Peabo said.

He watched as Peabo walked around to the side of the fenced enclosure that housed the lion. He saw there was a lockout connected to the cage. Peabo stuffed a package into the feeding tray, and watched as the enormous male lion padded into the small lockout area to investigate. As soon as he entered that section of the cage, Peabo reached up and released the rope that dropped the gate, locking the lion in the enclosure within an enclosure.

Jack's eyes were wide with fear and his heart started racing as he contemplated what was coming.

"He looks hungry, don't he?" Peabo said, as they watched the huge animal rip the package to shreds with his massive paws, quickly getting to the meat inside. In a few seconds, he had devoured the snack, and was turned around watching the two men with intense interest.

Peabo looked around and muttered, "That damn Shorty. We got to finish here and get back out to the beach. He's hell-bent on stealing that white serval." He looked down at Jack. "You know how much that thing's worth? $75,000—can you believe it? For a housecat on steroids. Shorty's found somebody that wants to buy him, so I told him that was his deal. I told him he could keep the money, but I wasn't messing with it."

Peabo produced a set of bolt cutters and cut a line spanning several sections of the fence enclosing the big cat. He pulled it back, bending it open enough to drag Jack through and into the enclosure. Joseph let out a roar that made the hair on the back of Jack's neck stand up straight, and he saw Peabo jump as well.

"Damn, never heard one that close. Scares the shit outta you, don't it?" he said, standing in front of Jack. Jack could see the moonlight reflecting off the lake behind Peabo, on the other side of the fence. He heard thunder—close, and rain started to fall. The breeze picked up and started to rustle the leaves in the trees overhead. *Where the hell was Tina?* He hoped she knew that Peabo and Shorty had separated.

Peabo kneeled down in front of Jack, reached out and ripped off the duct tape covering his mouth.

"Bet that hurt, didn't it? I took it off 'cause I want to hear you when he comes in the cage with you," he said, nodding in the direction of the lockout behind Jack.

"You think you're so fucking smart, don't you? Well, you don't look too smart right now," Peabo said.

Jack struggled with the ties binding his hands and feet, to no avail. "I was smart enough to let someone know I was going with you."

Peabo shook his head. "Nice try, but didn't nobody follow us. We was watching."

Jack wanted to keep him talking, to stall for time and give Tina a chance to find them.

"And, I figured out your pill game. I know all about you, Kirby, and Andrews."

Peabo shook his head and looked at Jack with something that resembled pity. "You're dumber than I thought, Davis. You don't have a clue, do you?"

"What are you talking about?"

"You think all that money was mine? I wish it was. This is way bigger than me and you."

Jack spat. "I know that. Andrews was the brains."

Peabo laughed and shook his head. "You really think Andrews was the big cheese, don't you?" He studied Jack as if deciding how much to tell him. "Andrews was just taking orders, like me. Think about it. Maybe you'll figure it out before the kitty over there has his dinner."

"You killed Andrews because he could identify you."

Peabo broke out laughing. "I just did what I was told to do. And, no, he didn't accidently fall into the pool, though he did have a weakness for the white powder."

Now Jack was confused. If Peabo didn't kill Andrews, then who was responsible? His head was spinning. Maybe he wasn't as smart as he thought, just like Peabo said.

Peabo's phone buzzed and he answered it, "Yeah?"

He listened a minute, then broke out with a big, toothy, tilted grin on his face. "Bring her back here to the lake," he said, and put the phone in his pocket.

"Well, well, Davis. Seems like Shorty has your little girlfriend."

The knot in Jack's stomach was back, bigger than before.

Chapter 32

"You really are a dumbass, bringing a girl along to do a man's job. Guess the kitty here's going to have a big dinner tonight," Peabo said.

In a few minutes, Shorty came into view, pushing Tina along by poking a gun into her back. She didn't have the other bag, and neither did Shorty.

"About damn time, Shorty. We're running behind," Peabo said.

Running behind for what? Jack thought.

Shorty made Tina crawl through the opening in the fence, and Peabo held his gun on Tina while Shorty tied her hands behind her back and bound her feet. When he was done, he pushed her down in the dirt next to Jack.

"You okay?" Jack asked her in a quiet voice.

She nodded.

"Who have we here?" Peabo asked. Tina stared at him and didn't respond.

"What did I tell you, Davis?" Peabo asked.

"It didn't make any difference, did it?" Jack said. "You were going to kill me anyway."

Peabo laughed. "Got a point. What's your name, sweetheart?"

She didn't answer again, and Peabo backhanded her, knocking her face down into the dirt.

"It's Tina," Jack said. "Dr. Tina Marshall—she works for Drager." Tina managed to pull herself back up next to Jack. Blood trickled out of her nose.

Peabo raised his eyebrows. "That so?" He undressed her with his eyes, and licked his lips. "A looker. Too bad we didn't get a chance to get you hooked up with the business. You could examine me anytime."

"Where's Molly?" Jack asked, trying to change the subject.

Peabo laughed. "Oh, she's safe, back in my room with that big-mouth bitch of mine." He turned to Shorty. "Let's get dinner going. We gotta get back before the others get there."

"Others? Who are you talking about?" Jack asked.

"They're coming to get them, take them away somewhere. Don't know, don't care—none of my business." He looked down at Jack and licked his lips. "That's why we need to get back—I wanna sample that some more. She's pretty tight. Got a nice body, too. I think she was beginning to like it the second time."

Jack lunged toward Peabo, but it was futile with his hands and feet bound. Peabo sidestepped him and he landed faced down in the dirt. Peabo kicked him in the ribs, and he saw stars.

Peabo pushed him back down next to Tina. Jack raised his spinning head. His eyes watered from the pain in his ribcage. He wished with all his might that he could get loose and go after this animal in front of him. He spit, and it landed on Peabo's leg.

Peabo looked down at his leg, then back at Jack. "For that, I might even let Shorty have a turn with her. He's a big boy, you know what I mean. That'd be fun to watch."

Jack snorted. "Fuck you, Peabo. At least you don't have the money, dickhead. Now who's the dumbass?" he said, sneering at Peabo and saying it with as much disgust as he could muster under the circumstances.

Peabo's eyes narrowed, a look of confusion on his face. He took a step closer. "What're you talking about?"

Jack grinned. "Did you check the bag, Peabo?" He was stalling for time, his only ally at this juncture.

Peabo stepped closer and grabbed the front of Jack's shirt. "What the fuck you saying?"

Jack kept smiling, but didn't answer, and Peabo punched him in the face, hard. He rolled his tongue around in his mouth, and felt a gap where a tooth once was, then felt the loose tooth. His jaw throbbed. Something wet trickled down over his lower lip and he tasted his own blood. He spit the blood and tooth out and said, "You don't have all the money, that's what I'm saying."

Peabo pushed him back down and stood up, taking a few steps back. The smile returned, but not as confident as before. "You're lying, just trying to get to me."

"I checked the bag, Boss. It was all there," Shorty said.

"Go get the bag and check it good. You'll see," Jack said.

"Shut up," Peabo said. He looked over at Shorty.

"I'm telling you, it was all there. You saw me check it in the car," Shorty said, more defensive now.

"Maybe Shorty made a deal here with Dr. Marshall. She had the other bag, the one with the real money," Jack said.

"He's lying, Boss. She didn't have no other bag. I caught her walking down the path back this way, but she didn't have no bag." Shorty sounded desperate.

Tina was smiling, but still silent, and Peabo noticed. Jack hoped she'd picked up on his plan adjustment.

Peabo stared at her, his black eyes burning. "You have another bag?"

"I did," she said.

"Boss, she's lying!" Shorty was getting flustered. "I swear to you, she didn't have no other bag when I caught her."

Peabo looked at Shorty and looked down at the gun the big man was holding. "Hand me your gun, Shorty," he said, holding his hand out.

"Boss—" he shook his head.

"Hand me the gun," Peabo said, this time a little louder.

Shorty gave Jack a look that could kill and handed the gun to Peabo, who put it inside his waistband.

Jack shook his head, and as he was about to speak, he saw movement behind Peabo and Shorty. He strained to see, then realized it was a tiger, in a crouch, stalking his prey and not making a sound. Peabo and Shorty had not heard a thing.

Jack tried to maintain his composure and hoped Tina had seen what he did. "He checked *your* bag, Peabo. We put the drugs and a few bundles of cash in it so that's what he'd see. In the bottom was nothing but newspaper. Tina had another bag with the real money in it."

He kept talking, not wanting Peabo to hear anything but his voice. *Come on, boy.* The tiger had slowed, each step measured and deathly silent as he closed the gap between him and the human closest to him, which was Peabo. Jack was rambling now, anything to keep talking and give the tiger a chance. He was afraid to look over at Tina, afraid he might telegraph what was happening.

"The bag's right outside the fence, Peabo, right where Shorty and I put it," Tina said. "I told him we'd split it with him."

The massive cat lowered his body, and Jack could see his muscles tense as he prepared to attack. He wanted to glance to his right and see how far it was to the opening in the fence, but he was afraid of signaling to Peabo something was amiss.

Peabo's eyes were now starting to smolder with the same intensity that Jack's had earlier. His fists were clenching and unclenching.

Jack laughed. "Your buddy fucked you, Peabo. When he caught her, she cut a deal—" the tiger made his move, and before Jack could finish his sentence, he was on top of Peabo, his jaws around his neck. Peabo tried to scream, his mouth open and eyes bulging, but all that emerged was a whimper.

Shorty staggered back against the fence, his mouth open with no sound coming out. He fell against the fence and clutched his chest, sweating profusely.

The powerful cat snapped Peabo's neck, jerking it to one side. Satisfied that the struggle was over, he started dragging the limp body of the man between his front legs like a doll as he walked back toward the water.

"Untie us, Shorty," Tina screamed. But the big man said nothing, his eyes glazed and breathing irregular.

"Come on, Tina, we've got to get outta here. Now!" Jack said.

Fueled by adrenalin, Jack rolled over and managed to get to his feet and hopped toward the opening, his feet still tied together, exhorting Tina to do the same. He kept his eye on the tiger, which was still going the opposite direction, his hunt successful. He watched as the big cat disappeared into the darkness, silhouetted by the moonlight.

They hopped to the opening and outside the fence, Jack tripped over the bolt cutters and went sprawling. *Bolt cutters.* He maneuvered his hands around the tool, and told Tina to turn around with her back to him. He positioned them so he could get the plastic ties binding her wrists between the jaws of the powerful device. He didn't know how much time he had left, but he knew it was limited, and he wanted to get the hell out of there before the tiger came looking for him.

His wrists slipped the first time he tried it, the blades of the tool digging into his arms as he fell backwards. He looked over at the cage. No sign of the tiger, but he remembered how quiet it had been when sneaking up on Peabo—and how fast. Time was running out.

He propped the bolt cutters up again, once more putting the plastic ties between their jaws. He leaned back with his elbows and felt the ties give way as the cutters did their magic. Tina shook her hands, grabbed the tool and cut the ties binding her feet. Then, she severed the ties binding Jack's hands and feet.

He shook his hands, and clenched his fists in succession, trying to restore the circulation. He found a pair of pliers and roll of cable that Peabo was going to use to repair the cut in the fence.

"We've got to get him out of there," Tina said, pointing to Shorty. "He's the only one that can tell us where Molly is."

He looked in the cage. Still no sign of the tiger. Or Peabo.

"Let me check him," she said.

He couldn't believe Tina was willing to go back in the cage, after what they'd just seen. But, Shorty was the only one that knew where the girls were.

"Hurry," he said. "I'll keep an eye out, but make it fast."

Tina crawled through the opening and checked on Shorty. He was unresponsive. She felt his neck and talked to him, asking where the girls were, but Shorty didn't say anything, but "To. Motel. To. Motel," over and over again.

"I don't think he's had a heart attack, but he's catatonic. His eyes are glassed over and he doesn't respond. He just keeps saying 'to motel' over and over."

They both jumped when they heard another roar from the back of the cage, but Shorty didn't flinch.

"Get outta there—now!" Jack said.

"We can't leave him in here! He's had some sort of psychotic episode, I guess from seeing the tiger get Peabo. He's totally zoned out."

He shook his head. He wanted to leave Shorty in the cage with the cats, hoping they would do to him what the tiger did to Peabo. But he couldn't do it. He crawled through the hole and grabbed Shorty's arms. "Get out, Tina. Get out, now."

She didn't argue with him and crawled back out through the hole in the fence.

Jack drug the big man through the hole in the fence and laid him down a safe distance away. Tina went over to check him, removing Jack's gun from the waist of Shorty's pants. She handed it to Jack, and knelt down to check the big guy.

Jack got down in Shorty's face. "What motel, Shorty?"

Shorty didn't answer.

Tina shook her head. "He's still unresponsive. We've got to get him out of here."

He pulled his phone out, but it was busted. "You have yours?"

She pulled hers out, held it up, and shook her head. Water dripped out of the case.

"Where's your car?"

"I left it at the McDonald's," she said.

"Let's finish repairing this, and we'll call an ambulance when we get back to the car." He finished securing the fence and shined the light to check his work. That was when he saw the other sign.

Nikita, Siberian tiger

Jack remembered the story about the reclusive tiger that shared an enclosure with a lion. *Thank you, Nikita. You saved our lives.*

"Let's go," he said. They turned to walk away when the deep roar of the lion startled him and he stopped. Tina looked at him as he peered through the fence. She didn't say a word and didn't try to interfere. He made his way over to the lockout and raised the gate, allowing the lion access to the full enclosure.

Joseph the lion quickly padded out toward the fence and looked at Shorty, lying motionless on his back on the other side. The lion stopped, his eyes unflinching, only a few feet away from Shorty's face. Only a few feet and a fence separated them, but Shorty didn't move and didn't say anything. Joseph opened his mouth and roared.

Chapter 33

Jack and Tina made their way back to the front gate of Big Cat Rescue as fast as possible.

"We've got to find Wren and Molly before the others get there," he said.

"But Jack, we don't know where they are. We've got to call the police."

Jack held his hands up. "What good would that do? We know it's a motel on the beach. Let's look in their car—maybe there's something there that will help." He was desperate.

"What happened to your bag—the one with the money?" he asked as they ran up to the Escalade.

"I left it at McDonald's."

"You did what?"

"I left it with the manager at McDonald's."

Jack shook his head. "You left a million dollars with a pimple-faced kid at a fast food restaurant! You've got to be kidding me."

Tina shrugged. "I figured it'd be safer than locked in my car sitting in the parking lot. Plus, I didn't want to carry it down the road when I didn't know where they were."

He opened the door on the driver's side. With no interior lights on he couldn't see a thing. He felt around where the ignition switch should be, and felt nothing but an empty opening where the key went. Leaning over the seat, he stuck his hand in the console, hoping for the keys to be there. Nothing.

"Do you have any clue where they might be?" he asked.

She shook her head.

He fiddled around until he was able to turn on the interior lights. He sat back in the seat, rubbing his wrists.

"Peabo said they were at the motel. What motel?" Jack wracked his brain trying to remember if he had heard the name of the place ever mentioned, but he hadn't. "There's got to be something in here with the name on it."

The inside looked as if someone had lived in it. There were all sorts of trash in the floor—empty beer cans, fast food bags, stale French fries—you name it. They searched through everything. Nothing, not even a scrap with a motel name on it.

Peabo's duffel bag was in the back seat. "You taking this?" she asked.

"Nope. Leave it for the cops, but take out the newspaper bundles." He looked across the small parking lot and saw the outline of a trash dumpster. "You can put them in there," he said, as he pointed to it.

She emptied the money bag while he finished searching the SUV. He found nothing.

"We've got to get to the beach," Jack said.

They ran back up the dirt road to the convenience store to get her car, splashing in puddles along the way.

Dripping wet, they went into the McDonald's and walked up to the counter.

Tina asked the young girl behind the counter for the manager. She went to the back and returned with a young man that Jack thought was maybe twenty-one, twenty-two, tops. The young man recognized Tina, nodded, and disappeared in the direction where he'd come from.

The manager returned with the duffel bag and lifted it over the counter to Tina.

"Thanks," she said, slinging the bag over her shoulder. "Will you call 911 and tell them there's been a break-in at Big Cat Rescue, and to send an ambulance?" She turned, and they walked out as quickly as they'd come in.

She threw the duffel bag in the back seat of her car, and they headed back toward Clearwater Beach. She drove as fast as she dared.

They got back to the marina parking lot and pulled in next to Jack's Mini.

"Now what?" she asked.

He grabbed the bag out of the back seat, put his gun in it and said, "Let's put this in a locker first, then figure out where to start."

As he closed the door, he saw a skinny, homeless man standing in the shadows between them and the marina. He looked around, and no one else was near. As the guy started toward them, Jack reached in the bag, trying to find the gun.

He found it and put his hand around the grip, his trigger finger alongside the chamber. Keeping his hand inside the bag, he pointed the gun in the direction of the man who was now only a few feet away.

The unkempt young man had a cigarette dangling from his mouth. He put his thumb and forefinger on it and took a deep drag. His hand was shaking.

"Ya'll from Kentucky?" he asked.

A smoker's cough rattled his lungs as he turned away from them, trying to catch his breath.

"What do you—" Jack said.

Tina put her hand on Jack's arm to say, *let me handle this*.

"No, we're from here. Are you from Kentucky?" Tina asked, her voice even, but gentle.

The man shook his head, coughing again. "No, ma'am."

Jack started to ask, "What the hell do you want," but felt Tina's fingers dig in.

"Where do you go to church?" the man asked.

Jack shook his head.

"I used to go to the Baptist church—when I was younger. Now, not much of anywhere. You?" Tina said.

"I was raised Baptist," he said, and seemed to be satisfied with her answer. "I just had to check. You're Wren's friend, aren't you?" he asked, looking at Jack.

Jack couldn't believe what the guy said. He kept his hand on the gun, but relaxed his grip. "Yes, I am. Me and my wife. Do you know where they are?"

The man nodded. "I can show you."

"You can?" Jack looked at Tina, then back to the man.

"We can pay you," Jack said, thinking the guy was trying to hit them up for money.

The man shook his head. "Don't want no money. Just want to help. Them boys from Kentucky is bad."

Jack took the bag and put it back in the locker where he'd stored it before, keeping the pistol with him. He got back and found out the man went by Bird. They got in Tina's car, Jack letting Bird sit in the front seat so he could tell Tina which way to go.

They got to the exit of the parking lot, and Tina asked Bird which way to go. When he didn't answer, she repeated the question, and he answered, "I'm not sure."

Jack put his head down and squeezed his face with his hands, frustrated. *I'm not sure?* This was not getting off to a good start.

"Do you know the name of the place, Bird?" Tina asked.

Thank God she had more patience than he did, Jack thought. He was encouraged when Bird nodded.

"Two something. I'll know it when I see it," he said. "They're in room 112. I do numbers good, but other stuff, I get confused sometimes."

Jack leaned forward, his head between Tina and Bird. "That's what Shorty was trying to tell us." The name of the place had "Two" in it, and Bird knew they were in room 112. They were closer. Now the problem was finding a motel with "Two" in the name. There must be a thousand motels on Clearwater Beach.

Out of habit, he pulled out his phone, only to remember that both of their phones were waterlogged and useless.

Clearwater Beach was really a series of long, skinny islands running north and south. *Where to start,* Jack thought. He told Tina to turn right and go north. At the first convenience store, he told her to pull in, where he went inside to ask for a phone book.

The clerk barely spoke English, and looked at Jack as though he'd asked for a spaceship. When he finally got the point across, all he got was a shrug and outturned hands, then a shake of the head.

Two stops later, Jack pulled up and saw an older, white-haired man behind the counter. *Maybe the third time was the charm*, he thought, as he walked up to the counter. He cut in front of a young guy with a twelve-pack of beer and said, "Excuse me, but—"

"Hey man, I was in line," the guy with the beer protested.

"I just need directions, it's important," Jack said, then asked the clerk, "Do you have a phone book?"

The clerk nodded, reached under the counter and handed Jack a dog-eared phone book that looked to be several years old.

"Thank you," he said to the clerk and to the customer. He stepped to the side, flipped to the Yellow Pages, and found motels. Running his finger down the pages, he scanned the listings for any that had *two* in the name. Thank God the keyword wasn't Palms or Ocean, he thought. There—Two Beaches Inn. He ripped the page out.

"Hey," the clerk said. "Don't be ripping pages out."

Jack ignored him and flipped the page, continuing to scan the listings. Two Harbors Motel. He ripped the page out.

"I'm going to call the cops."

Still looking at the listings, Jack pulled a twenty out of his wallet and handed it to the clerk. He scanned the remainder, and found one more—Two Palms Motel. He ripped the third page out, and handed the directory back to the clerk.

"Where are these places?" Jack said, pointing to the pages he'd torn out, repeating the names of the three motels. "Please," he added.

The clerk handed the young man with the beer his change, then took the three pages from Jack. He looked at the first page. "Two Beaches, ah, that's up on the north end of the beach, toward Caladesi. Pretty fancy for a motel. They call it Two Beaches because they have a beach on the Gulf and one on the Bay. It used to be—"

"Never mind," Jack said, snatching the page from the clerk. "What about the next one?" He couldn't picture Peabo and Shorty staying in a nice place, especially one on the far north end of the island. That would be too far from the clinic and pharmacy.

The twenty-something with the beer was looking over his shoulder.

The clerk shook his head. "Two Harbors is closed down. They've been closed for six months. It's up on—"

Jack snatched the second page from his hand. "What about this one? Two Palms?" He pointed to the third page.

The clerk shook his head, "No, not familiar—"

Beer guy was looking over at the page. "Hey, I know where that is."

"Where is it?" Jack asked.

"It's about two miles south of here, on the other side of the causeway. Kind of a dump. Lots of college kids stay there. Can't remember the name of the street, but it runs parallel to the main drag here. Two blocks east. Once you get past the causeway, cut over two blocks and head south. You can't miss it."

"Thank you," Jack said, already walking out the door.

Chapter 34

It took them another twenty minutes to find the place, but it was in the general vicinity of where the beer guy had said. Jack hoped he'd picked the right place.

The Two Palms Motel was a small, two-story structure that looked like it had seen better days. Only a few cars were parked in front of the building, and in typical motel-style, all of the doors opened to the parking lot.

"This is it," Bird said, his head bobbing. "Room one-one-two, room one-one-two." Tina turned in and drove past the building, looking for a door marked 112.

"There—there it is," Jack said, as they rolled past. No cars were parked in front of the room. He prayed they'd made it before the others.

She pulled into a parking place and switched the car off. It looked like the kind of place Peabo would pick. "We need to call the cops, Jack," Tina said.

Bird seemed to come out of his trance. "No, no. Don't do no cops," he said. "Gotta go, gotta go." He opened the car door.

"Hold on a sec," Jack said, reaching into his pocket. He pulled out a twenty and a ten. Disappointed that was all he had with him, he handed it to Bird. "Thanks for your help, man. Be careful out there."

Bird just nodded, got out and started shuffling back down the street the direction they'd come from. Jack got out, looked around, and got in the front seat. He didn't see any activity. Fortunately, the office was over to the right and didn't have a good view of where they were parked.

"Stay in the car. I'm going to the office to get the manager to open the door," he told Tina.

He ran over to the office, grabbed the office door handle and pulled. It was locked. He put his hand over his eyes and up against the glass. There was no one behind the desk in the dimly lit room. With his bare fist, he banged on the glass door. In a minute, an older man came shuffling through a door from the back.

"Open the door. I need you to call the cops. My wife's been kidnapped, and she's in room 112," Jack yelled through the door.

The old man shook his head.

"Call the cops—room 112."

The man looked scared and shook his head. He turned and went back through the door behind the desk.

Jack ran back to the car. "Go to the office and see if you can get the manager to call the cops. I'm going inside," he said to Tina. She started running toward the office.

He took one last look around, and saw no one. There were no lights on in the room. In front of the door marked 112, he paused and took a deep breath. Marshalling all the energy and hatred he could muster, he kicked the door as hard as he could. The first kick splintered the door jamb, and the second kick finished the job.

The door bounced back toward him as he pushed it aside. The room was dark, and it was hard to see.

"Molly?" he whispered. Nothing. "Molly, you there?" he said again, this time a little louder. Again, nothing. His heart started sinking as his eyes adjusted to the darkness in the room. *Maybe the others had already been here and left.* He could make out two beds in the room with lumps on each, but neither was moving. It could've been just the covers.

His hand shook as he reached for the light switch next to the door. Part of him didn't want to turn on the lights, but he had to know.

The overhead light came on and Jack blinked. On one bed, Molly was lying on her back, her wrists tied to the bed. Her eyes were closed, even with the light on, and she wasn't moving. Jack's voice caught, and the lump in his throat started to choke him.

On the bed next to Molly was Wren. She was also on her back, and like Molly, tied to the bed and motionless.

He ran back to the door and yelled for Tina, who was almost to the office.

She turned and ran to the room, following Jack inside. As soon as she saw them, she went to the bedside to evaluate them.

"Call 911," she said, with an authoritative voice.

He grabbed the phone and lifted the receiver, waiting to hear a dial tone. Nothing. He picked the phone up and the cord came with it. It had been pulled out of the wall.

"Shit. I'm going to the office to call." Not waiting for an answer, he left the room, running for the office. He'd hoped the manager had called the police, but he heard no sirens and saw no police cars.

When he got to the glass door, he started banging on it again, harder than the first time. The door behind the desk opened, and the little old man shuffled through the door and stopped, wide-eyed at the sight of Jack.

"We need an ambulance. Please call. Room 112," Jack yelled through the door.

The man looked frightened and confused, shaking his head. Jack was beginning to wonder if he understood English. "Ambulance, hospital, police," Jack shouted.

The old man flicked his hand, motioning for Jack to leave. Jack remembered the gun inside the waist of his shorts. He pulled it out and pointed it toward the man. "Call a fucking ambulance—now," he yelled.

That got the man's attention, and he picked up the phone behind the desk and called someone. Jack figured it was the police, but hoped they'd bring an ambulance, too.

He ran back to the room, where he saw Tina still trying to wake Molly and Wren.

"You call?" she asked.

"The clerk called somebody, probably the police. He wouldn't let me in."

A few minutes later, while he was sitting on the edge of the bed holding Molly's hand and talking to her, he heard the sirens. They were distant at first, then louder, until he heard them right outside the door. He jumped up to run out and meet them and almost ran head-on into a police officer pointing his gun at him.

"Hands up, where I can see them! Now!" the officer shouted.

Jack stopped in his tracks, put his hands up, and retreated a few steps back into the room. "We need an ambulance, call an—"

The officer's partner came around, his gun out as well, and looked into the room. "Hands up! Now!" he shouted at Tina.

She raised her hands. Jack heard other sirens outside in the parking lot, but couldn't see out the door from where he was standing.

"Where's the gun?" the first officer asked.

Jack said, "Over on the table next to the bed." Thank God he laid it there when he came back in the room.

"Move away from the bed—now!" the second officer said to Tina.

She did as instructed. "I'm a doctor. We need an ambulance, please call an ambulance."

Jack was amazed at how calm her voice was. The officer inside the room went over and picked up the gun with his free hand, keeping his weapon pointed at Tina and watching her.

As soon as he picked it up, the first officer shoved Jack down, and quickly frisked him before cuffing his hands behind his back. He then checked Tina for weapons. Finding none, he asked her for identification. She showed him her hospital ID. Satisfied, he didn't cuff her and told her to move over to the corner of the room.

"Okay, you're clear," the second officer said into his microphone clipped to his shoulder.

The paramedics rushed in, and took over, going first to Molly, then Wren. Tina stood there, telling the EMTs what she'd found. They quickly cut the ropes and put Molly on a stretcher. As they were taking her out to the ambulance, another crew came in, cut Wren's bindings, and placed her on stretcher. Minutes later, they took her out to the second ambulance and left.

Jack watched, and tears came to his eyes. For the first time in many years, he prayed.

Chapter 35

After the ambulances left, Jack tried to explain to the officers at the motel what happened. They apparently didn't buy his story, so now he was sitting in an interview room at Clearwater Police Headquarters. They placed Tina in a separate car, and he assumed she was also here in another room.

Once again, he recounted the evening's events for the detective seated in front of him. The detective was a large black man with a shaved head that seemed to rest directly on his broad shoulders. Under different circumstances, Jack would've asked him if he'd played football. The detective leaned back in his chair and locked his hands together behind his short, thick neck.

"So, let me get this straight," he said, looking at the notepad in front of him on the table between them. "You stole a bag containing cash and pills from this guy. Then, intending to swap his stash for your wife, you went with Watson and his sidekick Shorty to Big Cat Rescue in Tampa. Dr. Marshall followed you out there, where Watson double-crossed you and intended to feed you both to the cats?"

Jack nodded, tired of repeating the same questions and answers.

"Instead, a tiger killed him, and Shorty flipped out. You dragged him out of the cage, then went to a fast food restaurant and asked them to call 911. You and Dr. Marshall drove over to Clearwater Beach, where a homeless man named Bird told you where to find your wife and friend. You went to Two Palms Motel, where you kicked in the door on Room 112 and found your wife and her friend unconscious. Then you went to the motel office and threatened the night clerk with your pistol."

"Look, detective—whatever your name is—I'm tired, I'm exhausted, and I want to see my wife. Yes, yes, yes, I've told you this story and I've told the same story to the officers on the scene.

"And I only pointed my gun at the night clerk so he'd call someone, since the phone wasn't working in the room and he wouldn't open the office door."

The detective nodded, and leaned forward. "The manager at the McDonald's said Dr. Marshall left a duffel bag with him. He said the two of you came in, retrieved the bag, told him to call the cops and an ambulance, then left."

Jack didn't say a word. He figured they were asking Tina the same questions somewhere else.

"Where's the bag, and what was in it?"

"I've already told you, the bag contained cash and drugs. It was the same bag I stole from Peabo. We took it back to the Escalade at Big Cat and left it in the vehicle for the cops to find."

The detective nodded. "Why didn't you wait for the cops to get there?"

Jack shook his head. "Peabo said that some people were coming to get Molly and Wren and take them away. We had to get there before they showed up, and we didn't want to be driving around with cash and drugs in the car."

The detective stared at him. It was the same story Jack had told him twice before. He hoped Tina was giving them the same answer.

Jack told him that Shorty freaked out when he saw the tiger kill Peabo. They couldn't get him to respond, so they left him there.

"That's the part that puzzles me," the detective said. "Wouldn't it have made more sense to involve the cops? At that point, you didn't know where they were, right?"

Jack took a deep breath. "We knew they were in a motel on Clearwater Beach that had "two" in the name. Shorty told us that much. We didn't have time to wait on the cops and then explain what was going on."

The detective folded his thick arms across his chest and stared at him.

"I'll be back in a few minutes." The detective got up and left the room, closing the door behind him.

Jack was worried about Molly, and wanted to go to the hospital to see her. The detective had told him that she was in critical condition, but nothing more.

The detective who had questioned Jack walked back into the interview room with another man, a short, heavyset guy with thinning hair.

"We're releasing you," he said.

Jack went straight to the hospital. When he got to the floor, he told the nurse sitting at the desk that he wanted to see Molly Byrne. She repeated the name, and told him to wait a minute. She walked back into the office, and came out with a male nurse in scrubs that she introduced as the charge nurse.

"Are you her husband?" the charge nurse asked. Jack saw the badge clipped to his pocket. Mark Franklin.

"Yes," he said. He wanted to see Molly, even though he knew visiting hours were officially over.

"Can you step back here for a minute?" Mark asked. He led Jack to a door marked INTERVIEW, which had a window with a closed blind. He opened the door, and ushered Jack into a small room furnished with a sofa, several chairs, and a table with a lamp.

"Mr. Davis, if you'll wait here, I'll go get the doctor. Could I get you a soda or some coffee?"

"No, thanks."

Mark walked out and shut the door behind him. Jack surveyed the room. It was dim, with the only light coming from the table lamp. The walls were a muted green color and the carpet was thick and a similar shade. Jack noticed how quiet the room was, with not a sound leaking in from the hustle and bustle of the nursing station on the other side of the door.

A few minutes later, a young, short man wearing a white coat and glasses walked in alone and closed the door. "I'm Dr. Wilson," he said, extending his hand. "Boyd Wilson."

Jack stood and shook his hand "Jack Davis."

Dr. Wilson cleared his throat, and said, "Mr. Davis, your wife sustained serious injuries."

Jack's heart skipped a beat. *No*, he thought, *no*, please God . . . Dr. Wilson was having a hard time looking him in the eyes.

"We're doing everything we can, but her condition is critical. You need to understand that. She's unconscious, and the next twenty-four hours are critical."

"The other woman?" Jack asked.

Wilson looked relived to change the subject and held up his hand. "I'm really not supposed to discuss another patient's condition. However, I can tell you her condition is stable."

"What are . . ."

Wilson shrugged, anticipating the question. "I wish I could say, but in your wife's case, I don't know. The swelling is minimal and we've stopped the bleeding. Her MRI is clear, which is a good sign. Labs look good, and her vitals are stable."

Jack lowered his head and nodded. "Can . . . can I see my wife?"

The doctor shifted in his seat. "Let me check. Give me a few minutes."

Jack wasn't prepared for what he saw. Although they'd cleaned Molly up as well as could be expected, she looked horrible. Her face was black and blue and one eye was swollen almost shut. He could only imagine what she'd endured. It was a vision that would haunt him forever.

Chapter 36

He fell asleep in the chair next to her bed. When he awoke the next morning, a blanket covered him, and daylight was leaking through the blinds covering the window next to his chair. He looked over at Molly. Her chest slowly rose and fell, but her eyes were closed. The monitor beeped rhythmically. He reached over and put his hand over hers. It was cool to the touch. She didn't stir.

"Good morning." A nurse in scrubs walked into the room and went over to Molly's IV's and checked them.

"Morning," he mumbled. "Is she okay?"

The nurse nodded. "I think she's going to be fine. How are you?"

He stretched, getting the kinks out of his back. "Okay. A cup of coffee would be nice. Anywhere close by that I could get a cup?"

"Let me finish and I'll show you where the kitchen is. Coffee's not great, but it's hot and it's fresh."

She finished checking everything and entered her notes into the computer terminal next to the bed.

"I'm Janie," she said, as she motioned him to follow her out of the room.

"Jack Davis, but you probably already know that."

She took him down the hall and into the small kitchen behind the nurses' station. "Coffee, cups, and stuff for your coffee, if you need it. In the refrigerator, we usually keep water and juice. Anything you want, you can put it in there and leave it. Just be sure to label it, otherwise, everyone thinks it's fair game."

He laughed, for the first time in several days. "Thank you," he said, as he poured a cup of coffee. "Is she sleeping or unconscious?"

"No, she hasn't regained consciousness yet, but her body is healing, which is good."

A worried look crossed his face.

"Dr. Wilson will be making his rounds soon. He can give you an update, but I think the worst is over." She saw the doubt on his face. "I've been an ICU nurse for fifteen years. No one knows for sure, but everything looks good."

He asked her about Wren, and Janie told him that she was on the fourth floor, which was just a medical floor.

"If she's down there, she's doing well, but I don't know what the latest is," Janie said.

Jack took the coffee back to Molly's room and sat, holding her hand. He wanted to be there when she woke up.

Dr. Wilson stopped by and essentially said the same thing that Janie did. He also told him that the staff on this unit was the best he'd ever worked with, especially Janie Mason.

When Wilson left, Janie came back in with another person and told Jack to go downstairs to get some breakfast while they changed Molly's linens. When he hesitated, she told him that right now, the best thing he could do for Molly was to take care of himself.

He wasn't going to argue with Janie. He walked out, got on the elevator, and punched FOUR.

On the fourth floor, he walked over to the nurses' station and asked which room Wren Lawson was in. The unit clerk told him 4235 and pointed to his left.

The door was open, but he knocked, and smiled when he heard Wren's voice say, "Come in."

As soon as she saw him, tears started flowing down her cheeks. He walked over and hugged her, and Wren hugged him back fiercely, hanging on to his neck.

When they separated at last, he smiled. "You look good. How are you doing?" he asked.

She shrugged and said, "Okay. How's Molly?"

"Doing well. She's still unconscious, but her doctor came by a little while ago, and said the worst was over."

Wren put her hand over her mouth, and more tears appeared. "I'm so sorry."

He pulled her back to him, shaking his head. "Not your fault, Wren. She's going to be fine, don't you worry."

In the cafeteria, he went through the line, realizing how hungry he was. He couldn't remember the last time he'd eaten anything. When he got to the table with his food, he put the tray down, and was surprised to see Tina.

"Janie told me you'd be down here," she said, giving him a huge hug.

He held onto her for a long time, almost afraid to let go, and she just held him, making no effort to disengage. At last, he pulled back, his eyes moist.

"Thank you for coming," he said.

"Go ahead and eat. I'll get a cup of coffee, but I've already had breakfast."

He was famished, and he'd almost finished by the time she got back, holding two cups of coffee.

"I figured you could use a refill," she said, placing one cup next to his plate, and sitting opposite him.

"I ran into Dr. Wilson on the floor. He thought Molly was out of the woods."

Jack nodded. "I'll feel better when she regains consciousness."

"You doing okay?" She looked at him with the critical eye of both friend and physician.

"I think so. It's been a rough two days. And, thank you for everything."

"De nada," she said. "You two mean a lot to me. I just wish we'd gotten there sooner."

Tina told him what happened to Shorty. When the police got to Big Cat Rescue, they found Shorty still lying outside the cage, Joseph lying in front of him, only a few feet away, watching him curiously. The paramedics hauled Shorty out and took him to Tampa General for evaluation.

In the Emergency Department, an attendant with long brown hair and a full beard came to take him for an MRI. Unfortunately, the attendant must have reminded Shorty of Joseph. The big man went berserk, almost destroying the department. It took four aides and a physician armed with a powerful sedative to subdue him. Shorty was admitted to the psychiatric unit and still hadn't said anything.

He lowered his voice and leaned across the table. "The cops ask you about the bag?"

She nodded. "I told them it was the bag we left in Peabo's car."

"You and I are the only ones that know about the other bag. The question is, 'who does it belong to?' We thought Andrews was the head, but I'm not so sure."

"Does it matter?"

He considered her question, and for the first time since that night, he spoke the words that had rattled through his head. "Yes. Because that's the person who's responsible for what happened to Molly and Wren. I won't rest until I figure it out."

"Who do you think it is?"

"I keep coming back to one suspect, but I don't have anything concrete." He looked at Tina, wondering if he should tell her. "If someone else was heading the ring, it could've been only one person the way I see it. Devo Drager."

Chapter 37

At lunch, Jack went back down to the cafeteria to get some lunch. Molly was still unconscious. Dr. Wilson had said she could wake up at any time, or it could be days. There was no way to predict.

He'd turned on his phone, and the first message that popped up was a voice mail from Drager.

"Jack, it's Devo. Dr. Marshall told me that you're at the hospital, but please give me a call when you can. I don't want to bother you, but would love to come by when convenient. I've got a banquet tomorrow night, but other than that, I can be there most any time. If you need anything, please call."

He stared at the phone for ten or fifteen seconds, debating on whether to call Drager. He flipped through the rest of his messages, and decided they could all wait. He called Tony in Fort Myers and told him what'd happened. Tony insisted on driving up to see him, and Jack knew there was no stopping the stubborn police lieutenant.

He turned his phone off. Jack kept thinking he was missing something. Andrews and Peabo were dead, Shorty wasn't able to talk, and Patel had disappeared.

He was still haunted by Peabo's comments. Peabo was about to kill him at that point. Why would he say that Andrews wasn't the head? Peabo had nothing to gain by making that up. If Andrews wasn't the head of the operation, then who was? He was glad Tony was on his way.

"Something still nags me," Jack said. He and Tony were sitting at a small table outside the cafeteria at the hospital. The sun was out and it was a beautiful, sunny day in Florida. People were walking down the sidewalk on the other side of the hedge. *Business as usual*, Jack thought. Maybe for them, but not for me.

The retired Fort Myers police lieutenant looked at him, but didn't speak, waiting for Jack to continue.

"Peabo's last words were that 'it was bigger than us.' When I told him I knew Dr. Andrews was the head, he laughed. Before that, he kept telling me that I didn't have a clue. I thought it was a threat, but the more I think about it . . ."

"They found the money and drugs in the Escalade. I talked to the detective up here—he felt that it was consistent with the size of Peabo's business. They figured he was supplying Andrews with cocaine and killed him when word started to leak out. Looks nice and tidy. What about it bothers you?"

Jack looked at the detective. He'd not told him about the other money, not wanting to put him in a difficult position. He wondered if Budzinski's conclusion would be the same if he knew about it.

"Can I give you a hypothetical?" Jack asked.

Tony cocked his head and studied his friend. "Hypothetical, huh? You sure about that?"

Jack looked across the street and thought. He knew he was treading on dangerous ground here, but he desperately wanted Tony's opinion based on all the facts.

"I'm sure. Let's say, for sake of argument, there was more money involved."

"More money? What do you mean? How much more?" The detective was on full alert now.

"How much money did they find in Peabo's vehicle? A hundred thousand, something like that?" Jack asked.

The detective nodded. "How'd you know the amount?"

Jack shrugged. "I think I saw it in the news or something. What if it was, say, ten times more? Would that change your conclusion?"

"What are you saying, Jack?" Budzinski's tone was serious, and almost threatening.

Jack held up his hands. "Just speculating, Tony, nothing more. What if the amount of money involved was ten times what was found?"

Tony shifted in his seat. "You're talking about a million dollars. If that was the case, hypothetically speaking," he said, watching Jack for a reaction. "Two thoughts come to mind. First, this operation was a lot bigger than what Peabo was running, based on what I know about their operation."

"You said, 'two things?'"

Budzinski nodded. "Second, whoever's running it isn't going to forget about that much money. A hundred thousand dollars, he may write off as a cost of doing business. A million dollars—no chance. The person who has it or who knows what happened to it is in serious danger."

That was what Jack was afraid of. Only Jack and Tina knew about the other bag and how much money was in it.

The total cash in the second bag had come to just a little over eight-hundred thousand dollars. He'd decided that half would go to Wren, enough to give the young girl quite a comfortable cushion.

Tony looked at him carefully. "You hear what I said, Jack?"

Jack nodded. "Just thinking. What kind of danger?"

"Somebody like that won't rest until they get the money back. And they'll be willing to do whatever it takes. You have a lot of questions for a hypothetical situation. Are you trying to tell me something?"

Jack shook his head. "No, just speculation. Too much time to think."

Tony looked at him for an uncomfortable length of time.

"I've been a cop for a long time, Jack. You're not very good at concealing things." He paused to let that sink in. "I can't help you if you don't tell me what's going on."

He shifted in his seat, then shook his head. "Nothing to tell, Tony."

They sat there, in silence, for a few more minutes.

"You know where to find me," Tony said, standing. "I've got to run. You going to be okay?"

"I'm doing alright, good days and bad. Molly's doing well, and right now, that's all that matters. It gives me something positive to focus on."

When Jack went to shake his hand, the stocky lieutenant surprised him with a hug. "Be careful, Jack," he said. He pushed Jack away, and stepped onto the dock. "Call me sometime. Come down to Fort Myers. The wife would be glad to see you."

"I will, Tony. Give her a hug for me. And, thanks for coming."

Molly regained consciousness that evening, and the first thing she saw as her eyes fluttered was Jack. She squeezed his hand, and he cried like he'd never cried before.

"How long have I been here?" she asked.

He wiped his eyes and said, "A couple of days." He couldn't quit smiling. He was so glad to see her.

She had a confused look on her face. "I remember Peabo showing me a picture of Wren . . . is she—"

"She's fine. She's down on the fourth floor, but she's going to be okay."

She squeezed his hand again. "Thank God. I remember getting in the car with Peabo . . ."

Jack held his breath. He wondered how much she remembered.

"They gave me a shot. I felt the prick of the needle." She closed her eyes for a few moments, then opened them. "I don't remember anything else."

Her nurse called Dr. Wilson, who came by to examine Molly. He was pleased with what he found, and said she was going to be fine.

Outside the room, he told Jack that she would fully recover from the physical scars. The emotional scars were going to take much longer.

"She doesn't remember anything," Jack said.

"Not unusual. Maybe that's a good thing. Sometimes things come back—in bits and pieces, over time. I wouldn't worry."

Jack went back in to see her, not wanting her to be out of his sight. She smiled when he walked over and kissed her head.

When Molly had gone to sleep, Jack walked over to the atrium to call Tina and tell her the good news.

"That is wonderful, Jack. I'd like to stop by and see her in the morning, if that's alright."

"Please do. I know she'd love to see you."

After he hung up with Tina, he stopped by Wren's room on the way back upstairs.

"Molly woke up this afternoon. She's going to be alright," he said when he walked into her room.

A big grin spread across her face. "Oh, Jack, that's awesome. Can I see her?"

He smiled. "Of course, you can. She asked about you. She's asleep—she was tired, but maybe in the morning."

They chatted for a few minutes, then Jack said, "I need you to help me with something, Wren, but only if you feel comfortable."

"You know I'd do anything for you and Molly."

He sat on her bed and explained what he wanted.

Chapter 38

Jack was headed over to Big Cat Rescue. There was a benefit dinner there, awarding the Top Cat Award to the person in the community that had done the most to help the refuge the past year.

He wasn't invited to the exclusive gathering. When he got to the gate, the guard asked for his name and an invitation.

"I don't have an invitation, and I'm sure I'm not on the guest list. I work for Dr. Devo Drager." Jack held up a computer and his Drager clinic badge. "This is Dr. Drager's presentation. He forgot it, and called me in a panic to bring it to him."

The security guard, a young guy, looked around and scratched his head. He held his hand out. "Just give it to me and I'll take it to him."

Jack shook his head. "No can do. It's on his computer. I have to hook it up and make sure everything's working properly."

The guard hitched up his pants. "We've got somebody in there that can do that. I'll take it." Again, he held his hand out.

"Look, officer," Jack said, pumping up the guy's ego. "I understand you're just doing your job. But I'm doing mine, and if my boss in there doesn't get this," he tapped the side of the laptop, "I'm going to get fired and so are you. You want to take that chance?"

The guard thought about it, and reached for his radio, hooked to his belt. "I need to call my boss first."

"Time's a wasting," Jack said, in a loud voice. He pulled out his cell phone. "Forget it, I'm texting Dr. Drager and telling him you won't let—"

"Just pull over there and go to the building down on the right," the exasperated guard said, shaking his head.

Jack pulled over to the area where the guard pointed and got out. He ran down the walkway before the guard could change his mind.

Once out of sight of the guard, he slowed to a walk. He went up the steps to the house and through the door.

The room was dimly lit, and filled with people sitting at round tables. The men wore tuxes, and the ladies were dressed in evening attire. Up on the dais, he saw Dr. Drager sitting at a table with the other guests of honor. A bald man in a tux stood at the microphone addressing the crowd.

A young lady in a sequined evening gown walked up to Jack, looking him over. His jeans and tropical shirt were not the correct attire and she appeared concerned at the intrusion.

"Can I help you?" she asked, looking around as if expecting security to show up any minute.

Jack showed her his Drager Clinic badge. "I'm Jack Davis. I work for Dr. Drager. He hasn't started his speech yet, has he?"

"No, why?"

"Thank goodness." Jack held up the laptop. "He mistakenly took the wrong presentation. I've got the right one here. Can you take me to your audio-visual person?"

Obviously relieved by his explanation, she nodded. "This way," she said, ushering him through an interior door that led to a hall and out of the main dining room.

She came to a door marked *Projection*, tapped on it, and took him inside. A thin boy with a goatee was sitting in front of a console and three monitors, tapping away on a computer keyboard. He didn't even look up to see who'd entered the room. Jack noticed that one of the monitors had the same image he'd seen on the huge screen behind the podium.

"Freddie?" she said. "This is Jack . . ."

Freddie turned around, irritated by the interruption.

"Davis. Jack Davis." Jack held out his hand. Freddie gave him a slight nod, not offering his hand.

"He works for Dr. Drager, and brought his presentation," she said, backing out of the room.

"Thanks," Jack said as she closed the door. He turned his attention to Freddie. "Dr. Drager picked up the wrong presentation. The right one is on this computer. Can you get it loaded?"

Freddie looked at Jack as if he'd questioned his ability to breathe and nodded. "If anybody can do it, I can." Freddie held out his hand.

When Freddie finished downloading the file, Jack walked back down the hall to the main ballroom, his laptop under his arm. He cracked the door, and stepped in next to the hostess.

"Thank you so much. You think I could stand here in the back? I'd like to see Dr. Drager's presentation. I promise not to get in the way," he whispered.

She smiled and nodded. He backed up against the wall, close to the hall door leading to Freddie's room.

The next speaker took the podium to introduce Dr. Devo Drager. His introduction went on for several minutes as he talked of the doctor's accomplishments. At last, he introduced the man himself, to thunderous applause.

Jack smiled as Drager stood and bowed slightly, accepting the accolades. He looked good on stage, Jack thought. The man was charismatic, no doubt.

As the applause died, the speaker said, "Before I present Dr. Drager with the award, I'd like to show you this short video summarizing his accomplishments relating to Big Cat Rescue." His voice reverberated throughout the room. He picked up the remote control device, pointed it at the screen, and clicked it on.

The ballroom was quiet as the screen went dark. Then, Wren's bruised face appeared on the screen. She was sitting up in a hospital bed. The camera work was amateurish, but clear.

Wren's voice was strong and steady. She stated that over the last two years, she and others repeatedly obtained fraudulent prescriptions for OxyContin. These prescriptions were written by Dr. Winston Andrews at Bayview Clinic, and knowingly filled by the pharmacist at Bayview Pharmacy. Her boyfriend took the pills back to Kentucky to sell on the street.

The speaker frantically pointed the remote at the screen, punching the buttons, trying to stop the video.

Drager had turned to watch, and as soon as he heard Wren's comments, he rushed the microphone, asking that the video be stopped.

There was a murmur in the room as the guests tried to figure out what was going on. While what was disclosed was somewhat known to everyone, Wren wasn't done.

"I was present at a meeting between my boyfriend, Peabo Watson, and Dr. Andrews, where Dr. Andrews said that Dr. Devo Drager was the head of the entire operation."

"That's a lie," Drager shouted into the microphone. The room erupted in chaos, as the lights in the room were brought up to full intensity. The video continued.

Jack moved closer to the hallway door, noticing that several security guards appeared, blocking the main exit. Drager saw him at the back of the room. He jumped down from the stage and ran to where Jack was standing, pushing people aside to get to Jack.

He was out of breath when he got to Jack, but surprised Jack by shoving him to the side and entering the hallway. He was headed toward Freddie. Jack jumped up and followed him through the door, running.

He managed to get between Drager and Freddie's door just in time.

Drager's face was red with anger as he moved closer. In a low voice, he said, "She's lying. Anyone that knows anything is dead."

Jack stared at him with contempt. "Maybe, but I have the money." He moved closer, his face within inches of Drager's. "And you'll spend the next five years answering questions from every federal agency on the planet. Your pill peddling days are done."

Drager straightened his collar, and looked around. No one had come through the door, yet, but it was a matter of minutes.

"We could make things easier for each other, Jack. I'll split the money with you—consider it a tax-free bonus. You get to keep your job, life is good. You won't have to look over your shoulder. Help me deny all of this and repair the damage. She has no proof."

"Fuck you, Drager."

Chapter 39

Jack sat at the helm of the sailboat, with one hand casually draped over the large stainless wheel. The boat sliced through the calm waves of the Gulf of Mexico, the music of water rushing past the hull the only sound.

He felt the breeze in his face, and inhaled the salt air. Out of habit, he checked the compass heading and the trim of the sails. They were making good time. In another five hours, they'd be in Key West. There was nothing but water around them; not another boat in sight.

Molly was sitting on the leeward side of the boat, her head back and eyes closed, enjoying the breeze and sunshine on her face. She had a slight smile on her face, and she looked at peace.

Clearwater was behind them, permanently, Jack hoped. He wasn't sure what they'd do in Key West, but he wasn't worried. With the money from the sale of their cars and the "bonus" from Drager, they had enough to live comfortably for a while.

Taking their time, they'd worked their way down the west coast of Florida. When they got to Sanibel two days ago, they decided to spend the night at a marina on Fort Myers Beach. Their slip at the city marina was occupied, and they didn't want to go all the way up the Caloosahatchee River for one night. Tony and his wife met them out at the beach for dinner.

The conversation had been easy, with no mention of what had happened in Clearwater. They talked of earlier, more pleasant times in Fort Myers. After an early evening, the Budzinskis bid them safe travels, with a promise to visit once Jack and Molly had settled in.

Yesterday, after breakfast, they set sail for Key West. As they passed around the tip of Estero Island and turned south, Jack thought back to another sailing trip off of Fort Myers Beach.

It was the first time Jack had sailed the boat without Peter Stein, its owner. Peter was there—in spirit, at least—since his ashes were onboard. The occasion had been celebratory, in accordance with Peter's wishes. They listened to Jimmy Buffett music while enjoying Cuban cigars and Jameson Irish Whiskey. Once out of sight of land, Jack scattered Peter's ashes across the waters of the Gulf, while they were under sail.

Peter was the one who'd left him the boat, for which he was forever grateful. Though Peter's death had been unexpected, he was an old man, near the end of his days. Like most people his age, Jack didn't think too much about death, and was surprised when it ambushed him in unexpected ways.

His mind shifted back to the present, and he looked at the redhead sitting on the boat. She was the best thing that had ever happened to him, and he was grateful that she'd survived.

She was doing well; her body had fully healed and showed no signs of what had happened. Her mental health was more complicated. She was quieter, and still had difficulty sleeping. Her moods were like a roller coaster. A change of scenery and the passage of time were the best medicine for her. That, and sailing. She was most at peace on the water under sail.

Jack was also at peace, since showing the video at Drager's award dinner. Jack and Wren had made the video, exposing Drager's pill mill. Jack had warned her about the possible repercussions, but she insisted on doing it. "It's for Molly," she said.

While Drager probably would never serve time, at least he wouldn't be supplying the market with illicit pills. His reputation had been ruined, and his activities would be under scrutiny for years to come.

Jack had taken Wren's share of the money and set up a trust fund in her name with the majority of it. He'd given her fifty-thousand dollars in cash that he told her came from Peabo's bag. That was between them, he told her. It was only fair that she received some of the ill-gotten gains.

She wanted to take the money and get a small sailboat to live on. He'd helped her buy a good used thirty-foot Catalina for twenty-thousand dollars, and arranged for her to lease a slip in the Clearwater Beach Marina. Wren got her job back at the hospital and had enrolled in nursing school at the technical college, determined to follow in Molly's footsteps.

Wren cried when Jack and Molly left, but she understood. He told her to visit them anytime—she was always welcome—and she promised to keep in touch. Wren was doing well, and for the first time, he felt like she was on the right path. He knew Molly would insist on coming back for her capping ceremony, but that was a few years away.

Tina had also been there on the dock when they left. She'd promised not to cry, but when Molly hugged her, they both broke down in tears. With the three women crying and hugging, Jack tried his best to remain stoic. It didn't work, and soon he was in the circle, tears streaming down his cheeks.

Jack thought Tina and Wren looked like sisters, standing on the dock with their arms around each other, waving at them as they motored away from the marina. Tina planned to stay in the Tampa area, though not working for Drager. She vowed to keep an eye out for Wren, and Jack knew she'd be a good role model for the younger girl.

It made him think of his brother, Ray, who'd died so young. There was nothing he could do for Ray, but they'd saved Wren. That was a step in the right direction.

He smiled and nodded, then looked back out at the limitless waters of the Gulf of Mexico.

Acknowledgments

A special thanks goes to the following people for taking time to read my manuscript and offer much-needed feedback and support: Mary Jo Burkhalter Persons, Otis Scarbary, Cindy Deane, Shirley Scarbary, Clara Blanquet, Fred Blanquet, Barry McIntosh, and Jay Holmes.

Others who contributed and are gratefully acknowledged: Lt. Karl Steele, Ben Bollinger, Robert Duncan, Rick Brafford, and Tim McLaughlin.

A huge thanks to Carole Baskin and the wonderful people at Big Cat Rescue.

Another outstanding cover from Carl Graves. Thanks to Michael Garrett, who taught me a lot about writing.

Many thanks to my editor, Heather Whitaker. She pushes me to make my writing better, and I appreciate her advice and counsel. As always, any mistakes that remain are mine.

I made the "mistake" years ago of promising to buy books for my granddaughter, Breanna, who enjoys reading as much as I do. Rest assured that part of the revenue from my book sales goes to purchase books for her. She's still an inspiration in spite of the expense.

Once again, I thank my wonderful wife June. Thanks for supporting me and having faith in my writing. I couldn't do it without you.